She Felt A Comforting Warmth Spreading Through Her . . .

Brandy knew it was dangerous, this peaceful sleepy feeling. But it was so much better than the earlier pain of the cold. No, she wouldn't move now; it was so nice here. The snow went on about its gentle business of covering her.

Someone was pulling at her, shaking her, picking her up. Her blood poured like fire, searing its way back into her frozen limbs. She screamed in protest.

Grey's face was close to hers. "I've got to get you back."

She remembered the child lost in the storm, and the shivering started again, adding agony. "Missy's out here. I couldn't find her. Oh, Grey, I couldn't find her."

She slipped from the jarring pain of being carried into darkness. She did not feel Grey's strong hands holding her fiercely against his own warmth; she did not hear him repeating her name over and over.

The
Night Child

Celeste De Blasis

BANTAM BOOKS
NEW YORK • TORONTO • LONDON • SYDNEY • AUCKLAND

*This edition contains the complete text
of the original hardcover edition.*
NOT ONE WORD HAS BEEN OMITTED.

THE NIGHT CHILD
*A Bantam Book / published by arrangement with
the author*

PRINTING HISTORY
Bantam edition / March 1986

Songs quoted in The Night Child *are in the public domain but
are printed in the following books:*
"Simple Gifts," The Gift to Be Simple, *Edward C. Andrews,
Dover Pubications, Inc.*
"Katy Cruel," The American Heritage Songbook, *Copyright
© 1969, American Heritage Publishing Company, Inc.*

ISBN 0-553-27744-8

Published simultaneously in the United States and Canada

---

*Bantam Books are published by Bantam Books, a division of
Bantam Doubleday Dell Publishing Group, Inc. Its trade-
mark, consisting of the words "Bantam Books" and the por-
trayal of a rooster, is Registered in U.S. Patent and Trademark
Office and in other countries. Marca Registrada. Bantam
Books, 666 Fifth Avenue, New York, New York 10103.*

PRINTED IN THE UNITED STATES OF AMERICA

KR   14   13   12   11   10   9   8   7

With love and thanks
  To my parents
    for giving me space,
  To my grandmother
    for teaching me to see,
  And to my brother
    for believing.
Ciao, Captain Nirvana. Sail on.

Acknowledgments

I trust that the background research for this book does not intrude on the reader's pleasure. The story was written to amuse, not to present a lecture in history or in childhood behavior. However, when one writes outside one's own century, locale, and knowledge, debts of gratitude are incurred, and so it is with *The Night Child*.

To my friends in San Francisco, particularly to Jeffrey B. Leith, I owe much for their eternal pride in their city, their joy in its past and present, and their ability to make each day of its existence live in the instant.

To Kathy Poncy I owe my gratitude for her deep dedication to autistic children and for her generous sharing of her hard-earned knowledge.

But my deepest thanks goes to my aunt, Donna Pollard Campbell, and her brother, C. Owen Pollard, who began my love affair with Maine with the strange, beautiful cadence of their words and the luminous memories of their Down East childhood.

CHAPTER I

Brandy trembled from her effort to control the waves of laughter washing up toward sound. The voice of Mr. Ponsby droned on, speaking for the directors of the school, enumerating her sins against decency: She had taught unexpurgated Shakespeare, pouring ancient obscenities into young minds; she had stated that there were valid beliefs in religions other than Christianity; she had introduced Mr. Darwin's theory of the Origin of Species to the children; she had destroyed the discipline of Greenfield Academy, turning well-behaved students into disobedient fiends. And worst of all, she had been observed wearing trousers and engaging in horse racing on a Sunday.

The trousers and the racing were sins aplenty; the day of the week damned her for sure. She put her handkerchief to her mouth, trying to turn a giggle into a cough. It was absurd—all that destructive power attributed to her. They would never see that their collective narrow-mindedness and bigotry made them vulnerable. That was pathetic because it would be passed on to the children. But Mr. Ponsby's being the one to dismiss her, Lord, that was amusing! There he was, speaking ponderously in his good citizen's voice, the same paunchy little man who eyed every young woman hungrily, who terrified his wife and daughter, who tithed at church and charged double for the dry goods he sold.

Brandy tried to think of something sad, something which would lend her dignity of a serious expression. Her mind went back a year to her father's death, but it was no use. His legacy was what was tripping her up now, that constant appreciation of the foolishness of human behavior.

The voice had now moved to her general moral tone and was receiving a hum of agreement that it wasn't good.

Her eyes wandered over the faces in the small room. Most of the expressions were tight-lipped, forbidding, but here and there she saw friendly ones, translated into sadness because, though they did not believe her guilty, they would not risk anything to prove her worthy and keep her on.

She stopped her inventory. At the back of the room was a stranger, glaringly obvious because everyone in the smallness of Greenfield was familiar. He was leaning negligently against the wall; when he stood, he would be very tall. He was well dressed. His shock of black hair and his straight black brows did nothing to soften the arrogant sculpture of his face—the prominent cheekbones underscored with hollows, the high-bridge nose, the heavily carved mouth, and the decisive angle of chin. Harsh lines had etched away youth. He looked like the devil come to a church social. The distance between them was short enough for Brandy to see that he too was amused. Her own impulse to laugh died abruptly.

Ponsby's voice was impatient; he must have asked the question several times. "Well, Miss Claybourne, what have you to say for yourself?"

Nothing would do any good. They had no intention of allowing her to remain. They simply wanted to hear an apology which would confirm their charges. Brandy wasn't sorry. Her voice was quiet and even, words dropping like stones into the silent room.

"Mr. Ponsby, ladies and gentlemen. Ignorance is excusable when there has been no opportunity to remedy it; pride in one's ignorance is never excusable. This is eighteen hundred and sixty-nine, the Dark Ages ended years ago in most places; apparently they are to continue at Greenfield. New ideas, new theories, and knowledge of foreign cultures and alien ways of thought are not harmful, but suppression of them is. The bloodiest wars in history have been fought because of intolerance. And unfortunately, there will always be people such as you who are willing to continue the wars.

"There is no hope for you—your minds are rigid with the hate and fear of anything new. The tragedy is that you will inflict your narrow visions on your children, and they will perpetuate your ignorance. Even had I the opportunity, I would not continue to teach in such an atmosphere. You have done me a great service by dismissing me."

Voices rose in outrage as Brandy made her way out of the room. Her height served her well. She held herself proudly erect, walked slowly, and stared coolly down at the contorted faces. She heard the comments and did not flinch. "What, that slut, how dare she?" "To think she has been allowed near our children." "Should never have been hired. She's from the West; just goes to show you how uncivilized they are out there."

At the door she stopped and turned, making her voice loud enough for all to hear. "By the way, I am sure you must be wondering about the race. I won."

She heard a shout of laughter amid the angry buzz, but she did not pause or look his way. Once in the corridor, she felt her knees giving way, but she made it outside to lean against one of the massive pillars of the portico, thinking irrelevantly that the Greeks would have hated their architecture to be used in a place of so little enlightenment.

Well, now you've really done it, she thought. *There will be references all right, all bad. Just try to find another teaching post. How delighted Aunt Beatrice*

*will be that I finally got my comeuppance—that's what
I can't bear to think about—leaving the Adamses' house
to go back to live with Aunt Beatrice.*

She was startled by the voice beside her. "Miss
Claybourne, I am Grey King." His voice was deep with
a strange drawl which sounded almost British. His
handshake was firm, and even though she was eight
inches over five feet, he towered above her. His eyes
were so dark, pupil and iris merged. The devil indeed
and still looking amused, at her expense.

"I hope you enjoyed my performance!" she snapped,
and glared at him.

"I did. I wouldn't have missed it for the world. But I
did not follow you out here to congratulate you. I would
like to offer you a job."

Brandy stared up at him suspiciously. "Doing what?"

"Teaching, of course," he said impatiently, and Brandy
was about to ask him if he was mad or just cruel, but
the change in him stopped her. All humor was gone,
the lines cutting deeper, his face a graven mask with
glittering eyes. Brandy felt a tremor of fear and resisted
the impulse to step back.

The sound was harsh. "I'm not offering you another
Greenfield. I'm offering you what I think is an impossible
job with one pupil. I have a daughter. Melissa is five
years old, but she has not spoke since my wife died two
years ago. She does not play; she does nothing but rock
and stare. I have taken her to doctors, and they all
agree it is hopeless. They think it would be for the best
if she were put in an asylum. I have had a succession of
governesses, but none of them has been able to reach
her, and they have all left with great relief. My home is
in an isolated spot in the state of Maine. I will pay you
double what you've been paid here, but if you come,
you must agree to stay for at least six months. Do you
want the position?"

Brandy tried to sort it out—a strange offer to work
with a deranged child in the middle of nowhere or
going back to live with Aunt Beatrice in her cheerless

house in noisy Boston. And how had this man known she was to be fired?

He saw the question before she asked it; maybe he was more than a little like the devil. "George Adams is an old friend. He's seen Missy, and he knows the problems I've had keeping anyone to work with her. I saw him in Boston yesterday and told him I was trying to find another woman. With reluctance he told me about your situation. He too thinks Missy's condition is incurable, and he made it clear that he would prefer you did not get involved. But in fairness, he thought you should have the chance to decide."

Brandy was getting her wind back. Unconsciously she assumed what her father had called her "let's find some trouble stance"—head up, chin out, eyes wide and deceptively innocent, feet apart and planted firmly in unladylike strength to meet all comers. "Mr. King, you sound as if you hope I will not take the job, but you're out of luck. I accept, and I agree to the six months' clause. But you must understand that I have never taught a child such as yours, and there is every possibility that not only may I not be able to help her, but I might make her worse. If that is the case, I'll not hold you to the time limit if you wish me to leave."

Satisfaction gleamed in the obsidian eyes, and he said, more to himself than to her, "Perhaps I've finally found what Missy needs, someone who is willing to fight for her." Then in a brisker tone: "Can you be ready to leave by tomorrow?"

"Yes," she said without hesitation, not asking how they were to travel or whether she would be properly chaperoned. The quirk of his eyebrows told her he had noticed the omission. She reflected glumly that she would never look or behave like a governess. She liked the feeling of moving freely like a colt sure of quick-springing muscles; sedate steps were beyond her. On her neck she could feel the tendrils of hair which had escaped from the briefly decorous chignon. Her hair was the color of her name, a rich red brown, a strange combination with her tawny eyes, wide-spaced and almond-long under arching brows. Her nose was straight, her mouth full and red. She always felt too earthy, too brightly colored around the small, round women of fashion.

Mr. King's eyes moved over every detail of her appearance and gleamed suddenly as though in appreciation of a private joke.

She broke his silence. "Well, have you finished your survey? Do you think I'll do? You look as if you're buying a horse."

His smile softened the grim lines, but Brandy was aware again of her uneasiness. Under the disciplined exterior there was a volcano, and though she wasn't afraid of many things, she guessed his anger, if it were ever unleashed, would be terrible. "I apologize, Miss Claybourne, my mind was wandering."

He escorted her back to the Adamses' house, making arrangements for the next day as they walked. He would return with a carriage to pick her up, and they would leave Boston on his schooner for the trip to Maine. *Private schooner,* thought Brandy, *what am I getting myself into?* But outwardly she accepted the instructions calmly.

The Adamses' house was a rambling affair which had been built on a farm and had then seen Greenfield grow into a stately little village with easy access to Boston. The oaks and maples around it were bright with autumn, and Brandy felt a pang about leaving. The Adamses had become family, and Hugh would have liked the relationship to be closer than that. But she could not take advantage of them, remaining there without a job. Dorothea was all the help her husband, George, and son, Hugh, needed in dealing with their patients. And no school for miles around would hire Brandy now.

Dorothea saw them coming up the walk and came out to greet them. The number of carriages and horses indicated that the doctors were having a busy day, as usual, but Mrs. Adams invited Grey to stay for the evening meal, telling him he could relax in the library until then.

"Thank you, Dorothea, I would like to accept, but I brought a guest with me. She's been shopping in Boston and will expect me to dine with her tonight."

"Ruth?" asked Mrs Adams.

"Who else?"

"Grey King, why don't you marry that girl and make a decent woman of her? You've had long enough to get to know each other." Trust Dorothea to say what she was thinking. She spoke to him as though he were a young boy; obviously they had known each other for years, and he did not frighten her.

"What a novel idea. I'll think about it," he said sarcastically.

"You're impossible, and I'm busy." She gave him a hug and went back into the house.

He had left his horse hitched to the rail, and when Brandy saw the beautiful bay, she gave a low whistle of appreciation and saw Grey's renewed amusement— a governess who whistled. It was a wonder Greenfield had not listed that among her sins.

"Yours?" she asked, running her hands gently over the horse's face and rubbing behind his ears as she spoke softly to him.

Grey's amazement showed plainly. Calaban was not a friendly animal and usually rolled his eyes and nipped at strangers, but now he was hanging his head with an idiotic look of contentment.

"He's out of my stock, but he belongs to a friend in Boston who is kind enough to let me use him when I'm up this way. Sorry, but I can't lend him to you for any races," he added as he mounted in one easy movement from ground to saddle.

Brandy stepped back, and Grey looked down at her. "I'd better get him back before he falls asleep and I have to carry him. See you in the morning."

She watched him leave, watched the road for a long thoughtful moment before she went in.

Her packing did not take long. She was not in the habit of collecting things casually. Her books and music went in first, followed by her small wardrobe. Defiantly she put her Levi's on top of the dresses. Her special treasures from the West went on top—the gown from Pearl, the jade pendant from Chen Lee, and the watch and gold nugget from her father.

She saw Dorothea first in the hour before supper, but her questions were forestalled. "My dear, you've decided to take the post Grey offered. I can't say I'm pleased about it; I would like you to stay with us, with Hugh especially, forever, but you are as stubborn as ever either of your parents were, and I know it would be useless to try to dissuade you. And I know there are things you would like to know about Grey, but I'm not the one to tell you. Let George do it."

Mrs. Adams was not the crying sort, but she gave a surreptitious wipe at her eyes as she bustled off, and Brandy realized how much of a mother this busy little woman had been to her.

She saw Hugh next as he came down the hall which linked the office with the rest of the house. Hugh, blond, laughing Hugh, dependable and kind, favorite with all of his patients from the youngest to the oldest. He look so safe after Mr. King. Why couldn't she love Hugh, settle down with him, have his children?

He caught her by the shoulders and held her, looking at her with the same penetrating gaze he used when he was diagnosing a case.

"I haven't got the measles or any other contagion," she protested, feeling uncomfortable under his eyes.

"I know. You haven't caught me either, and I've done my best to make sure you did. I can tell, you're really leaving us, leaving me. I am going to try to be civilized about the whole thing, but it isn't easy. I love you, Brandy, you know that. I want you to marry me, and that's nothing new either. I don't want you going off to the wilds of Maine to live under King's roof with his incurable child. I haven't seen her, but Father has, and he doesn't think there is a chance she will ever be normal.

"Please stay. I'm sure we can find another job for you, and I promise not to push about us. I am responsible for your losing your position. If I hadn't let you race Blue, this would never have happened."

"Don't be silly, Hugh. It was my idea, and besides, the race was just the last in a long series of my sins. I'm quite certain they were already thinking of letting me go at the end of last year. They're just so slow that it took them until now to add everything up and decide. Anyway, I'm determined to take this new job, and I won't be told that the child is hopeless until I've seen for myself. But from the way you talk, there's something I ought to know about Mr. King which no one has told me yet."

Hugh shook his head ruefully. "No, it's just plain old jealousy. Oh, I've heard he's been a bit of a rakehell but never with anyone who wasn't willing. I don't know him that well. He's nine or ten years older than I, and Father knows him much better than I do."

He kissed her gently on the forehead and drew her against him. "Darling, I am going to let you go because I haven't any choice in the matter. But I'm going to hope that you won't like it there, that you'll come back. I want you to promise that you won't hesitate to get in touch with me if you need me or if you want to come home."

He tipped her head back, and Brandy saw the concern in his eyes. She smiled at him. "I promise I'll give a yell that you'll hear down here if I need you."

He kissed her on the mouth, not gently, and let her go. "That's to remind you of how I feel," he said, his voice suddenly rough. He left her standing there wondering why such a marvelous man stirred no more than feelings of friendship in her. *Be honest, Brandy, he's too safe, and life with him would be much too even and easy, and you must be mad not to want that*.

Nine or ten years older than Hugh—that meant Mr. King was thirty-five or thirty-six. Her mind supplied the figures automatically, quickly dismissing Hugh, intent on Grey King.

The evening meal lacked its usual casual conversation and gaiety. Brandy's imminent departure hung so heavily in the atmosphere that she thought if something didn't happen soon, she was going to burst into tears like a child and flee the table. But what happened did not make things any easier.

In the middle of the meal, Mrs. Ponsby and her daughter, Judith, came to tell Brandy good-bye, bringing with them a bouquet of late flowers and a letter signed by her pupils saying how much they would miss her, how much they had liked her as a teacher. The letter was written in Judith's careful hand, and Brandy recognized the individual signing of each child's name. She was speechless, not only from the sweetness of the children's gesture, but because Mrs. Ponsby had had the courage to come. Her husband would make life hellish for her if he found out.

The nervous little woman saw her concern and rushed into speech, giving Brandy time. "Miss Claybourne, I just had to come. Judith and the other children thought of the letter all by themselves. They are so distraught that you are leaving. And I'm ashamed that it was my husband who did it."

Brandy answered huskily, "You have no idea how much this means to me. As long as the children were happy and learned something, none of the rest matters. And your husband was only the spokesman; the decision was made by several people. You aren't to blame. I have a new job already. I'm leaving tomorrow, but I won't forget you."

She saw the tears welling in Judith's eyes, and she knelt down and drew her close. "Judith, you have a wonderful mind. Go on learning everything you can, and try to like your next teacher. As long as you can read about new places and new ideas, you'll be free and nothing can really hurt you." Including your father, she added silently. She stroked the little girl's hair, and the tears stopped. Judith gave her a quick, shy kiss, took her mother's hand, and they were gone.

Brandy had no stomach to finish the meal, and Dr. Adams didn't either. He rose from the table and took Brandy with him to his study, leaving Hugh and Dorothea looking preoccupied and sad.

Brandy loved old Dr. George. He was nothing like her flamboyant father except that they both carried about them the same air of authority and concern for the well-being of their patients.

He settled himself in his chair, rumpled his white hair in his characteristic way, and lit his pipe before he began. "My dear child, I am not going to try to talk you into staying; I'm sure Hugh and Dorothea have already covered that ground thoroughly. But I am going to claim a sentimental old man's privilege to be maudlin for a minute.

"Your father was ever a direct man. When he persuaded you to come East, he knew he was dying. I had not heard from him more than a few times since he and your mother headed for California, but I loved them both, and it was a personal loss when I learned that your mother had died so soon after their arrival, so soon after your birth.

"Of you I knew very little. When his last letter arrived, I didn't know what to think. He said that because of family ties, he was sending you to your mother's sister, Beatrice, but that he was quite sure it would not work. Kathryn was never like Beatrice; she was always wild and willful, enchanting, and ready for any adventure. Beatrice has been purse-lipped and frightened of God's wrath since birth. Your father knew you resembled your mother too much to get along with your aunt, but he felt honor-bound to give her the first chance of providing you with a home. You see, he considered it a privilege, he loved you so much. But he was honest. The letter to me explained that he had reared a girl who was as wild as the country she was born in. Dorothea and I didn't know what to think, and frankly, we dreaded the day when we might become responsible for you. When you got in touch with us because you were unhappy with your aunt and had gotten the job at the academy, our hearts sank. But the rest you know. Within twenty-four hours we had both fallen in love with you. We always wanted a daughter, and we could not love you more or be more pleased with you even if you were our own. We will always feel that way, and this will always be your home."

Brandy sat quietly with her hands in her lap, making no effort to wipe away the tears.

Dr. George continued: "Of all that they gave you, Brandy, the finest gift from your parents is your honesty. You laugh and cry and love with no pretense. What happened at the academy should leave no stigma on you, only on the power that caused your dismissal. Some people find honesty and an open mind intolerable affronts, but that is their loss, not yours. And you have my deepest gratitude for the way you have treated Hugh. Perhaps in the future you will come to love him, but you do not now, and you have not led him to believe that you do. To choose the truth over a comfortable offer of marriage is something few women do. Kathryn did." His voice had a sudden tightness, and Brandy glanced at him quickly, trying to see him clearly through the blur of tears. He swallowed and went on more evenly. "She was wise to do so. She liked me very much, but she adored your father. And I learned to love Dorothea deeply, to know that she was the woman to share my peaceful existence, to be happy with one place and never want to cross the mountains. Your mother and father were both born wanting to know what was on the other side."

The silence stretched on, but it was not uneasy. Brandy's tears had stopped with her startling new knowledge of Dr. Adams. She could see his face clearly now, and she knew he was seeing her parents as he remembered them, with love. His voice was pensive when he began to speak again.

"King and his daughter seem to be your next mountain, a very difficult climb. I knew Grey's father, and I've known Grey since he was small. He is a man of great wealth and power, but little joy. Too many things have happened to make him bitter. But I knew him when he was young and full of laughter and high spirits, in spite of the fact that his parents died of cholera when he was only eighteen, and he had to step into his father's shoes. His mother was always frail, but the death of his father was a real shock. Now all his energy goes into his empire. He owns shipyards, textile and lumber mills, granite quarries, breeding farms for fine horses, and just about anything else you could name. He drives himself relentlessly, probably because he doesn't want to think too much about his daughter or her mother." His face assumed the brooding expression of the times when he had patients who were beyond his help.

"Grey's wife was a girl named Jasmine Lavelle. She was from New Orleans." He saw Brandy's expression of surprise. "Oh, yes, strangely enough, because of the cotton trade, the ties between Maine shipowners and the South were very strong before the war, closer in many cases than between Maine and the rest of New England.

"Grey met Jasmine in New Orleans, fell in love with her, and married her against her family's wishes—they had no use for Yankees, and she was only seventeen. He brought her north to live and as far as I know, she never visited the South again. Of course, the war came and broke communications, but from what little I know, Jasmine had no desire to see her people again anyway. I met her only once when Grey brought her to Boston. She was very beautiful, but not likable. She was one of those women who radiate discontent. She had nothing but contempt for the provincialism of Maine, and she talked incessantly about how much she missed a civilized social life. Grey bore it in good humor because he loved her and because he believed that love would be enough to make her happy.

"Then when the war came, Grey was nearly killed at Gettysburg. He was sent home to die, but he was just too stubborn. And about a year later the little girl was born. I don't know too much about those three years with Missy, but from what I gather, the marriage went along with the child as the center. At least in that Jasmine was normal. Mutual friends said that both parents adored the child, whatever their personal problems were. But those problems certainly existed. Grey has a brother, Raleigh, and he seemed to have been involved. He's younger, gay, charming, and financially dependent on Grey. He didn't go to war, and perhaps he kept the home fires burning too brightly. There were rumors that he and Jasmine were much too close in Grey's absence. I've met Raleigh a few times, and he is a hard man to hate, so I have no idea whether or not there was any truth in the gossip. Jasmine was the type who would have liked to create a scandalous reputation whether or not it had any basis in fact.

"What is important is that what little remained of Grey's youth after the war was shattered in one night. I don't think anyone will ever know what actually happened. Grey had been home, but apparently he was not when the fire started."

"Fire," echoed Brandy stupidly. She was having a difficult time connecting everything Dr. George was saying with the man she had met so briefly and accepted a job from so quickly.

His words were steady. "The fire that killed Jasmine. God knows why she was in the stables late at night when they burned to the ground. No one knows how the fire started. What is known is that Jasmine died that night, and the little girl has not spoken since. Whether that is simply because her mother died so suddenly or because she saw her die in the fire is not known either. But I've seen the child, and my diagnosis is that she will never be healed. Maybe in the future we will discover how to persuade such children to come back into the world, but we don't know how yet, and all I can foresee for you is frustration and sorrow."

All Brandy could see at the moment was pity for Mr. King, and the last part of the gruesome tale brought him into even sharper focus.

"I would rather not tell you, but I think you ought to be warned. The stableman swore that Grey did not arrive until the fire was roaring and that he made valiant attempts to save the horses and thus found his wife's body. But the story persists that he murdered her. I do not believe it; from what I know of Grey, it is impossible. But even I must allow that strong emotion can make the sanest man unstable."

His voice died away. Brandy got up and put her arms around him. "I love you as I loved my father," was all she could manage, but by his look it was enough. She went up to her room without seeking out Dorothea or Hugh; there was no sense in making the parting harder by more anxious time together.

She was exhausted by the events of the day, but she did not sleep peacefully. She had learned too much too soon about Grey King, and it was impossible to reconcile the separate images of that arrogant devil of a man with one who had suffered so much and might have committed murder out of desperate love.

CHAPTER II

By the time Mr. King arrived the next morning Brandy
was anxious to be on her way. It was one of the things
her father had emphasized from the time she was
small—to make decisions courageously and, once having made them, not to fret. She was going to Maine,
and nothing would be gained by prolonging her departure or wondering if she was doing the proper
thing. She kissed the Adamses good-bye, ignored
their looks of concern, promised to keep in touch,
and gave Dr. George a note to be delivered to her
aunt when next he went to Boston. She had no
intention of hearing her aunt's opinion of what she
had decided to do.

Beyond a brief "good morning," Mr. King said very
little, though Brandy had felt him watching as she
made her farewells. Now driving out of Greenfield, he
confirmed this. "Are you sure you want this job, Miss
Claybourne? Obviously Hugh Adams feels more than
brotherly affection for you. Or perhaps that is why you
are putting such a distance between the two of you?"

Brandy's compassion for the man evaporated. "Mr.
King, I have taken the job with no regrets. I am
looking forward to teaching your daughter. But my
private life is entirely my own, and I'll thank you to
keep out of it."

His reaction was not what she expected; she suspected

his responses would never be predictable. He laughed, turning his attention from the horses he was driving to her. "Point taken. And I knew you wouldn't wear a bustle."

The *non sequitur* amused her, and she joined his laughter. She knew very well that the russet of her traveling costume set off her coloring and that there had been approval, not offense, in his comment. "Silly things, I hate them," she said. "They make women so impractical; even sitting down is a chore. You talk more like the Western men I knew than an Easterner. Most of the men here are afraid God will strike them dead if they so much as think about an undergarment, let alone mention it."

"What kind of men did you know in the West?" he asked, and she started to bristle again but then realized he was really curious, not just prying, and that he had a right to know something about her background.

"I knew miners, gamblers, sea captains, farmers, horse thieves, doctors, and lawyers, just about any kind you could name, good and bad. But most of them shared one thing—they were kind and gentle to me while I was growing up, and a lot of them helped to raise me. You see, my mother came with my father to California in forty-nine, and she was already carrying me when they boarded the ship, but she didn't tell my father for fear he would cancel the trip. He was a good doctor, but she was over thirty, and up till then there had been no sign of a child, so perhaps that made it easier to keep it from him. It was a long, hard voyage, and it ruined her health. In spite of all he could do, she died in childbirth a few months after they arrived. Women and children were as rare in San Francisco as the mother lode in those days, and the few there were treated as exotic creatures who needed protecting. Father used to tell stories of miners who offered gold dust just to kiss a woman or hold a child because they missed their own families left in the East.

"I think you have the right to know something else. The first women who arrived in any numbers were what you would expect, prostitutes and dance hall girls, and many of them helped bring me up, too. One in particular who called herself Pearl Orient was the closest thing I had to a mother." Brandy caught his look of sympathy. "Oh, don't think that! Pearl was wonderful, and so was my childhood. As far as I know no one knew Pearl's real name or where exactly in the East she had come from, and nobody cared. She ran a saloon in front of her building and had rooms with girls in the back. Her house was clean and honest, and even the girls who worked for her liked her. We stayed there when we were in San Francisco. Father never set up a practice; he was sort of a traveling medicine man going from one isolated camp to the next, and how glad they all were to see him. Pearl gave us a home when we were in the city; we wouldn't have had one otherwise. When I left two years ago, she had long since retired and was living in a beautiful house overlooking the bay, and Father still stayed with her when he was in San Francisco. She was the one who wrote to tell me that he was dead, that he had died peacefully in her arms."

Two years ago, that was when Grey's wife had died, not peacefully but in an inferno. Brandy went on quickly.

"Pearl must have come from a special background. Her English was very proper; she could speak French perfectly, too, and even learned passable Cantonese in San Francisco. She had a well-stocked library, and most ships coming in brought the additional volumes she coveted. She played the piano, and her customers loved to hear her play and sing. She taught me how. She taught me a great deal more than I learned when I finally started my formal education. Even when so-called modish society became a reality in the city, my father and I preferred Pearl and the others like her, the people who had faced the first hard years and survived.

"I thought it only fair to tell you while you still have time to change your mind about me. You might not want someone with my background around your daughter."

He hesitated so long that she thought he was indeed disturbed by the prospect. His voice was leaden. "What I want is for the day to come when Missy can understand well enough for you to tell her about Pearl and the West."

Brandy was touched, and she didn't know what to say. She was relieved when he continued on a lighter note. "Two more questions, both of them personal, but permissible, I hope. First, how did you happen to be named Brandy?"

"That's simple. My father drank the stuff for a week after my mother died and then decided that his child had better be as strong as the liquor if she were to survive. I guess it was like giving me an Indian medicine name, and Brandy's better than Eagle's Wing or Bear's Claw."

That drew a smile from him. Amazing what a difference it made in the hooded face.

"Next question?"

"Did Pearl ever want you to follow in her footsteps?" he asked.

Brandy gave a peal of laughter. "Good heavens, no! She was perfectly happy herself, but she had no intention of letting me become a prostitute. She said some were cut out for it, but I wasn't. She was stricter than the most straitlaced matron about some things. When her girls were entertaining the customers in the back rooms, I was either asleep or doing lessons in her study. But she was always open and answered any questions I asked. She just made it clear to the men that I was not part of her business, that I was to be treated as a daughter of any respectable woman would be. I only remember a couple of men misbehaving, and they both ended up on the street, forbidden to visit Pearl's place again. She was the one who started my father on the notion that I should come East. She said both coasts should be tasted."

They finished the ride in companionable silence. Mr. King seemed to use words only for extracting or giving information; small talk was not one of his habits, and Brandy agreed with him.

It took them scarcely more than an hour to reach Boston and the harbor from Greenfield. The sounds of the city closed in, and the peculiar smell of the wharves grew stronger—tar and hemp and the thousand strange things being handled there. Brandy was becoming ever more aware of how important Mr. King was. An agent was on hand to take the carriage and pair back to their Boston stable. And when Brandy discovered which ship they were to board, she stopped dead and breathed, "Now that's a yacht!" More than fifty feet long, the *Isabella* rode proudly with every surface gleaming from constant care.

Grey was amused. "No, actually she's not. *Isabella* isn't used solely for pleasure; she's a working vessel, does coastal trading when she's not transporting me or Raleigh. On her normal route, her arrival is quite an event in the small ports. She doesn't match up in size; there are many ships which are twice as big as she is, but she's appreciated nonetheless. Why, right now her hold is full of goods bound for Wiscasset. Most of it is special orders such as a rare blend of pipe tobacco for Joe Samuels, a bolt of fine cloth for Jane Alman's wedding dress, and if I remember correctly, a new whalebone corset for Mrs. Pettigrew." Brandy giggled at the picture of Mrs. Pettigrew waiting anxiously for her new corset to sail in.

Captain Hackett, a broadly built man with white hair and sea-faded eyes surrounded by permanent squint creases, greeted them as they came on board. Besides the busy crewmen, there was a woman on deck. She was pacing impatiently when Brandy first caught sight of her, but she stopped when she saw them. The old come-to-me trick, thought Brandy cynically as they walked toward the figure. Grey introduced her to Ruth Collins.

There was no denying that she was beautiful. She was a good head shorter than Brandy, slender-boned and elegant but round in the right places. Her blond hair was carefully coiffed under a charming blue hat trimmed with tiny roses. Her matching blue dress was finely tailored with a bustled skirt and fitted jacket. Stupid wide skirt to wear on a ship, decided Brandy irreverently. Ruth's eyes were long-lashed under delicate brows. Her nose was small and straight, her mouth a perfect rosebud. She looked younger than the thirty years Dorothea Adams had put to her credit.

And there was no denying that she disliked Brandy on sight. Her eyes widened in surprise quickly hidden. She forced a smile as the introduction was made, but her voice was tense in spite of her efforts to make it casual. "Why, Grey darling, Miss Claybourne hardly looks like a governess. She's terribly young. What will she find to do in our backward state?"

Brandy's temper flared. She hated being talked about as if she weren't there. She spoke before Grey had a chance. "I wasn't aware that governesses are all cut in the same pattern. I am nineteen and have already taught school for over a year. And I'm going to Maine to work, not to be entertained."

She was instantly sorry for her outburst. She saw anger flash on Ruth's face, but it was followed by a faint shadow of fear. Poor Ruth, from what Brandy gathered, she had been in love with Grey for years and hopeful of marrying him, so why shouldn't she be suspicious and resentful of a younger woman who was joining Grey's household? She put out her hand impulsively. "Please, let's be friends. I'm sure there is so much you can tell me about Missy that would take me a long time to discover on my own."

Ruth took her hand, and this time she really smiled. Grey seemed satisfied that they were not going to start pulling out each other's hair, and he walked off to talk to the captain and so missed the change in Ruth's expression and her words.

"There's nothing I can tell you about Melissa that you won't know the minute you see her. I can tell you that she was a normal, laughing little girl before. Even her mother, the most hateful woman I have ever known, loved her. But all that is gone. The child is an empty shell, and she's ruining Grey's life. That's awful to say, isn't it? But it's true. He is so guilt-ridden that sometimes I wonder if he's sane. He can shut himself so far away that he resembles his daughter. Miss Claybourne, the best thing you can do for him and for me is to agree that the child belongs in an asylum so that we can get on with our lives."

Brandy still felt sorry for her, and for a moment she had thought they might be friends, but nothing could excuse such a callous attitude toward a child; surely if there was love between Grey and Ruth, they could make a life which included Missy. Brandy felt her facial muscles tighten with dislike, and Ruth saw it.

Her voice was harsh. "You are too young to understand how desperate love can make one. And you will not cooperate. You will struggle and fail like all the others, but it will take you months to admit it. If you took my advice, you could save yourself and me a lot of wasted time."

"Thank you for your concern, Miss Collins," said Brandy stiffly, and was relieved to see Grey coming back their way. He asked if she would like to see her quarters, and she agreed with alacrity. Ruth watched them go, her polite smile frozen into a grimace.

The crew's sleeping quarters were forward; the passenger cabins aft. Though the *Isabella* was fairly broad-beamed, the living space below deck was cramped, and Brandy could see why everything was so carefully stowed in its proper place. Her quarters were small but neat and comfortable. She saw Grey's cabin and Ruth's and noticed the connecting door. How convenient.

But in spite of her feelings about Ruth, the trip

proved a pure delight for Brandy. She had little experience of ships beyond her passage East by steamer, and she found to her relief that she was a good sailor. She loved the gentle undulating motion, the singing of the lines, the snap and rustle of canvas, the faint bell sounds. The weather held clear and fairly calm, so there was no rough water to contend with.

She persuaded one of the crew to tell her why Grey had referred to going up to Boston while going to Maine was going down, clearly a reversal of the actual directions. He told her that it was on account of the wind—you sailed up the prevailing winds to Boston, down back to Maine. From him she began to get a better idea of how closely Maine was tied to the sea— his own family had been bound to it one way or another as far back as anyone could remember, being either builders of boats, members of a crew, or fishermen. And in his voice she heard the strange broad vowels, soft tones, and hesitant, careful use of words peculiar to his state and much more intense than in Grey's speech.

Beyond mealtimes, she spoke little with Grey and never without Ruth present. Captain Hackett took his meals with them, and Brandy enjoyed his company, though she suspected that Grey had asked him to eat with them to reduce the tension between the two women. The captain told wonderful tales about his days on the clippers, and Brandy envied his wife who, like many of the clipper captains' wives, had voyaged with him, staying at home only when the arrival of a child was imminent. When she told him so, the captain shook his head sadly. "Ayuh, those were th' days, but they're fast passin', an' I'm thinkin' my Samantha misses 'em more'n I do. She hates steam for doin' in th' sails."

He and Grey went on to talk about the new Suez Canal, another sure blow to sailing ships, for now the steamers would be able to cut down the distance between coaling stops, and the less fuel they had to carry, the more profitable cargo space they had. And the newly completed transcontinental railway would also bring a change. Brandy listened in fascination, thinking of how vast a seaman's boundaries were—a change half the world away affected him as if it had happened next door. Ruth did not bother to hide her yawn of boredom.

Grey spent most of his time with the captain or members of the crew. He was well liked and respected for his seaman's knowledge, something the captain said most owners sorely lacked. And the sea was good for Grey; he looked younger, less careworn, almost at peace.

Brandy was perfectly happy exploring the ship and watching the seabirds, other vessels, and the changing shoreline. They were within sight of land most of the time, and she watched sandy shores of New Hampshire change to the rough granite of the Maine coast jutting out from tall stands of pine and spruce. Here and there isolated houses, compact and practical, looked out on the sea, each with a boat tied close by, and there were a multitude of tiny harbors. The ruggedness reminded her of the West, and already she felt a kinship with the state.

Ruth made no attempt to speak about Missy again, and that suited Brandy. She caused a stir on the first morning out by appearing in her fitted denim trousers. Grey's mouth twitched, and some of the crew were startled enough to forget what they were doing for a moment of frozen wonder. But only Ruth felt impelled to reprimand her. "Do you think those are quite proper, Miss Claybourne?" she asked, her judgment clear in her tone.

Brandy returned her cool stare. "Yes, I do, quite proper for climbing around on a ship; much more sensible than trailing skirts or those idiotic Turkish trousers which are bound to trip me. Besides, my figure is hardly enough to be called indecent, whatever I wear." Ruth was flushed with anger and shock, Brandy noticed with satisfaction.

"That's a matter of opinion," Grey said, his eyes taking in every detail of her appearance, the long, slender lines softly rounded. Brandy had always dismissed her figure as too boyish for fashions; apparently Mr. King did not share her view.

Ruth's face was rigid as she took Grey's arm possessively and asked him to escort her back to her cabin. She was not as easy with the boat's motion as Brandy was. Brandy felt the little tremor of fear again—Grey was not a man to tamper with or try to bind too closely. Poor Ruth, she should have learned that by now.

On the third day, they sailed up the wide Sheepscot River to Wiscasset, where Grey had his major shipyard. Brandy was delighted with the lovely white sea captains' houses, many of them complete with widow's walks around the roofs. The port still looked very busy to her, but Grey said that the war had changed things radically, and now that steam was so popular, many shipyards were closing down because they could not compete with the British builders of steamships. Brandy saw his hardness again; he had no pity for men who could not anticipate new trends and prepare for them.

Not far from where they docked, a man was waiting with a wagon. Grey accepted it as a matter of course that he would be there, but Brandy thought rebelliously that far too many people seemed to spend their lives waiting to do Mr. King's bidding. Either that or he had an uncannily accurate sense of timing which he passed on to his employees.

Grey went to speak to the man and returned with him. Ruth gave a small, cold nod of recognition; obviously she did not like him. As Brandy was introduced to Raphael Joly, she wondered if Ruth's dislike might stem from fear, for his appearance was not reassuring. Such a soft name for a hard-looking man. He could be anywhere from forty to fifty years old. He was not as tall as Grey, but he was much broader, and his skin was as brown and grained as bark, his hands as gnarled as the wind-warped trees she had known on the coast of the Pacific. But none of that was difficult to accept. Brandy had seen men shaped by the elements before. It was his face which gave him a baleful aspect. He had heavy brows, a hooked nose which had encountered fists often enough to be bumped and off center, and a heavy-lipped mouth. And his face was set in a perpetual, twisted leer because a puckered scar pulled skin and muscles tight from the outer tip of his left eyebrow to the corner of his mouth. Raphael Joly did not get along well with his fellowman, that was certain.

Brandy found it difficult to look away from the scar as they were introduced. She forced her eyes to meet his and experienced a shock. His eyes were a clear brown, and they were as gentle and innocent as a child's, completely out of place in the contorted face. She smiled at him and, hearing his thick accent, acknowledged the introduction in French.

His eyes gleamed with pleasure, and he said, "Please, it is better for me in English. I have still much to learn."

Brandy wondered where Grey had found him and how he had got the scar. It was not that old, probably no more than a few years. No matter; Brandy already liked him because of his eyes and because of his manner with Grey. There was no subservience in it, and obviously Grey expected none. They treated each other as equals. Brandy wondered what bond they shared.

The wagon they were to travel in had been built for durability, not style, as had the matched pair of ponderous grays hitched to it. Brandy had a good idea of what the road was going to be like by looking at the equipage. She envied Mr. King, for there was a sleek black horse tied to the wagon, saddled and ready for him to ride. She wished she had worn her breeches instead of her civilized clothes, then she might have had a fighting chance of riding horseback part of the way.

She was amused by Ruth's reaction. With all of Ruth's luggage, her own trunk, and sacks of supplies, they did look like tinkers on the move, and Ruth's face showed clearly that she would have preferred a carriage and pair even for so short a trip. She lived in a trim white town house, and they stopped to let her out. Grey wanted to be at his own house by nightfall, so there was no question of tarrying. But Ruth made her position known.

She reached up and kissed Grey deliberately, and her voice carried to the wagon. "When will you be back, darling?" And Grey's answer must have pleased her, for she smiled and said, "I'll have your favorite supper ready."

Grey rode along beside the wagon. People hailed him now and then, and he paused courteously but made it clear that he had little time to spare. Brandy returned the curious stares she was getting with her own.

She was amazed by how swiftly the road changed. For some distance it was suitable for carriage travel, but soon it degenerated into a track of connecting ruts. Grey still rode beside them, but there was no conversation, and Brandy didn't find the silence offensive. She was concentrating on seeing everything while maintaining her seat on the hard planking of the wagon. After the civilization of the port, she was astonished by the wildness of the country. There were trees everywhere—maple, oak, spruce, and pine—making a quilt of autumnal color: the reds, golds, and yellows made more brilliant by the dark-green emphasis of the evergreens. There was an abundance of water; rivers, lakes, and the small threads of wetness on their path flashed silver in the sun. The land rolled from one hill to another, and here and there were solitary farmhouses, small patches of cultivated land stolen by endless toil from the woods.

The farther inland they went, the more puzzled Brandy became. For a seafaring family, the Kings certainly lived far from the sea. She asked Grey the question, turning to look at him as she did. Her voice trailed away, but he did not seem to notice. As the countryside had changed, so had his face. He looked ten years older, all traces of humor gone. His mouth was a rigid line, his words as mechanical as the steady beat of the dray horses' hooves.

"My great-grandmother lost her youngest son to the sea, and after his death, she wanted to be out of sound and sight of the tide. My great-grandfather built King's Inland for her the following year, in seventeen hundred and ninety. But he kept a house in Wiscasset, and my brother, Raleigh, lives there. The country is much too quiet for him. And now if you will excuse me, I will trust Rafe to deliver you safely."

He touched his hat politely. The great black horse sprang forward, and they were soon lost in the trees.

Brandy stared after him blankly. The change to cold formality had been so abrupt, the shutting down of all warmth so sudden. She turned to Raphael. "What in the world was that all about? I can understand how anxious he must be to see his child, but lordy, that wasn't a happy man who just rode off."

Raphael said nothing for a moment. The sunlight of his eyes regarded her intently. She felt him probing her mind, sorting through the impulses of her heart. She had never felt so open to judgment or cared so much about the verdict. Finally he spoke.

"You are to live in his house, you should know. That one, he has many demons with him, but always the most difficult is his child. She fears him above all things. She is a child of the silence, but when he is near, she cries out. He does not go often to her. I do not know what the infant thought she saw that night, but she has the fear of her father since then."

Brandy's heart beat loudly against her silence. Children saw things so clearly, judged so ruthlessly until they were taught that civilization required a certain blindness for survival. What if it had been Grey, what if the child had seen it—the deliberate murder of her mother by fire? That was the worst possibility of all, that fire had been used as a weapon. There was more savagery in that than in a gun or knife or even bare hands. Brandy knew. She had seen San Francisco in flames often enough to realize fully the horror of dying

that way. But Dr. George had said that Mr. Joly had
testified to Grey's innocence, so surely it was true.

Her courage flooded out of her, and she wanted to
ask him to take her back to the port; she would get
passage back to Boston somehow. But something stayed
her. "Why, damn you for a coward, Brandy Claybourne,
if it is true, then the child needs you more than ever."

Raphael reached over and patted her hand clumsily.
She had not realized she had spoken aloud. "It is good.
And this one, Rafe, he would like to be your friend," he
said, and urged the grays to a faster pace.

The sun was going down by the time they reached
King's Inland, and Brandy had been seeing everything
through a haze of weariness for the past hour. She
never wanted to sit on a wagon seat again; it was going
to be difficult to sit on anything comfortably for several
days. Not even the occasional herds of deer leaping the
track held any appeal for her now. But her first view of
the house enlivened her senses in an instant.

She didn't know what she'd expected, certainly not a
hovel, but not this magnificence either. Three stories of
elegant simplicity rose from the clearing at the end of
the treelined lane. Golden light flowed from the many
paned windows of the first floor. Even in the semidark-
ness, Brandy could see the richness of the exterior, the
weathered wood lovely in itself without the coats of
white paint which seemed the rule in Maine. To the
right and some distance from the house was the barn
with its two low-lying side wings which Brandy guessed
to be extra stalls for the horses Grey raised. The barn
and stables were glaringly new. Of course, the fire.
Brandy looked away.

Rafe broke the silence. "It is like a magic place, no?
And there is the enchanted princess. Perhaps you will
break the spell." A strange man this, Brandy thought.
He looked like the product of years of saloon brawls,
and yet his ways were gentle, his speech was courtly.

He pulled the wagon up to the front door, and
Brandy climbed down stiffly, thankful to stretch her

limbs. The door opened, flooding the entrance with light, silhouetting the woman who emerged. She was of medium height. Her gray hair was dressed neatly in a bun; her blue eyes sparkled with benign curiosity behind gold-trimmed spectacles; her tendency to plumpness eased the lines of sixty years or so. She took Brandy's hand in her own capable ones and greeted her.

"I am Mrs. Bailey, Grey's cook and housekeeper. Welcome to King's Inland." She regarded Brandy intently. "Well, my dear, you are younger than I expected, but perhaps that will be good for Missy." Her accent was of New England but did not have the peculiar Maine sound.

Rafe broke in. "Eh, that one, calling herself housekeeper, cook. She is *la châtelaine*. One must stay always on her good side, or it is great trouble. She has been here a hundred years, I think."

"Away with you," said Mrs. Bailey, flapping her apron at him. "Where is Grey? I thought he was coming in with you."

Rafe's face pulled, and he shook his head. "He came before us. I thought he would be already here. He must have need to be alone."

Mrs. Bailey sighed. "Well, poor man, he has problems enough to fret him. Come, Miss Claybourne, I'll show you your room so that you can freshen up, and then we'll have supper."

"Please, call me Brandy."

Brandy's laugh was cut off by a gasp as she got her first look at the interior of the house. She had never seen such opulence. The floors were of shining, inlaid wood with intricately patterned carpets spread here and there. There were beautiful pieces of furniture, and the woodwork of the house itself carried fantastic carved designs. Porcelain, jade, and sculpture in metals and stone rested on tables and behind the glass doors of cabinets. And yet the large rooms bore it all without being cluttered. It would take days to explore the whole house.

Mrs. Bailey smiled at her obvious wonder. "Sea captains are compulsive collectors, and this house holds almost eighty years of booty." She ran her hands lovingly over the wood of one of the cabinets.

Brandy was so busy catching glimpses of the rooms that she did not see the girl standing shyly at the bottom of the staircase until Mrs. Bailey introduced her. "Brandy, this is Persia Cowperwaithe. She lives with her family on a farm a few miles from here, but she comes in five days of the week to help me keep this place in order. Two people can scarcely do it all, but I prefer that to an army of servants who just clutter the place and break things."

Persia was not as tall as Brandy, but she was large-boned and well fleshed. Brandy guessed they were probably of an age. Persia looked as if she had been conjured out of the autumn woods. Her hair was a fiery tousle of red, her eyes were leafy green brown, and golden freckles ran over her fair skin. Her smile was wide and infectious, revealing white, slightly crooked teeth. She was intensely alive and sturdy-looking, conveying the impression that hard work and joy went together with no conflict.

"Persia, please show Brandy her room. I'll have supper ready in a trifle. Rafe can bring her trunk up when he has Grey to help him," said Mrs. Bailey, and Persia turned obediently to lead Brandy up the stairs.

She hesitated. "Shouldn't I meet Missy first?"

Both the faces took on that expression of sadness which Brandy already associated with any mention of the child. Mrs. Bailey shook her head. "No, tomorrow will be soon enough for that. She's asleep now, which is a blessing. Sometimes she lies for hours with her eyes open. It wouldn't do to wake her."

"No, of course not," agreed Brandy, following Persia up the stairs, but inwardly she was feeling more doubt-

ful than before. What had she got herself into? The
child didn't even sleep as other children did.

The staircase wound up and to the right from the
middle of the hall, and when they reached the second
floor, Persia explained which rooms were which. Brandy grinned to herself; Persia's accent, like that of the
schooner's crew, was so strange-sounding to her ears
that she had to listen very closely to understand.

There were seven rooms, three on each side of the
hall and one at the end, which was Grey's. Missy's room
was the center one on the right-hand side; Brandy's was
across from it. The house had been built to hold a large
family and many guests; on this floor alone there were
four unoccupied rooms. Persia explained that Mrs. Bailey had her own suite of rooms on the first floor, toward
the back of the house.

"And there's a whole floor above this one!"

"Yes, ma'am, but kept mostly shut an' used for storage an' such."

"Oh, Persia, please don't call me ma'am. It makes me
sound a hundred years old."

"Yes, ma'am," said Persia, and they both started to
laugh, trying not to make noise that would wake the
child.

Persia opened the door to Brandy's room, and Brandy gave a low whistle of pleasure. The room was large,
and in spite of the glow of several lamps and the fire
burning in the open hearth, there were shadows. But
she could see enough detail to be stunned that this was
to be hers. The walls were covered with Chinese
wallpaper patterned with pairs of brilliantly plummaged
birds. It was old, hand-painted, and had nothing in
common with the modern monotony seen in most
houses these days. Persia pointed out the owl—the only
bird without a mate—and explained that the paper fit
the saying "Love and beauty walk hand in hand, but
wisdom stands alone." Brandy felt an immediate affection for the lonesome little fellow staring saucer-eyed
from the wall.

The bed too was old-fashioned, huge and canopied in heavy yellow silk which matched the window draperies and one of the predominant colors in the wallpaper. The chair by the fireplace had side wings to screen the heat and was covered in lavishly embroidered figures of flowers, trees, and fantastic beasts.

The ample desk had ornately carved, curving legs and a chair to match, but what intrigued Brandy most of all was the traveling desk on top of it. Intricately inlaid with mother-of-pearl and the initials "M.K.," it had obviously been designed for a woman, yet it was larger than any she had ever seen. It must have belonged to someone whose correspondence had been widespread, whose household paperwork had been demanding even when she was away. Brandy lifted the lid and peeked inside. The drawers and pigeonholes were empty, though under the writing surface the bottom held an ample supply of creamy writing paper of the finest quality. A long rectangular space with a separate lid formed the back of the box and held steel pens, an inkwell, fine sand, and some old quills. As Persia put it, the house was "full o' other folks' things." She made it sound as if the previous generations of King's Inland had just stepped out for a stroll and would come collect their belongings later.

Everything gleamed with the evidence of good care, and the air smelled pleasantly of cedar, lavender, and burning wood. "It's heavenly!" exclaimed Brandy. "I can't believe I'm to stay here."

Persia smiled proudly, and Brandy knew she must have had much to do with getting the room in order. "Thank you, I can see your hand in this," she said, and the girl blushed with pleasure.

Then she said briskly, "There's water in th' pitcher if you're wantin' to have a wash. I'd better be along to help with supper."

"I'll hurry," Brandy promised.

She took off her bonnet, bathed her face and hands, and was brushing her hair back into some semblance of order when she heard a door shut softly in the corridor. She wouldn't have heard it at all except that her own door had been left ajar. She froze for a second, then gave herself a mental shake. What in the world was she so jumpy about? It was probably just Mr. King coming in. No, he would have made more noise than that; he wasn't the type to creep about in his own house. The child then. Brandy went into the hallway. There was no sign of anyone, and Missy's door was shut. She went and opened it carefully.

She was stunned. There was a lamp burning beside the bed, and she could see the child clearly. In all the things she had been told about her, no one had mentioned how beautiful Missy was. Her hair was sun gold, thick and curly. She was tiny for her age; everything about her was petite and exquisitely formed except her eyes. They were large and dark in her small face. Brandy's heart missed a beat. In color and shape, the eyes were Grey King's, but there the similarity ended. The child's eyes were absolutely blank, wide and seeming to be fixed on some object through and far beyond Brandy. Brandy was surely in her field of vision, but not by the slightest sign did the child betray that she saw her. It was far worse than looking into physically blind eyes. Brandy steeled herself against a nervous shudder. It must have been the child at the door; therefore, she could not be totally withdrawn if she had heard the voices and responded with curiosity.

Brandy went and sat on the bed, making no attempt to touch her. The eyes remained fixed. Brandy spoke slowly. "Hello, Missy, I'm Brandy. I've come to stay with you. I hope we'll be friends and that someday when you feel like it, you will talk to me."

She got no further. Missy's body did not stir, but something moved for an instant in her eyes, and she started to scream. Brandy whirled around, and there stood Grey. His voice was as expressionless as the eyes of his child had been. "I see you've met my daughter," he said, and walked out.

The piercing wail of terror tore at Brandy's heart. She knew she might make it worse, but she gathered Missy into her arms anyway, crooning to her and rocking the frail body gently. It was another thing outside her experience—the child's body remained rigid, her muscles not relaxing at all in response to being held. But some contact must have been made, for the screaming gradually died to whimpers, then ceased altogether. Either that, or simply having the object of fear gone was enough.

The weariness of the day washed over Brandy; she felt totally incapable, and when Persia appeared, saying that she would sit with the child until she slept, Brandy could have wept with relief. Persia insisted she go downstairs and get something to eat. "'Tis a bit much to take in all at once. Missy an' me, we get on all right. Don't fret. She'll be fine."

Grey met her at the bottom of the stairs, and she wanted desperately to reassure him, but she could think of nothing to say; Missy's behavior left no doubt about how she felt toward her father.

Grey spoke first, his voice oddly gentle. "I know better than to appear in Missy's room, but somehow I always think this time will be different, for once she won't be afraid. I have as many delusions as my child. Rafe and I had just brought your trunk up, and I wondered if you were with Missy."

They were in the dining room now, at the back of the house. It was connected to the kitchen by a pantryway, and Brandy could hear Mrs. Bailey moving around in the kitchen. Impulsively she put her hand on Grey's arm. "Don't worry. There must be a way to change her. And perhaps it is a good sign, though terribly difficult for you—at least she reacts to you; she doesn't seem to see me at all."

"Thank you," was all he said as Mrs. Bailey bustled in carrying a tray heavily laden with covered dishes.

Brandy moved to help her, but she refused. "No, this is my bailiwick. You looked starved to death and tuckered out anyway, wouldn't want you falling over and breaking the best china. Now sit."

Brandy laughed and did as she was told. The table would have seated twelve people easily; it looked bare with only three places set, but the candlelight from a pair of silver candelabra softened the scene. The walls were hung with tapestries, and the padded cushions of the chairs were covered in burgundy-red velvet. Brandy didn't think she would ever become accustomed to the richness of King's Inland. She felt very countrified in contrast with the grandeur.

"What about Persia and Rafe, won't they be eating with us?" she asked, thinking she would be very glad of their earthy presence.

Grey was much too quick; he read between the lines easily, and she knew he was aware of her reaction to her surroundings. "No," he said. "Rafe only comes under the pressure of formal occasions. He has his own cabin in the woods, and he guards his solitude fiercely. Persia was raised in this country, and she thinks nothing of walking home after dark. I've offered her the use of a horse, but she insists her legs are much more trustworthy than any beast's, and she is probably right. She likes to be with her family in the evenings. She'll probably be down soon and on her way." The shadows crossed his face.

Brandy knew she owed some explanation for being in Missy's room. "I really am sorry for all the fuss; I'm to blame. But the oddest thing happened—I heard a door shut in the hall, and I thought it was the child, so I went into her room. She was wide awake, so I told her who I am. It seemed hopeful. I mean, she was curious about the new arrival, so she can't be totally oblivious to what goes on, can she?"

She could not judge whether or not the small space of silence held any hope; if it had, it was overcome by doubt. "Brandy, we all want to believe, as you do, that there is a normal child hidden somewhere in Missy and that she peeks out now and then, but it is impossible that the noise you heard was caused by her. She does not go out of her room by herself," said Mrs. Bailey. "You must not get your hopes too high; the disappointment could be dreadful."

Grey nodded wearily in assent but said nothing. Brandy felt her temper rising and hoped it didn't show. How could the child ever improve if everyone around her accepted her as ill forever? Come on, Missy, come on, she pleaded silently, I'm sure it was you, and you know I'm here. Let's show them, let's show them soon!

But outwardly she shrugged and let it go, making a polite comment about the food which she could hardly taste because she was so weary. Persia stuck her head in briefly and bid them good-night. The only conversation at the table was between Grey and Mrs. Bailey concerning various problems at King's Inland. Late apples and early colts swam together in Brandy's mind, and her muscles protested the day's wagon ride. She was just considering going to sleep right there when Grey said, "Miss Claybourne, if there is anything I cannot bear, it is a pretty woman with blueberry pie on her forehead, and that is exactly what you are going to be if you fall asleep. You are excused."

She felt like a child, but she answered his smile with a rueful one of her own. Any humor he showed in this house was a good sign. He walked with her to the foot of the stairs.

"Unless you are an extremely early riser, I'll be gone when you awaken. If you need anything, ask Margaret or Persia. I've already given orders to Rafe that you are to be given a horse if you wish to ride. And there is a piano in the music room if you wish to use it. Good night and good luck."

He turned and left her. She was amazed by his memory for details, that out of the rush of his daily life, he had remembered she liked to ride and to play the piano. She was glad she had not followed a perverse impulse to ask him to give her best to Ruth.

She had a thousand things to ask, to think about, but

she considered none of them. She barely got her clothes
off and her hair down before she collapsed in bed and
fell asleep. She did not hear her door open or see the
small figure of the child watching from the shadows.

CHAPTER III

Brandy roused briefly in the predawn when she heard Grey come up to his room. She was vaguely satisfied that at least he was going to get a few hours of sleep, but he left again almost immediately. Poor man, she thought as she drifted back into sleep, he can't even rest peacefully in his own house.

When next she opened her eyes, it was to full sun and Persia peeking in the door, trying not to let the dishes of the breakfast tray rattle. "Oh, I'm sorry, I wasn't to waken you, but I reckoned you might be up an' hungry by now," she explained.

"Heavens, I am embarrassed! I've nearly slept the clock around, and now I'm being waited on. You shouldn't have let me be so lazy."

Persia shook her head. "You'd no choice, Mr. King's orders. He said you were to sleep as long as you might after yesterday's journeyin'."

"Is he still here then?"

"No. He left word with Mrs. Bailey last night. I expect he pried up the sun this morn."

"Oh," said Brandy, trying to sound surprised, unwilling to admit she had been so attuned to his movements. She patted the bed. "Can't you stay a minute? I've so many things to ask you."

Persia put the tray within Brandy's reach and sat carefully on the bed. As she did so, Brandy heard a soft

39

mew, and then two cats, one after the other, landed on the bed. "Why, you rascals, followed me right up, didn't you? Shall I put them out?"

"No, don't. They're lovely. Introduce me, please. I've never seen cats quite like these," said Brandy, staring at them. One was mottled white, orange and black, and the other had a lovely coat of soft gray faintly ringed.

Persia laughed. "Cats in the state o' Maine are more spoilt than th' children. Th' captains collected them an' brought them back like all th' other oddments from th' world. Th' spotted one, Tiger, she's a money-cat, an' they're always female. T'other, she's Iris, an' she's a coon-cat. Some say they come from wild coons an' house cats gettin' together, but I don't believe it. We've a tom here too, his name's Horace, but he don't like people much, 'ceptin' Rafe, so he's usually there." The way she said Rafe's name made Brandy glance at her quickly, and she saw the telltale flushing of the fair skin. Well, well, so that's the way the wind blows, she thought, but she didn't want to embarrass the girl by commenting on it.

"What about dogs?" she asked instead. She liked cats well enough, but she preferred dogs. "I didn't hear any bark when we arrived."

Persia's face fell, and Brandy knew before she spoke that it had something to do with the child. "Mr. King won't allow any on th' place, even though he fancies 'em himself. Missy's scairt to death of 'em." Her face brightened. "But we've quite a passel at our farm, an' one o' th' best bitches is fixin' to whelp any day now, so you can come there if you get lonesome for a good dog. I'd be pleased to have you meet my people anyway, if you've a mind to."

"I'd love to," Brandy said, but she wanted the talk to turn back to Missy. She was beginning to suspect that though the people of this region probably kept track of everything, they were disinclined to gossip with strangers. She approved, but she needed information. "Persia, what else is Missy afraid of and do you know why?"

Persia hesitated; then she shrugged hopelessly. "She's scairt o' so many things, you can't hardly keep track o' 'em. She's scairt o' goin' out o' her room, o' th' dark, o' th' outdoors, o' dogs. She hates things to be moved about, an' she's scairt o' fire, even in th' hearth, but most o' all, she's scairt o' her father. Now some o' that, like th' fire, that makes sense, but th' rest's beyond me."

Brandy wondered if she also thought Missy's fear of Grey was reasonable, but she knew she would not say. "How do you know about her being afraid, does she scream like she did last night?"

"No. She only screams when Mr. King's about," Persia said sadly. "For th' other things, she rocks an' stares. Sometimes it gives me th' collywobbles to watch her. You'd think she'd be tuckered out, but she just goes on an' on. An' th' oddest thing, there're things she should be scairt by, but she's not. She don't hear loud noises—you could drop th' roof in an' she wouldn't jump, an' she can stay in a cold room an' not seem to feel it at all."

Brandy stared pensively at a pair of birds on the wallpaper, her half-eaten breakfast forgotten. Persia saw her abstraction and was not offended by it. "I'd better be about my chores," she said, picking up the tray. "Missy's awake, so just go on in when you want, but try not to be too down-hearted by what you see."

Brandy brought her attention back for a moment. "Thank you. I'm awfully glad you're here." Persia's ready smile flashed, and she bobbed her head as she left the room.

Brandy dressed quickly, her mind whirling with what she'd been told. If so many of Missy's fears were unreasonable, could it not also be true that her fear of her father was equally unfounded? She sighed; she wished it was so, but she doubted it. The child's terror was so specific toward Grey.

When she went to the room, she found Missy sitting motionless on the floor. There were dolls and toys spread temptingly about, but not by the child. She did not play. Her hands were in a strange position—elbows out, wrists dropping, fingers curled uselessly.

Brandy settled down on the floor beside her. She began to talk, telling the child again who she was and why she was there. She changed the pitch and volume of her voice constantly so that Missy could not slip away easily from a monotonous sound. She kept at it for more than an hour, watching the little girl for any sign that she heard. There was none, and Brandy was exhausted. She made a rule for herself then. She must allow herself time away from her charge; otherwise she knew the lack of response would make her angry and frustrated, and that would be a victory for the child. She would be groping her way blindly toward helping Missy; she knew no sure methods, but some things she was already beginning to sense—the child had rigid control over what she saw, heard, and touched, and somehow that must be broken.

Brandy got up stiffly. "Missy, I'm going now, but I'll be back. I'll be back again and again because I want to help you."

There was no danger in leaving the child alone; she never did anything. As Brandy headed down the stairs, she met Persia coming up with a tray of food. The food was cut into small pieces and arranged precisely.

"Does she always eat in her room?" asked Brandy.

"Yes, an' always at th' same times."

"Does she feed herself?"

"I don't reckon so. I've left th' tray sometimes, an' once I thought she might've taken a mite on her own, but I couldn't tell for sure. You see, she don't seem to get hungry, but she'll open her mouth an' eat a little when I feed her."

Brandy continued down the stairs mulling this over. To her it was one more example of the child's control, and this too had to be changed. She wondered if they had ever let the child go hungry enough so that her body would compel her to eat.

On her way outside she saw Mrs. Bailey, who was busy polishing a cabinet in the hall. She offered to help, but the housekeeper shooed her out. "I'll call on you if I need help, but I'm terribly fussy about the treasures in my charge. If anything's to happen to them, I'd better be to blame. Not that I'd judge you clumsy," she added. "But with the burden you've taken on, you're going to need all the free time and fresh air you can manage. Go explore the grounds and get Rafe to show you the horses. Grey said you are a good rider." She said it with no hint of mockery, so Mr. King must not have told her about the disgraceful race—that was thoughtful of him.

The day was perfectly golden, and she skipped a little as she walked. She saw the flower beds in front of the house. They were bare of blossoms now but would be beautiful in the spring, she guessed, for gardens seemed to be important in Maine. All the houses they had passed the day before, even the most isolated ones, had had pots solely for flowers. Nice to know that Maine women considered beauty as essential as food.

She found the spring- and smokehouses and the vegetable garden in the back, finished save for the bright pumpkins and plump ears of corn yet to be harvested. Beyond it lay the brown stubble of a hayfield, a small orchard, and then the woods. She marveled again at the pervasiveness of the forest, guarding its darkness, surrounding every patch of cleared land which had been wrested from it. She could see a path leading from the field into the trees, and she looked forward to following it. She liked the wildness of the growth and wanted to see the creatures whose voices drifted to her from the shadows. But first she wanted to see the horses.

She found Rafe cleaning out stalls. His eyes brightened in welcome, and he was happy to take her on tour, obviously proud of his domain. He had a right to be; the horses were beautifully groomed, their tack meticulously kept. The center part was the true barn, high-ceilinged with a long loft piled with hay over several box stalls. Chickens scratched and chuckled in the hay. There were five additional stalls in each of the two wings connected to the barn. And behind the building was a paddock where the horses could be exercised. Brandy inhaled the sweet hay and warm horseflesh smell with delight.

There was one cow which supplied King's Inland dairy needs, and there were five horses in addition to Pete and Polly, who had pulled the wagon. Two of the five were yearling colts in training. That left three—Prince Lucky, Tally, and Lady—to choose from for riding. The only horse which was off limits was Orpheus, Grey's stallion, but in any case, he was usually gone as now with Grey.

Brandy looked the three over carefully. They were all magnificent, long-legged, satin-coated, high-strung aristocrats of their species. She chose Lady without hesitation. Lady was a chestnut, a little larger than the other two, but just as finely built. Brandy appreciated all the points of her confirmation, but she chose the horse for a certain look in her eyes. They were large, wide-set, and gentle, but there was just enough mischief gleaming in them to make Brandy want to try her. She told Rafe she'd go riding the next morning and asked him what she ought to expect.

"She is good, but she has only three years, so sometimes she plays as a child. But already you have seen that, no?" Brandy smiled and nodded, and Rafe continued, "Now, for the jumping, she is agreeable to it but in that still an infant. She needs more working to make the grand ones. Go carefully, yes?"

Brandy agreed, and they went on talking as Rafe led her out and around to the back where the two colts were playing in the paddock. Brandy settled herself contentedly on the warm, stubbled grass, and Rafe sat beside her.

"I thought Mr. King raised a lot of horses. Are these all he has?"

Rafe gave a deep chuckle. "All here? Oh, no, there are many more in other places, more south and warmer with more persons for training. And at the finish of the summer, we have sold many that were here, fat on the fine grasses. Not that the winter here is too bad," he amended hastily. "It is not as in the north." Brandy saw the sudden tightening of his muscles as he said it—a winter in the north and the north country itself, something that had happened there? She did not know him well enough to ask. Instead she questioned him about Missy.

"Rafe, was the little child normal when you first came? Did she like the outdoors?"

Whatever his other thought had been, it vanished in his concern for the child. "Like the butterfly she was beautiful, laughing, dancing, running every place, as from flower to flower, fearing nothing. Like that I knew her for a short time before the fire. Often I would take her with me on the horse, and she had not fear, only joy."

Brandy swallowed the lump in her throat. The way Rafe spoke English made everything sound strangely beautiful and profound. How deeply he had loved the child, and this too Missy had relinquished.

Brandy thanked him and walked back to the house, going straight up to Missy's room. The child was in the same spot, and she wondered if she had moved at all. She went patiently to work again. She quit when her voice began to get hoarse. Nothing stirred in the blank eyes.

That night after supper Mrs. Bailey invited Brandy in for tea in her rooms across the hall from the dining room, and Brandy liked what she saw. Mrs. Bailey had a sitting room and a bedroom, both of ample proportions. The quarters provided her with some privacy as there was a back room leading outside. She smiled softly in remembrance as she pointed out the special conveniences of her apartment.

"Mr. King, the boys' father, hired me and brought me

to this house to be housekeeper and companion for his wife more than forty years ago. The grandparents were still living then, too, and all four of them, the old and young people, were people of strong character. Mr. King knew that, and he wanted me to have some life of my own, so he gave me these rooms and declared them off limits to the family. No one was allowed to trouble me here, and I was most grateful. I was only twenty when Mr. King hired me, but I was already a widow; I had lost both my husband and my baby son. They died of typhoid fever."

"Oh, I'm so sorry!" exclaimed Brandy, knowing the words were inadequate but at a loss for others.

"It was a long time ago, and the Kings gave me a new life, a new family. When Grey and later Raleigh came along, it was as if they were my own boys, though I must admit Grey wanted no confusion about it. He used to tell visitors, 'This is not my mother, but she takes good care of me.' I think he felt some sort of misguided pity for his mother when in fact, Mrs. King was glad to have help raising them; she was frail, and they both had more than a touch of high spirits and mischief in them."

As Brandy sipped her tea, Mrs. Bailey showed her some of her special treasures—pieces of ivory, jade, porcelain, and silver given her by the generous Kings of several generations. But it was a much humbler article which caught Brandy's interest. It was difficult to imagine Grey as a child, even when she held the tiny ship carved from a single piece of wood and initialed "G. K." There was something vulnerable about the patient care which had been lavished on the figure. She shifted her mind away from the inexplicable sadness it gave her.

"Does Raleigh ever come here?" she asked.

Mrs. Bailey's face lighted with joy. "My, yes, he does. I give him a good scolding when he stays away too long. But Grey and he don't get along at all. It's just one of those things. So he only comes when Grey is gone." She explained it with complete acceptance that sometimes brothers did not feel the blood bond, but Brandy wondered how much the estrangement had to do with Grey's wife.

She rose to go. "I've taken up enough of your time, but I do thank you for showing me everything. And now, if it won't disturb you, I would like to try the piano."

"Disturb me? Mercy, no! The music room is clear in the front. Besides, it will be nice to have music in the house again. Come along, I'll show you the room, and tomorrow I'll take you on a full tour."

As they walked down the hall, Brandy asked who used to play.

"Why, of course, you wouldn't know. Jasmine was the last one." Mrs. Bailey's voice held no rancor when she said the name. "I swear I don't think that girl could have baked a loaf of bread if her life had depended on it. She didn't do that sort of thing, but she could play the piano, dance, and ride, things like that. And she was good to Missy."

"It's awfully difficult to get any clear idea of what she was like," mused Brandy.

Mrs. Bailey opened the door to the room. "Maybe that will give you a better view." She pointed to a painting hanging on one of the walls.

The room was lovely, its gilt chairs exquisite, the piano magnificent, all of the decorative touches perfect. But nothing was as beautiful as the portrait of Jasmine King.

Brandy stared speechlessly at the image of Missy's mother. With the crinolined skirts of her time billowing around her, she looked like an exotic flower come to life. The fitted bodice of her dress accentuated her slim, yet sensuous figure, leaving her creamy shoulders bare. Her neck was long and slender, her face a perfect oval framed by the sunlit wealth of her hair, Missy's hair. Her eyes were enormous, their unbelievable violet-blue depths fringed by surprisingly dark, long lashes. The mouth was full, the lips slightly pouting. But despite its great beauty, there was nothing vapid about the face. There was a recklessness, a lurking mockery, and above all, a determination to have her own way in her expression.

Brandy had a sudden vision of the burning—the exquisite face distorted by pain, destroyed by flames—and she spoke quickly to erase it. "Was she really that beautiful? It seems impossible."

"No painting could do her justice, not even that one."

"No wonder Mr. King loved her!"

"Yes, any man would." There was no sarcasm in Mrs. Bailey's voice, only admiration.

"Did you get along with her?" she asked hesitantly.

"Well enough. Even though I have been in this house for a long time, I have no illusions about my position. The wife of the house is the first lady. Jasmine was. She was quite content to let me run the day-to-day business since she had no interest in housekeeping. When the child came, Jasmine didn't want me to have much to do with her, but that was all right, too. I was already getting too old to keep up with a youngster." Brandy made a gesture of protest, but Mrs. Bailey forestalled her. "No, that's the truth. Missy was so full of energy, I could not have kept track of her properly. How I wish she was still like that." She hurried on. "I expect Ruth Collins will be first lady soon, and that will be fine with me and good for Grey. The house needs a mistress."

Brandy had a better knowledge now of how much the house and the King dynasty meant to Mrs. Bailey, who had spent most of her life helping to keep both going. "Well, now," she said briskly. "I'll leave you to your music."

It gave Brandy an eerie sense to be in the room with Jasmine's portrait, as though she were not alone, as though the painting were a living presence. She shivered a little, imagining an echo of mocking laughter. Then she chided herself. In a way, the picture was a good sign; Grey had not destroyed all traces of his wife. She did not want to consider the idea that he might be punishing himself.

She pushed such thoughts away as she touched the piano. It was a wing-shaped grand some ten feet long. She recognized the famous name of Jonas Chickering of Boston. There was no finer piano to be had, and she was awed to be allowed to play it. Its tone was full and perfect; it had been kept in good tune.

She did not know how long she had played when her muscles finally protested enough to make her stop. She was tired and content as she rose, taking the lamp with her. She did not look at the portrait as she left.

She was halfway up the stairs when she heard them, light footsteps running down the hall, a door closing with a careful click.

It had to be Missy. Missy alone in the dark of the hall? Brandy moved as swiftly as she could carrying the lamp until she put it down impatiently and ran the rest of the way. A light was burning in Missy's room as always, and the child lay on the bed, eyes closed.

Brandy stood looking down at her, seeing the racing pulse beating under the thin skin at the base of the tiny throat, and was shocked by the swift impulse to anger which flowed through her. She wanted to shake Missy until the child had to cry out to her to stop.

She was instantly ashamed, and her voice was gentle as she sat down on the bed and gathered the tense body into her arms. "I know it was you; I heard you. Did you come out to hear the music? That was very brave. But I'll play for you anytime you wish. All you have to do is ask me." *Ask me, that's a good one! Missy, if you asked me out loud, in a real voice, to jump up and grab the moon for you, I'd try, and I'd be so happy, I just might be able to reach it.*

She continued holding her, talking to her, stroking the fair hair. The pulse slowed, and the slight relaxation of muscles, of which Brandy was already so aware, came, telling her the child was truly asleep.

She went wearily to her room, the peace of her music lost. She lay awake for a long while, wondering what had caused Missy to creep closer to the sound—was it because it reminded her of her mother or simply because the music pleased her?

She awakened once to find she had slept so restlessly that she had pulled the pillow over her face and tangled the bedclothes. She fell back to sleep still fretting over Missy.

By the next morning she had decided several things. First she met Persia bringing up Missy's breakfast. She held out her hands for the tray. "Please, I'd like to take over feeding her, if you don't mind."

Persia's eyes filled, but she handed the tray over obediently. Brandy hastened to reassure her. "Please, don't look like that. It isn't because of anything you've done. I know how patient and good you are with her. It's just that I want to get as close to her as I can. If I'm to do her any good at all, she's got to recognize me as an important part of her world. And eating is pretty basic for all of us, even Missy, I suspect."

Persia's face cleared. "Well, just look at me, won't you? Here I am going green an' tetchy over such a thin'. I surely can use th' extra time to redd up this house. But you call on me sometimes, if you're too busy, won't you?"

"I certainly will," Brandy assured her, loving her for her concern for the child.

Missy, already neatly dressed by Persia, was sitting in her usual spot on the floor. Brandy looked at the snowy fabric of her dress, the gleaming gold of her hair, everything so still and doll-like. She nearly laughed aloud at herself; here she was hoping for the day when Missy would be dirty and mussed from playing, a state most governesses abhorred in their charges.

She settled down beside Missy. She couldn't tell exactly what it was, but something warned her that Missy was aware of the change in her schedule and resented it. "Persia and I are going to take turns, darling," she explained, holding out the first morsel of food.

Missy's action surprised Brandy so that she nearly dropped the fork. Her hand came up, and Brandy thought for a moment she was going to strike her, but instead she held her hand in front of her face and started flicking her fingers. Brandy stared at her, at the relentlessly mechanical motion of the fingers, at the dark eyes fixed on them, and she realized that the child must feel the need for an added barrier against her.

"No, Missy, don't do that," she commanded, reaching out and taking hold of the hand. The flexing continued in her grasp, and she knew that she had done the wrong thing—Missy was winning the point, for as soon as Brandy let go, the hand would screen the little face again. She let it happen, and then she brought her own hand up in front of her face, copying Missy's actions exactly. She could hardly breathe, so desperately did she want to win the battle of the wills.

It worked. Missy's hand dropped to her side. So Missy was normal in this. Brandy had learned in her teaching experience that children hated the ridicule of being imitated; she had seen her younger students do it to each other, often to the point where she had to intervene before someone got a bloodied nose.

For the first time, the strange eyes were looking directly at her, with anger or hate, she didn't care which. She offered the bit of food again. Missy's mouth opened, and she took it. Brandy was amazed at the wild rush of blood she felt from such a minor victory.

She was still beaming when she handed the tray to Persia downstairs. Persia grinned back at her. "I'm so glad it went well, on th' first try, too! Mr. King will be pleased."

"Oh, is he coming back so soon?" Brandy tried to keep the anxiety out of her voice; she wanted to have much more than this morning's work to show him when he returned.

Persia understood. "No, I don't know when he'll be

back, but don't you worry, you're doin' fine with Missy. Little things mean so much with a child like that one."

When Brandy arrived at the stables, Rafe took one look at her face and said, "So it is a good morning?" He eyed her trousers with approval. "Better than a dress. Now you will not need the foolish lady's saddle."

He readied Lady for her and gave her a leg up. She asked about riding in the woods, and he said it was fine as long as she kept to the trail and did not lose her bearings.

Lady snorted and shied playfully. Brandy reined her firmly, speaking to her quietly, letting the mare know her rider could be trusted. Rafe nodded. "I will not fear. It is well between you."

She waved her thanks as she rode off. They crossed the meadow and entered the woods, and Brandy drew breath at the beauty. Sunlight fell in delicate patterns through the gold and red leaves; the singing of the birds surrounded her, and she inhaled the sharp pine scent until she knew the farthest boundaries of her lungs. Lady was willing and obedient, and Brandy let her canter on the smooth parts of the trail. She took a slight detour on a well-trod path and discovered the tidy little cabin which had to be Rafe's. He took great care of his place; everything was in repair, and neatly cultivated land surrounded the building.

She went back to the main trail and found a lovely little pond deep in the woods. It would be a good place to bring Missy someday. A herd of deer, startled by her approach, escaped in graceful leaps as she watched with pleasure. She found a couple of low log falls and tested Lady's jumping ability and judged Rafe's opinion to be correct—with patience and practice the mare could be trained to be a fine jumper. She felt utterly content by the time she turned the horse for home, keeping her at a slow pace to match her own dreaming state.

Lady's start and her snicker of welcome jolted Brandy out of her daze. Another rider was coming down the trail. Grey King on a big bay. Where was Orpheus? She raised her hand in greeting, then dropped in confusion as he came closer. His grin was wide and mischievous; all the same features were there, but much more lightly drawn on the youthful face. Brandy blinked and stared.

"Sorry to disappoint you," he said, tipping his hat to her, "but my big brother is still in town, so I thought I'd sneak out to meet the new addition to the household. I'm Raleigh."

His dancing black eyes took in everything about her at a glance. "My, my, I thought you must be special; the fair Ruth turns green at the mere mention of you. But special is hardly adequate. My brother is becoming a connoisseur in his old age. I must congratulate him."

She knew she ought to be insulted, but Raleigh's gaiety was infectious. She shook her head in mock disapproval. "Are you always so full of flattery? That has to be some of the worst nonsense I've ever heard!"

"My dear Brandy—Miss Claybourne is too formal—you wound me. I am a sincere fellow driven to flowery speech by your surpassing beauty."

They laughed and chatted all the way back like lighthearted children. Raleigh was so easy to be with that Brandy could not get over the contrast in personalities between him and his brother, made so much more noticeable by the physical similarities. It gave her a strange sense of double vision, as though she were looking into Grey's face of ten years ago.

When they got back to the stables, Brandy was startled by Rafe's reaction to Raleigh. He was polite and willing to take care of Casco, Raleigh's horse, but his manner was distant, all light in his eyes extinguished. *Why*, thought Brandy, *he's so protective of Grey that he resents Raleigh's even being here, or maybe for being with me*. She felt a faint flicker of fear in a sudden new thought—as gentle as Rafe might be in most things, she had no doubt that he would be savage in defense of Grey. She suppressed a shiver; fanaticism in any form was dangerous.

If Raleigh's reception at the stables was cool, it was

not so at the house. Mrs. Bailey heard them come in, and her face was joyous as she came down the hall. Raleigh lifted her right off her feet and kissed her, leaving her blushing like a young girl as she tried to make her voice angry. "You incorrigible boy, I'll have you remember that I am a dignified old woman!"

"Not my Margaret, not if I can help it."

"It's no use," said Mrs. Bailey, "he's been like this since he was born, even with all my efforts to bring him up right."

She prepared a light meal for them, and Brandy ate hers quickly and left to take Missy's tray up despite Raleigh's protest. She knew they wouldn't miss her. They were talking rapidly and laughing when she left, obviously old favorites with each other.

Her morning's victory held; Missy ate without any problem. Brandy set the tray aside and talked to her about her ride and what she'd seen.

She was interrupted by Raleigh saying from the doorway, "Mind if I come in and say hello to my niece?" There was nothing to say since he was already coming toward them. Brandy could see no change in Missy, but her own body was tense, and she realized she wanted Missy to react to Raleigh as she did to Grey. Why? To show there might have been some mistake? She didn't understand her motives for wanting it.

But Missy did not oblige. She didn't scream or move when Raleigh picked her up and kissed her. "How's my little one, now that the nice lady has come to stay with you?" Brandy knew he expected no answer, but she was touched by the kindness in his voice. She put away the wish that it was Grey instead of Raleigh holding the child.

When she came down for dinner, she was pleased to learn that Raleigh was staying for a few days. She was too honest to deny that his company gave her pleasure.

After the meal, Mrs. Bailey and Raleigh took her on the promised tour of the house. There were endless cabinets of silver, gold, porcelain, jade, and ivory. There was a collection of tiny, fully rigged ship models representing every vessel built by the Kings. Brandy recognized the *Isabella* with delight and could almost see a tiny figure on deck, Grey looking out to sea. And even the pieces of furniture were by famous makers, proudly listed by Mrs. Bailey. Brandy recognized some of the names—Chippendale, Sheraton, and Hepplewhite—but she felt very ignorant as Mrs. Bailey elaborated on the different joints, finishes, and woods used to make the articles, touching each piece as gently as if it were a beloved child.

Treasure after treasure passed before Brandy's eyes until she was dizzy with the richness of it all. Without stopping to think, she asked impulsively, "Do you ever mind being the second son, not having King's Inland for your own?" She gasped as the rudeness of what she'd said assailed her. "Oh, I am so sorry! What a dreadful thing to say!"

Raleigh smiled easily. "Don't be embarrassed. It's a fair question, and I like your directness. No, I don't mind at all. What would I do with this lot except gawk at it as we are now? And being second relieves me of a lot of responsibility. I don't want to be old and grim before my time, like Grey. Besides, Margaret has always spoiled me terribly, probably to make up for it. It has its compensations."

"You are a wicked young man," chided Mrs. Bailey.

"Can't help it, all second sons are, you know, way they're raised," he teased, but Brandy suspected that her question had hurt more than he admitted, especially since the formidable Mrs. Bailey's eyes rested on him with such troubled intensity. It made her feel guilty, and she was especially nice to him for the rest of the evening.

CHAPTER IV

Brandy had to curb her tendency to do everything too fast in her dealings with Missy, but her knowledge that the child did leave her room at night gave her courage for the next part of her plan. Missy's lack of response except for terror had gradually defeated everyone so that they allowed the child to keep to the safe prison of her room. Brandy thought it was one of the unhealthiest things of all, and she wanted it changed immediately. It was Saturday, one of Persia's days off, and Raleigh was taking Mrs. Bailey out for a ride in the wagon to visit some of the farms, so only Rafe would be around. That suited Brandy perfectly. In case of a disaster, she did not want extra spectators.

Despite the frosty mornings, the Indian summer still held and softened the edges of the days, and Brandy couldn't wait to be outdoors. And so when Missy had finished eating, Brandy picked her up. She was so slight that her weight was easy to carry; only the rigidity of her body made it difficult. "I know you go out of your room sometimes, so now you're going to go out with me. It's time you saw the sun again."

The trembling didn't begin until Brandy had carried her down the stairs. She steeled herself against giving in to it; it was pathetic—the little body quivered in her arms as if touched by deadly cold. When she finally got outdoors with her burden, she felt as if her own teeth must be chattering from mere contact, but she didn't put Missy down until they were out by the paddock where the two colts were already busy teasing each other. She settled herself and the child on the ground, keeping her arm around her. The cats ran up, mewing for attention, and Tiger rubbed against Missy. The child did not reach out to touch the animal, but it did not seem to add to her fright.

The shivering slowed, then stopped altogether. Missy's eyes had been tightly shut since Brandy had picked her up; now they opened and Missy's head turned slightly. Brandy nearly crowed aloud with delight. The colts were in the child's line of vision, and Brandy knew she was seeing them, really seeing them, not looking through to some invisible point beyond. Brandy sat very still, watching every small movement which told of new things being looked at, one by one.

She heard a step and looked up to find Rafe staring at them, mouth open in amazement. Missy gave no sign that she was aware of him, and he recovered quickly. He sat down beside Brandy. "It is a beautiful day to be under the sky. I am glad to see you, my little friend." Just that, nicely said. Brandy could have kissed him for it—no mention of the long time past, no demands on the child. They sat for a good while, Brandy and Rafe talking about the animals, not letting Missy's silence become their own.

Finally, Rafe excused himself to go back to work, and Brandy said to Missy, "We'd better go in now, too. I am too tired to carry you. Will you walk, please?" Gently she stood the child upright and then put out her hand. Nothing was offered in return, but when she took hold of the small hand, it was not withdrawn, and when she started off, Missy walked stiff-legged and clumsy but obediently at her side.

So much had been accomplished that Brandy nearly lost her nerve for the next step, but it was important to try it while Persia was gone—Persia was so tender-hearted that she would suffer more than the child.

Brandy brought Missy's midday meal up and set it before her, explaining firmly, "Missy, I fed you breakfast. People have been feeding you like a baby for a very long time, but I want it to stop. You are five years old, and I know you can feed yourself. I'm going to leave this; eat what you want." She left quickly because she felt if she looked one second longer at the frail body, she would go right back to hand-feeding the child.

She found she didn't want anything to eat at all. *You are as bad as Missy,* she accused herself, and tried not to feel so anxious. When she went back to get the tray, it had not been touched. "All right," she said, picking it up, "you are probably not hungry now, but perhaps you will be by supper time."

Apart from another talking session with Missy, she spent the afternoon writing letters to the Adamses and to Pearl, and she was very happy to hear Mrs. Bailey and Raleigh coming in. She went down to meet them. Raleigh eyed her and said, "We had a very nice day, but it doesn't look as if you did. You look like a fox caught in a hen house. What have you found to do around here that's as bad as that?"

Brandy laughed louder than she meant to, but her protest was sincere. "No, I've had a marvelous day!" She told them about Missy's excursion, and after their first stunned disbelief and Mrs. Bailey's protest of "It can't be!" they were properly joyous. She didn't mention her experiment with Missy's eating, and she had to fight the wild impulse to say, "Oh, yes, and I'm seeing if I can get her to eat by herself. I'm starving her."

When she took Missy her supper, she repeated her earlier words. The eyes did not flicker; the body rocked slowly, steadily. She knew what she would find when she went back for the tray. She looked at the untouched food, then at Missy. "I know you can do it, I know you can, if not for your hunger, then for mine because I am not going to eat until you do. So if you care about me at all, you will do as I ask. We'll try again tomorrow."

Out in the hall she fed bits of the meal to Tiger and Iris. She had let them follow her up; she could see how cats could come in handy sometimes. She did not want Mrs. Bailey to see the full tray.

It wasn't difficult to refuse food at supper; she wasn't hungry. She felt as if she could go for days, but Missy couldn't, not tiny Missy.

When Mrs. Bailey asked if she was feeling all right, she laughed and said she certainly was, so much so that she'd been an awful pig when she made her midday meal. Raleigh was skeptical and teased her about being lovesick. In truth, she did feel a little feverish with anxiety about whether or not she was doing the right thing. She was relieved when they asked her to play the piano. Her music had always brought instant escape, but now as she played, it was difficult not to think of a hungry little girl huddled at the head of the stairs, listening.

And when she finally slept, it was to wake again tangled in the bedclothes and feeling suffocated—a strange thing since she usually slept so quietly. Work with Missy was taking its toll of her, she admitted as she tried to sleep again. But another thought struck her, and she sat bolt upright. Now that she was more fully conscious, she thought she remembered hearing her door click shut just as she had awakened. She crossed her room swiftly, yanked the door open, and looked up and down the hall. There was no one there. She shrugged and went back to bed. Waking from bad dreams often leaves one unsure of what is fantasy, what is truth.

Breakfast brought no change. Iris and Tiger ate well. Brandy looked at Missy and sighed, amazed she could still be rocking. "I am sure you're hungry by now; I know I am. We'll try again midday."

She skipped the morning session with the child,

hoping the solitude would make her hungrier. She went for a ride with Raleigh, feeling light-headed and reckless, drawing repeated warnings from him about going too fast and trying impossible jumps. She settled down only because she might endanger Lady.

Raleigh was puzzled by her behavior, but his only comment was: "I thought you had some bee in your bonnet, but it seems to be a granddaddy hornet instead."

By the time she took the next meal to Missy her hands were shaking so that she could hardly carry the tray. It had to work; she had to win, but she couldn't go on this way much longer—Missy's control might be enough to bring death by starvation.

She put the tray down before the child without hope and turned to go. The clink of silver on china turned her unbelieving eyes. Not with her fingers but with the calm precision of a longtime use of tableware, Missy was feeding herself.

Brandy swallowed her tears and made her voice steady. "That's very, very good. I knew you could do it. Thank you. Now I can eat, too. I'm awfully hungry."

Of course, Missy paid no attention to her, but Brandy was completely satisfied, watching the competent movement of the small hands. When Missy had finished, Brandy kissed her. "I am so proud of you. How I love you!" The rocking was not resumed.

Her relief that the battle was over and won left her bemused, and she was not aware of the voices until she reached the bottom of the stairs; then the words broke over her in an angry wave. Grey was home.

He was facing Raleigh in the hall. His whole stance was one of violence barely restrained. "Can't you ever do a man's job? You were supposed to be there when the *Lisbeth* docked. You knew that. Instead I find you in my house, amusing yourself with my servants. Now get out!"

Neither heard Brandy's outraged gasp.

Raleigh grinned mockingly at his brother, and his voice was lazy. "There are plenty of other men there to check in the cargo; another useless job to keep me occupied, wasn't it, big brother? Bit possessive of your belongings, aren't you? Guess I would be too if I had such good taste in governesses."

The tray crashed to the floor, startling both men, and before she knew what she was doing, Brandy was between them screaming, "Stop it, stop it! You're behaving like horrid, hateful children. And I belong to no one!" She had a glimpse of their stunned faces before the world tipped crazily and the light whirled away.

She was aware of the rough weave of Grey's coat; that was nice, he must have caught her as she fell. He was carrying her. She looked up into his white face. "Well, I'll be damned," he said.

"I'm sure you will. Now put me down!" snapped Brandy, remembering the scene that had caused all this.

Grey placed her carefully on the sofa in the drawing room. His anxious, guilty expression made him look momentarily younger, more like Raleigh. Raleigh was hovering in the background. They reminded Brandy so much of ten-year-old boys caught in a prank that she had to smile.

Grey's face eased. "That's better. You are not the sort of woman I would have thought suffers from the vapors, even though I've heard it's fashionable. Do you faint often? May I get you some whiskey?"

"No to both. I never faint, well, never until now, and the last thing I want is whiskey. It was hunger, not fashion, which caused that bit of idiocy."

His eyebrows rose in bewilderment. "You certainly don't wish to be any thinner than you are?"

Brandy laughed ruefully; he had none of Raleigh's talent for a compliment. But then her joy in Missy's progress welled up again, and the words tumbled out in explanation.

When she had finished, she saw incredibly that his face was not nearly as pleased as she had expected. It was more than a little angry. "That," he said, "was a very foolish thing to do."

"Oh, I know it was a risk, but I had to try it. I wouldn't have let any harm come to her, you know that, don't you?"

"I'm not talking about Missy. I would agree to anything which would help her. But for you to go hungry on her account is beyond my understanding."

"Don't you see, I promised!"

He eyed her curiously. "Did it never occur to you that she would not have known?"

"That would have been dishonest. Promises I make, I keep. But you're missing the whole point. I think she really cares about other people. I think she finally fed herself for my sake, not for her own. That means she is still capable of feeling something besides terror, of loving."

Grey's face was old again. He shook his head wearily. "I think it means the child finally got hungry enough to do something about it. But I am, of course, pleased with her progress, whatever the motives. And I apologize for my behavior with my brother." He looked around for Raleigh, but there was no sign of him, and Grey shrugged. "We don't see eye to eye. My words about servants were unforgivably rude, but I ask your pardon anyway."

Brandy smiled at him as she stood. "Apology accepted because if this goes on any longer, I never will get anything to eat."

Grey smiled back at her, but it never reached his eyes. She had a sudden lonesome wish for Raleigh's blithe presence.

Brandy would not have mentioned it, but Grey told Mrs. Bailey what had happened, adding that she'd better keep an eye on Miss Claybourne, who seemed unable to take care of herself. Before Brandy could make a nasty retort, Mrs. Bailey said, "I think she's quite capable. Just think, she managed to do what I've been trying to accomplish for years—she ended one of your dreadful rows. It would be so much simpler if you boys got along." Grey's mouth tightened, but he said nothing.

Mrs. Bailey asked Brandy to play the piano again that night, saying that she was getting quite spoiled by having music so readily available once more. She led the way to the music room, and Brandy hesitated, putting her hand out to stop Grey. "If you'd rather I didn't play, I can say I'm still feeling too wobbly." She didn't know how else to approach the subject, but her meaning was clear to him.

"You take me for more of a sentimentalist than I am, Miss Claybourne. My wife played the piano, rode horses, danced, and did many other things. I still enjoy all of them." His voice was calm, but his expression was grim, and Brandy wondered how he could bear to have the picture of Jasmine in his sight.

There was no easy slipping away with Grey present. Brandy was acutely conscious of him sitting where he could watch her hands. He could also see the portrait. She could not resist stealing occasional glances at him as she played, nor could she deny the feeling of triumph when she saw his absorption in the sound, the easing of his guard. She played well, her fingers finding the keys not only without fault but with passionate conviction, offering the best she could without knowing why it was so important.

She didn't know what warned her—it was like picking up the small changes in Missy—and she played the English suite to the end without faltering. But she saw it all—the sudden shifting of Grey's eyes to the painting, the mocking lift of his eyebrows, the twist of his mouth, his whole sardonic salute, as though he had said aloud, "All right, Jasmine, you have reminded me; I cannot forget."

Brandy felt sick, as if she had been spying on an intimate scene between lovers. She rose after the last note. "Thank you for your patient listening. I must go to bed now; it has been a long day. Good night." She was thankful for the steadiness of her voice. She left swiftly, hearing Mrs. Bailey's words trailing behind her. "She does look worn out. It was thoughtless of me to ask her to play tonight." Brandy did not hear Grey's reply. Instead, as she made her way without a lamp, she heard the sounds of Missy in the darkness, deserting her post, scurrying down the hall, shutting the door.

She was very desperate to sleep, but every time she shut her eyes she saw Grey and Jasmine, mocking, hating, loving each other. She concentrated on the night sounds. A loon's hysteria rose to meet the chuckling bark of a fox. She did not hear Grey come up to his room, and in the morning he was gone. He had only come to King's Inland because he knew Raleigh was there. But even so, his precise attention to details had not faltered. Mrs. Bailey told her he had taken her letters to start them on their separate journeys.

Persia was late, but when she arrived, she was in even better spirits than usual. The new puppies had arrived that morning, and she had tarried to make sure the bitch was all right. "Five little ones she had, all perfect. Now, you'll have to come visitin' right soon, so you can see 'em while they're wee." She thought a minute. "How 'bout tomorrow afternoon? I could finish early, an' we could get Rafe to take us in th' wagon. Then you could both stay to supper."

Brandy hid her amusement; she guessed how much Persia wanted Rafe to be included in the plan. It was fine with her, but she hesitated, not wanting to leave Mrs. Bailey out. The housekeeper saw her doubt. "Don't go mothering me! I've been in this house more than double the years you've been alive. And I'm perfectly capable of giving Missy her evening meal, especially now."

Persia's puzzlement turned to incredulous pleasure when she heard about Missy's accomplishments. Her laughter and tears were in what she termed "a regular tangle."

Later, when Brandy carried the child down the stairs

again, Persia had control enough to say, "Good morning, Missy," as though it were normal for her to be out of her room.

As soon as they were outside, Brandy put the child down and took her hand. She seemed less awkward than she had the day before, but Brandy realized she was setting her steps toward the stables. Even this Missy was trying to form into a pattern. There was a moment of resistance when Brandy resolutely started in the direction of the orchard behind the house, but then Missy started to walk again. When they had settled down beneath an apple tree, Brandy took Missy into her lap, cuddling her, talking, and singing nonsense rhymes. By the time she was ready to take her back to the house she thought she could feel a slight bending of the body to fit her own.

The next day she made her walk from her room and was amazed that there was no problem. The stairs were awkward for her; she went down them with infinite care, making sure that both feet were firmly planted on one step before she tried the next, but as far as Brandy was concerned, she could take all day if she wished, as long as she kept going. Beyond a slight hesitation as they passed the door to the music room, Missy did not even protest walking through the house. And she made no attempt to determine the direction of their walk, apparently accepting the fact that it would be different and Brandy would decide. Brandy's heart was singing as she led Missy into the beauty of the woods, and she enjoyed every minute of their time there.

Persia finished her chores at three, and Brandy went to see Missy before they left. She checked at the doorway, wondering what was different, and then it hit her. Many of the dolls, books, and various toys so long untouched had been moved. She was so attuned to this room that she could see clearly that things had been picked up, and though there had been some attempt to put them back in their usual places, either the time had been too short, or in the excitement of touching them, Missy had forgotten how they had been arranged. And as added proof, a brightly painted rocking horse still swayed back and forth slowly, as if a hand had given it a sly push.

Brandy had a moment of vicarious pleasure, of knowing what it must be like to touch all sorts of different objects, to feel the various shapes and textures after so long a time of nontouching, of dead hands. Her eyes flew to Missy's hands. The fingers were no longer curled; the wrists no longer dropped; the strange bend of the elbows was gone. The hands rested naturally in her lap.

Brandy swooped her up in her arms, laughing her joy and telling her how marvelous she was. She hated to leave her after such a discovery, but Persia's family was expecting them, so she explained carefully, telling Missy that Mrs. Bailey would bring her supper but that she, Brandy, was going away only for a short while. She hoped Missy understood, but her reaction wasn't encouraging; her body was rigid again as though ice had suddenly frozen where blood had flowed.

Brandy was quiet for most of the wagon ride, disinclined to mention the latest developments until she understood them better herself. She knew what was happening was good, but also one-sided. Missy was reestablishing contact with objects but only indirectly with people. At least she made no violent protest to being touched. Brandy sighed and brought her mind back into focus. Rafe and Persia had not minded her lack of attention; they were engaged in a silence of their own. Rafe had been very polite and willing to be their driver, but Brandy could see the wariness in his eyes, the tenseness in his body, holding away as if afraid to touch Persia, who sat beside him. Through Missy, Brandy was learning a great deal about the ways a body could whisper and shout without uttering a sound. Persia's face was more open, anxious at Rafe's coldness but nonetheless blissful because she was with him.

They reached the Cowperwaithe farm in less than an

hour, but on foot it would have taken quite a bit longer. Brandy asked Persia in wonder, "Do you really hate horses so much that you'd rather walk all this way twice a day than ride?"

Persia grinned. "Well, that's part of it, though I always know Rafe'll give me a lift if I need it. But you see, things are lively in our house, an' my walkin' time is peaceful like."

As soon as she met Persia's family, Brandy could see her point. The house overflowed with cats, dogs, and children. Mrs. Cowperwaithe was short, round, red-headed, and energetic, a good thing seeing all she had to manage. Lean and lantern-jawed, her husband gave a first impression of dourness, but it was soon belied by the wry good humor in the far-seeing blue eyes. When Brandy complimented him on the beauty of the farm, he said, "It'll do till somethin' better comes along."

Persia's older brother, Ben, was a youthful copy of his father. Hank and Amos, the other two boys, were still in the toddler stage; what the family called "the gaggle of girls" came in between. Persia had two sisters, India and Ivory, both younger than she. Ivory, in spite of her name, was dark-haired and brown-skinned; India was another of the fiery-haired Cowperwaithes. The richness of the girls' names was another reminder of the legacy of a seafaring state.

The family greeted Brandy with diffidence but no servility. They were proud and warm, tempered into strength by their unceasing battle to wrest a good life from the unyielding ground.

Brandy duly admired the new puppies and stroked the head of the mother who seemed to think it her just due for a job well done. But it wasn't until she saw the outcast that the idea came to her. He was not a member of the new litter. He was past weaning but every once in a while he would wander hopefully over and try to creep in among the puppies until the bitch would send him away with a low growl and teeth bared. He was small and liver-colored with floppy ears and a potbelly.

He looked as if he were made of random parts of several breeds.

Brandy picked him up, and he snuggled gratefully against her. "Where did he come from?" she asked.

"Well, we aren't rightly sure," drawled Mr. Cowperwaithe, face straight, eyes dancing, "that's why we call him Mebbe, 'cos mebbe he's a dog, mebbe not. Th' others that came with him, they are dogs all right, an' we've given 'em all t'other farms. But him, well, we aren't extra-proud o' him, so runty he's a shame to th' family."

Brandy regarded him with admiration; she bet he could spin tall tales by the hours. She put the dog down and tried to put him out of her mind.

Time passed much too quickly. Brandy had a merry time, and even Rafe relaxed, helpless against the atmosphere of goodwill.

Brandy resisted almost until it was time to go, but then she picked Mebbe up again. "Please, may I buy him from you?"

"Nope, but you can sure have him so long as you don't let on where he came from," said Mr. Cowperwaithe.

"Thank you, thank you," she cried, hugging Mebbe. But she saw the doubt in their eyes; they knew about the no dog rule at King's Inland. "Don't worry. It will be fine. I'm sure it will. Missy needs something alive to have as her own. I don't think she'll be able to resist him."

"If it don't work out, just send him along home with Persia," said Mrs. Cowperwaithe practically.

The family saw Brandy and Rafe off, telling them to come by anytime. The lanterns hanging on the wagon cast shards of light, and Rafe kept the pace slow so that Pete and Polly wouldn't stumble. The creak and rumble of the wagon, the warm weight of the puppy asleep on her lap, and the quiet man beside her filled Brandy with peace. She sighed contentedly. "They're a very special family, aren't they?"

"Yes, good people they are, all of them." Brandy

heard the wistful note in Rafe's voice and tried to think of a way to shift the subject casually to Persia. She turned her head to see Rafe more clearly, and out of the corner of her eye, she caught sight of wide-set green eyes pooling the lantern light. She started, grabbed Rafe's arm, and woke the puppy in the process. "Good grief, what's that?" She tried to point out where the eyes had been, but nothing glinted.

Rafe laughed softly. "You will see him again. He is following us. It is the lynx cat. They are full of a great curiousness about people and light, but they will not harm."

The opportunity for talking about Persia was lost, but Brandy decided it was just as well; she probably would have made a bad job of it. As Rafe predicted, the cat stalked them most of the way, jade eyes gleaming and then disappearing, but Brandy didn't mind; now that she knew it was just a bobcat, it seemed rather comforting, like having a woods' guardian.

Mrs. Bailey met her in the hall when she got home. Her welcoming smile died at the sight of the puppy. "My dear Miss Claybourne, I am sorry you didn't understand. Dogs are not allowed in this house. Missy is afraid of them, and Grey forbids them. He got rid of his kennel on account of the child."

Brandy didn't want to be defiant, but small points were so important. She was also reluctant to suggest that perhaps Missy had feared Grey's dogs simply because they were his. Instead she said, "I am sure I'll make many mistakes, but one thing is clear to me— Missy's world must be changed, her fears overcome each in turn. I think the dog will be another small beginning, but if not, I will send him back."

Mrs. Bailey shook her head ruefully, her smile returning. "Miss Claybourne, under that meekness, I detect an iron will. But it's not me you have to answer to, it's Grey. I admit you are making remarkable progress, though, and that should please him. The child ate her supper like a perfect lamb."

Brandy thanked her, and carrying Mebbe, she went to see if Missy was asleep and found her sitting up in bed, eyes wide and staring, body rocking. She rushed to her, putting the puppy down and taking the child in her arms. "Poor darling, did you think I'd left you forever? I went to meet Persia's family, and they sent you a present. Isn't he beautiful? His old name was Mebbe, but that isn't nearly good enough for him." *A maybe dog for a maybe child; no, not nearly good enough*. "I think we ought to call him something special like Panza. There was a man named Panza, and he was a fine friend." *To another human being who lived in a fantasy world*, she added mentally. She hardly dared breathe as she waited for a reaction, any reaction.

The golden head turned, the black eyes focused and widened, a shiver ran from the child's body to Brandy's. *Please, please*, Brandy prayed silently, *let the fear pass*. Panza looked up at Missy, whined and wiggled closer, rolling on his back and begging to be petted. A small hand was extended tentatively, and Panza licked it shyly. The hand drew back a little, and the puppy lowered his head as though sure he had done something wrong. For one awful moment, Bandy thought the child might strike him.

Missy put her hand out toward him again, holding it uncertainly over him, and then gently, gently she touched his face. He licked her hand again, squeaking joyfully, and this time there was no withdrawal. With infinite care and complete absorption, Missy touched his ears and the soft skin of the little round belly and ran her hand down his back. It was too much for Panza; he snuggled closer, then climbed clumsily into Missy's lap, ecstatic with acceptance, reaching up to lick her chin. Her head bent to him, her arms held him close. Brandy's vision blurred as she hugged them both to her. The first miraculous contact had been made; of her own accord, Missy had reached out to touch something warm and alive, to touch it gently with awareness of its vulnerability.

Brandy wished the moment could go on forever, but she was well content when she left the pair. Missy was asleep, her body not rigid but slightly curled to provide the hollow where Panza dozed contentedly close to her warmth.

CHAPTER V

When they went walking the next day, Panza followed at Missy's heels, and Missy turned her head every once in a while to make sure he was there. The child walked independently, no longer needing a hand to keep her going. Brandy saw her own idiotic grin of delight reflected on the other faces at King's Inland, Rafe's especially noticeable because his scar distorted his countenance so much when he smiled.

Brandy brought food this time, having decided they would picnic in the woods if Missy did not seem too tired to keep wandering. They ambled along under the trees, Missy walking gracefully now, and it was Panza who showed the first signs of weariness, his short, fat legs having to trot to keep up. Brandy picked him up to give him a rest, and Missy reached out to touch him every now and then, though she was careful not to touch Brandy. Brandy put Panza down at intervals, and at one point he saw a squirrel and gave chase, barking in his ridiculously small voice, tumbling over a log in the way. He looked so funny that Brandy laughed and glanced at Missy in time to see a small lift of her mouth. In other children it would have been nothing; in Missy it was the tiniest beginning of a smile. Brandy could not imagine how beautiful she would be if she truly smiled.

A short distance from the pond, a muffled growl and

the rising hackles on Panza gave her a first warning. The puppy shivered in her arms. Brandy stopped and looked around carefully. At first she could see nothing, but then a faint snorting grunt gave her direction. She stared hard at the shade- and sun-dappled thicket and saw, as if he had appeared in an instant, a great brown bear, sitting up on its haunches, its beady eyes watching them, its nose twitching as it tested their scent. The rush of fear made her giddy, and she looked around wildly for refuge—looked around to see Missy walking toward the beast. Brandy was beside her in an instant, holding her firmly but trying not to communicate her terror.

The instant of panic seemed endless to Brandy, as though time had stopped while her mind worked crazily at high speed. Run? No, how far would she get carrying a child, and what would be more likely to start the bear after them? If the bear came after her, could she keep it busy until Missy could get away, would Missy run on command, would she know the way? *Oh, Grey, I never thought!*

The bear gave a low, snuffling growl, followed by a human-sounding snort of disgust; then it dropped to all fours and shambled into the brush, leaving only a faint trail of sound to tell Brandy it was moving away from them. She stared at it in disbelief, and her knees gave way so that she sat down abruptly, pulling Missy into her lap, bringing a squeal of outrage from Panza, who had barely avoided being sat on. Brandy heard her own laughter rising hysterically. *Must get a grip on yourself, mustn't frighten Missy.* She stopped with a choke and offered a shaky explanation. "Well, he was something to see, wasn't he? I'm glad you weren't afraid of him, but you must be awfully careful around bears. You never want to get too close to them; they're big and strong, and they might squash you flat just trying to give you a friendly hug." *Friendly hug, my soul and body*, thought Brandy as she held Missy, *more like a predinner preparation.* She knew the truth now of another facet of

Missy's strangeness; though afraid of something as harmless as a dog, she would have walked right up to the bear.

Brandy drew a deep breath and got to her feet, helping Missy up. Resolutely she headed for the pond rather than home, making herself let go of Missy's hand in deference to the child's new independence. Having faced what seemed the ultimate calamity and having escaped unharmed, Brandy decided it was foolish to change plans, and she felt rewarded for her conviction by their time at the pond.

It was so peaceful there with the water reflecting the embers of the trees' autumnal fire. Bare branches etched the sky, and heavy drifts and fallen leaves rustled with the busy scurryings of mice hard at work to make winter a time of plenty. Two otters played ceaselessly on the mud slide on the far bank, and Panza rolled and bounced and yipped through his explorations while Missy watched him. Brandy got the food out, and Missy ate with good appetite, and with no prompting, she gave Panza a piece of meat when he begged. Brandy didn't care how spoiled he became as long as he provided a living link with Missy.

When they passed the thicket on the way back, Brandy was relieved to see no sign of the bear, but sometime later she was not so sure they had been lucky. Missy stopped and stiffened, and at her heels, Panza sat down and cocked his ears, whining a question. Then Brandy too heard the hoofbeats, and as soon as Raleigh was in view, Missy relaxed. She knew the difference between her father and her uncle, even to the horses they rode.

"At last I've found the pilgrims," Raleigh said as he reined Casco to a stop, and Brandy was very happy to see him, even though it might mean more trouble with Grey.

He dismounted, saw the puppy beside the child, and comprehension dawned in his face. "Well, I'll be, introduce me to the new member of the family, won't you?"

He caught on to the name too. "Very apt, trust a schoolmarm to find the right word."

He squatted down so that his eyes were level with Missy's and put his hands on her shoulders. "Hello, little flower, you look all rosy from your walk, very pretty, in fact. Would you like to ride a ways with me on Casco?"

Brandy watched her carefully—her eyes were looking directly at Raleigh, and she did not rock or flick her fingers to provide a shield. Brandy decided it was worth a try.

"Why don't you get on, and then I'll give her a boost up?"

Though Missy did nothing to help the plan, she did not hinder it, but once she was in the saddle in front of Raleigh, she put out her hands. Brandy thought for a moment she was actually reaching out to another human, wanting to get off the horse, but then Panza's jumping and whining told her what was going on. She handed the puppy to Missy, and the child's thin arms held the fat little weight firmly. Raleigh steadied her with one arm. He kept the pace slow, and Brandy walked, which, according to Raleigh, was the way things should be. Brandy stuck her tongue out at him, but she agreed with the situation; Casco might not be so gentle with an unfamiliar rider.

When they arrived home, Rafe was so pleased with the procession that he even greeted Raleigh warmly, and he treated it as the greatest privilege to be allowed to lift Missy down. The little girl's lack of protest at being touched by several different people and at being on a horse was wonderful, and Brandy gave full credit to Panza. It was as though the sensation of the soft body under her hand had given Missy back the knowledge that physical contact with living things was a pleasant and necessary part of existence. If only her part of it, the reaching out, could be extended beyond Panza's warm fur to a human hand.

The child was fast asleep by early evening, proving to

Brandy that much of her tenseness and her hours of wide-open eyes had come from what lack of exercise had added to the illness of her mind. Brandy resolved that under her regime that was one problem which would cease.

Raleigh's presence made it easier. For the next few days he walked and rode with them. When they rode, they took turns holding the child and the puppy, and Brandy was amazed by the sedate behavior of Lady and Casco, who acted as if they knew how precious the added burden was. The busy days had the desired effect on Missy, and some afternoons she even napped, Panza snoring beside her. She made it clear she did not want the puppy out of her sight, looking around anxiously when he was gone.

As much as she loved the child, the afternoons when Missy slept were a delight to Brandy because of Raleigh. She would check in with Persia or Mrs. Bailey, and then she and Raleigh would go for long rides, letting the horses behave with more freedom than on the careful mornings. Brandy tried to suppress an eerie feeling about the whole situation, but it kept returning. It was not helped by the fact that Persia, Mrs. Bailey, and even Rafe appeared to be reconciled to it. She, Raleigh, and Missy felt like a family. They fit comfortably together, and Grey's dark image was an intrusion. Brandy dreaded his return; he brought with him mockery, anger, bitterness—a barely controlled universe of violence.

Her feeling was stronger than ever one afternoon as she and Raleigh sat on the grass in a clearing beside the road which led to King's Inland. They had ridden out on it because it provided better places for jumping than the more overgrown woods trail. They had ridden hard, and Brandy was pleased with the way Lady was coming along, not refusing jumps, sailing over them easily.

The days were cooler now, but the afternoons still held the sun, and Brandy was relaxed and content resting on the warm earth. She turned her head slightly and saw Raleigh watching her, his smile lighting his face as her eyes met his. He reached out, and she was in his arms. He kissed her slowly, thoroughly, and she responded; there was no urgency or clash of wills in the act, only a gentle sharing of a perfect moment.

Silently she cursed Grey for it as she drew away. She countered Raleigh's puzzled frown by putting her hand against his cheek in a gesture which reassured, yet told that the magic was, for now, finished. She shut her eyes, trying to destroy his presence, but he was there still—Grey, enraged by the kiss, jealous of his child, of her, willing and capable of doing harm to anyone who displeased him. She tried not to shiver, not to show Raleigh how cold she was in spite of the warmth of the glade. She rose swiftly, mounted Lady, and called to him to hurry before the good light for jumping was gone.

She knew his male pride was enough. Though he was still confused by her reaction, his expression showed that he was rapidly deciding her withdrawal had come from an excess of emotion and maidenly confusion. *Maidenly confusion, hell,* thought Brandy, but she was grateful he did not suspect that his brother, though miles away, was with them.

She wanted to outride his image, and her urgency communicated itself to Lady. They were off before Raleigh was in the saddle. She heard his shout of surprise and asked Lady for more speed, heading for another clearing ahead, wanting the difficulty of the obstacle there.

She heard Casco thundering behind her, but she knew she could clear the jump well before him. The log fall loomed ahead. She collected herself and the mare. Lady left the ground just as the shout rang out. Brandy felt the midair jerk of the horse's body, the front legs fumbling on the logs, the girth giving way, her own body flying through the air.

Rough hands were poking and prodding, a voice telling her to wake up. She said very clearly, "Keep your filthy hands off me!" and looked up into Grey's strained face. He was standing now, his body taut with rage. She sat up abruptly and cried out at the excruciating pain shooting through her shoulder. Her left arm hung uselessly. She clamped her good hand over it and looked around desperately. "Lady, is Lady all right?"

She caught sight of the saddleless mare placidly nuzzling Orpheus just as Grey snapped, "She's fine."

Brandy decided to attack first. "You fool, don't you know better than to startle a horse in mid-jump? Where did you come from anyway?"

For a minute she thought he might accomplish what her fall had failed to do. His hands flexed involuntarily, and she was sure they itched to encircle her neck.

"You stupid little bitch, if you want to commit suicide, do it on your own time and your own horse somewhere away from here. You should know Lady isn't good enough to take a jump like that," he snarled. "And I come and go from my home as I please."

"Lady's good enough if her rider knows how to ask her. We would have made it anyway if the saddle hadn't come off," she said, but her voice lacked conviction. Things were fuzzy at best, but it was becoming clear that Grey didn't give a damn about the horse, that he was masking his concern for her with anger. Suddenly she could see the reason—she was the only one who had got anywhere with Missy; what would happen if she died as abruptly as the child's mother had?

"Where's Raleigh?" she asked, still trying to sort things out.

"I sent him to get Rafe and the wagon," he said, dismissing his brother with a few words. Then he was kneeling beside her again. He took her hand away from the injured shoulder, and she closed her eyes as his hands explored the damage.

"Don't think it's broken, just dislocated," she gasped through clenched teeth, opening her eyes in time to see him nod.

His own face was as rigid as hers as he laid her back

on the ground. She shut her eyes tightly again as he braced her shoulder with his boot and took hold of her arm; she had seen her father do it often enough. The jerk came, snapping the bone back into the socket, and Brandy was disgusted by the sound she made. She rolled over onto her good side, swallowing convulsively. Being sick in front of Grey would be too humiliating.

She was so accustomed to dueling with him that she found his gentleness difficult to accept. His arms held her firmly until she was breathing regularly again. Her shoulder still ached as if badly bruised, but the sharp pain of the displaced bone was gone.

"Thank you. I'm fine now. I'd like to get up, and I'm sure I can ride home."

His face eased and his habitual mockery was back as he helped her to her feet. "I am convinced you could ride home, but I won't allow it. Lady isn't really hurt, but she's bruised and probably getting stiffer by the minute. She doesn't need a rider on her back. You'll ride in the wagon."

"Yes, sir," Brandy said, and admitted privately that she would be quite happy to go back via the wagon. She still had a case of Persia's collywobbles, and falling off of Lady a second time would complete her disgrace.

When the wagon came into sight, she froze and rubbed her eyes, but the vision remained. Raleigh wasn't with Rafe, but Missy was; Missy outside for the first time without her. Joy shot through her; she gave Grey's hand a quick squeeze and then ran to the wagon. She expected Missy to sit composedly as she usually did, but when she got there, the little girl put her arms out, and Brandy responded with her own, swinging the child down, holding her, feeling no pain at all from her shoulder.

"My brave Missy, my brave, wonderful girl! You came all the way with Rafe. And I'm fine, nothing is the matter. I just did a silly thing and fell off Lady. Oh, I am so proud of you!"

Missy's hands were around her neck, her head hidden against her. Brandy looked up at Rafe and saw the sun rising in his eyes. His face was warped by a huge smile. For once he spoke in French to explain. When Raleigh had gotten back to the house, Missy had seen him from a window. At the anxious, tugging insistence of the little girl, Persia had taken her downstairs earlier—now it made sense. Missy had wanted to be able to see toward the stables, had wanted to be that much closer to them, and when she had seen Raleigh, she had flown to the front door. Persia had let her out, and she ran to Rafe, grabbing hold of him, insisting without words that she be taken along. Rafe finished by telling Brandy that she had been right all along: Missy did know what was going on; she had known something was wrong with Brandy.

He added in English, for Missy's benefit, "The little one, she is a good one, yes?"

"A very, very good one," agreed Brandy, stroking Missy's hair. She would have liked more than anything else to hand the child to Grey. She looked around for him. He was standing a little ways off, holding the broken saddle and the reins of the horses. He looked utterly forsaken, his face drawn with the acceptance of the fact that even in her triumph, Missy barred him from her world. Brandy sighed; she was sure Missy knew exactly where Grey was, for she was keeping her head turned away from the spot, and Brandy felt her muscles tensing. But at least the screaming did not start.

Brandy met Grey's eyes, trying to keep the tears out of her own, and gave a small shake of her head. Grey turned away and mounted Orpheus without a word. Then he said, "I'll lead Lady home so you won't have to worry about her." His words were so tightly controlled that Brandy could feel his throat muscles closed around them. He looked at Rafe. "Where's Raleigh?"

"Eh, that one, he does not like the trouble. He has left in a hurry." His accent, the long e's and rolling r's added extra contempt to his opinion of Raleigh. Grey merely nodded, staring thoughtfully down at the saddle he had dropped on the ground. He asked Rafe to pick it up and started for home, urging even poor Lady into a brisk trot. Brandy knew it was because he could not bear the sight of Missy with her and Rafe, with no place for him. Rafe understood, too, and waited until Grey was out of sight before he helped them up onto the high seat.

For the first time, Missy spoke eloquently with her body, and Brandy was so happy she hardly noticed the absence of words. Missy patted her every once in a while as though to reassure herself that Brandy was still alive and with her, and she reached out and touched Rafe occasionally as if to thank him. When Brandy put her arm around her, the child snuggled against her.

Orpheus was in his stall when they arrived home, but Casco was gone. Though Rafe attributed Raleigh's disappearance to cowardice, Brandy believed he had left to avoid another scene with Grey because she had left no doubt about how she felt when they shouted at each other.

She still felt dizzy from her fall, but something in Rafe's manner as he picked up her saddle from the back of the wagon brought her pause. His motions were normally slow and steady, but he was in a clumsy hurry to get the saddle into the barn.

"Wait!" she commanded, taking hold of the girth. For a moment she thought they were going to have a tug-of-war, but then he stopped, his eyes not meeting hers.

Turning it, she stared at the place where the strap had broken. Broken! Her heart thudded uncomfortably. It was possible that the leather had just given way but unlikely. Tack was so well cared for at King's Inland. And the break was odd—ragged and fibrous on the top side as if torn, but sharp and clean on the back. Her hands shook as she held it. There was no way to prove it, but she was quite sure someone had cut it so that with enough strain it would give way. Her mouth went dry at the thought of Missy in front of her on the saddle. They had ridden slowly, so a fall might have left them unhurt, but it would have undoubtedly terrified the child and reversed much of the progress they had made. Or perhaps the damage had been done just for her own hard afternoon rides. Everyone at King's Inland knew about them; everyone except Grey—unless he had been home before she knew, unless he had found out about the time spent with Raleigh. Perhaps the shout had been an attempt to prevent his own plan from working. Then why had he looked so carefully at the saddle? Her mind spun with all the possibilities. Someone wanted her at the very least injured, at the most dead. She shook her head to clear it.

"Please, forgive me. It is my fault that such a thing should happen. But I do not understand; I am very careful with all of the leathers." Rafe's voice was anxious, pleading.

Brandy looked at him, her face empty of expression. Did he really not suspect it had been deliberately done or was he covering his own crime with feigned innocence? He would do nothing unless she threatened Grey, and surely he did not think that of her. No, she could not believe it. She trusted him too much, loved him too much. Her face softened, and she put her hand on his shoulder. "It was my fault as much as yours. I saddled Lady myself this afternoon, and I am a good enough horsewoman to know how to check my own tack."

She turned to look for Missy and found her sitting on the ground with a frantic Panza licking her face. Persia was with them. "That pup went near crazy when she left him." She looked closely at Brandy. "Are you all o' a piece? What a terrible thing!"

Could she have done it? No. Brandy managed a smile. "I'm fine. I've taken quite a few tumbles before, and I'll probably take many more before I'm done." But not because of a cut girth, she added mentally.

She did not believe that something good always came of something bad, but in this case it had. Missy's new responsiveness was not a transient phase arising out of an interval of shock. When Brandy went to her, Missy reached out as though the barrier had never existed, and hand in hand they went into the house.

Grey was probably in his study, and Brandy hoped he stayed there because she did not want this delicate new part of Missy to be cut off by terror. As they went up the stairs, Missy ran her hand over the smooth wood of the banister and touched everything within reach on her way to her room. Once there, she picked up one toy after another, openly savoring the texture of each as Brandy knew she had done secretly.

Brandy left her to wash the dirt of her fall away and met Mrs. Bailey in the hall. Mrs. Bailey? No, not her either; her normally serene face was white and tense with worry. "My dear, I am so glad you were not badly hurt. I don't think any of us could have borne it; you have become so much a part of us. And I have never seen Grey so upset. He wants to see you immediately in his study."

Brandy thanked her for her concern, but some inner defiance moved against Grey, and she said, "Please tell Mr. King I will be down as soon as I have had a chance to freshen up and to give Missy her supper. And will you ask Persia if she would bring the tray up to me?"

Mrs. Bailey was obviously surprised that Brandy would defy Grey, but she complied.

Brandy brushed the dirt out of her hair and surveyed the damage. A fine bruise and an aching shoulder were all the fall had given her. She knew how lucky she had been. She shivered and dressed hurriedly.

Missy was calmly holding Panza when Brandy went back to her. She stayed with her until she had eaten her supper and fallen asleep, and then she went down to see Grey.

He was working at his desk, and he rose politely when she entered. He made no comment on her defiant lateness, but his face was forbidding, and he scrutinized her carefully before he spoke. "I am glad to see you in one piece, Miss Claybourne. You might easily have broken your neck."

"I know that, but I've had enough experience to know how to fall."

She expected him to be amused, but he wasn't. "I have no doubt of that. Anyone who mismatches horse and jump like that must be prepared to fall quite often. But it is difficult for me to understand Raleigh letting you attempt it. He must be even more empty-headed that I thought."

Brandy's temper flashed, but she tried to keep her voice even. "That's unfair, both ways. I told you before, I've been doing a lot of work with Lady; she's taken that jump easily on several occasions. Your shout and the girth breaking were to blame, not the horse. And Raleigh had nothing to do with it. I went ahead of him and chose the jump." She blushed at the sudden memory of Raleigh's kiss, and Grey's mouth curled sardonically as if he were seeing it.

"I can't say I have much respect for your choice of companions, but then, Ruth was probably right, there is so little to amuse a young woman here." Brandy kept her hands clenched in her lap because she wanted to slap him. But when he continued, his voice was weary, the sarcasm gone. "I will take you back with me tomorrow. I will pay you for the full six months plus your passage back to Boston."

Brandy stared at him incredulously. "You'll what? You'll send me packing just because I fell off a horse?" The image of the cut leather rose again in her mind.

"Not because you fell off a horse, but because you might have been killed. And the very last thing I can afford is to have another woman die accidentally at King's Inland."

Brandy heard the emphasis on "accidentally" and met his eyes squarely. "All right, so it might not have been an accident. I saw the strap, too, and it was either a very odd break or someone cut it. I will be more careful about checking my tack in the future. But I'll not leave. We made a bargain, a six-month bargain, and I'm going to hold you to it. The only way you are going to make me leave is to haul me off bodily, and I'll kick and scream all the way. I've thought about it, and I can only find two people who might have a motive for wanting to be rid of me. One is Ruth, but unless she has someone hiding in the woods to do her work, she can hardly have managed it from miles away. The other is you, and if it's true, then it's very strange indeed. Missy now goes outdoors; she is no longer afraid of dogs or horses; she feeds herself; she touches not only objects, but people; and she sees, really sees. In a very short time, we've made tremendous progress, she and I, and I'm proud of both of us. I have no doubt that she will speak one day, and I want to be here to hear her. Now, the only reason I can find for your wanting me gone is that this whole business of your wanting to help her is a sham, that what Miss Collins told me is more of the truth than even she realized—that you and she would be much better off without the burden of the child."

She had never seen such blazing anger. She noticed the details with an odd detachment. His eyes were narrowed to mere slits of darkness; a vein pulsed in his temples; the lines in his face looked deep enough to have been carved with a knife. But when he spoke, his voice was devoid of emotion, flat, dead. "That will be all, Miss Claybourne. Right now I would not mind in the least if you broke your neck or if someone did it for you. I myself am more than tempted. Get out."

Mrs. Bailey was puzzled by Grey's absence at supper, but Brandy did not enlighten her. Brandy's anger lasted through most of the meal until she heard first the study and then the front door opening and slamming shut, and Mrs. Bailey shook her head, saying, "He's off on one of his wild rides on that great black devil. It's a wonder to me he ever comes back whole."

Brandy's anger dissolved, and the dismay that had been creeping around the edges of her mind flooded in.

She felt so guilty she could hardly bear it. If anything happened to Grey on his ride, she would be to blame. She desperately wanted to drown her consciousness in music, and she wanted no audience. Mrs. Bailey accepted her explanation that she wished to do some practicing without anyone there to hear her mistakes.

She played classics, popular tunes, and the haunting melodies of lonely ballads she had learned in the West. She played until her hands ached and her injured shoulder throbbed with a life of its own. And then she played past the pain until she felt disembodied, as if she were listening to someone else making the instrument ring.

She did not hear him come in, did not know how long he had been standing at the doorway before she felt his presence. The music died abruptly as she spun around to face him.

He was dust-grimed, and his face was bleached with fatigue except for the scarlet lines across one cheek where a branch had hit him. She could not meet his eyes, afraid of what she might see there. Her voice was queer and choked to her own ears. "Mr. King, I am so ashamed about what I said. I made accusations for which I have no proof, and I don't even believe them anyway. I spoke out of anger because I care so much about Missy I could not bear the thought of leaving her. I can't bear it now. Don't you see, she is the most important consideration. She will be ready to let me go someday, but not yet. And there is no proof that the strap was cut, no reason in spite of what I said that anyone would want to harm me. I'll just be more careful. But I'll never be more sorry than I am right now, and I have never wanted anything more than I want your pardon."

Silence filled the space which had held so much music minutes before, and finally, Brandy could not forbear looking at him. He was staring at her, a queer light which was not anger in his eyes. She had never heard so kind a voice from him.

"I hired you because I thought you had the spirit to fight for Missy. You have proved you do to a much greater degree than I would have guessed. I would be a fool to dismiss you; God knows what it would do to the child. But if you ever feel frightened enough to want to leave, my offer still holds. Good night, Miss Claybourne."

Threat or concerned promise—she could not decide.

Her sleep was broken once more by the hot choking feeling which was becoming distressingly familiar. She checked the hall and found it empty, and as far as she could tell, Missy was truly asleep.

CHAPTER VI

Brandy had become so accustomed to Grey's quick exits that she was astonished to find he was still at King's Inland the next day. Missy knew it too; she was tense, her eyes were fixed again, her body rocked rhythmically.

Brandy picked her up, speaking gently but firmly. "No, you mustn't do that anymore. You are all right; I won't let anything happen to you."

The dark eyes focused, the rocking stopped, and Brandy felt the childish body relaxing, curving to fit her own. She wondered how much Missy might have heard the night before; her return to old ways might have been from the fear that Brandy was leaving as much as from her father's presence.

She spent the day outdoors with the child. The weather was much colder now, and that was a good excuse for being very active. Brandy wanted Missy to be weary by nightfall. They even ran together down one smooth stretch, and Brandy was pleased to see that the child's new coordination extended even to this; she ran gracefully, though without the smile and playful gestures which were so characteristic of normal children.

Grey was obviously making an effort to stay out of sight, and Brandy thought of how painful that must be and wondered how much he was observing from the shadows. That evening when Missy was blessedly fast asleep, and Brandy was eating dinner with Mrs. Bailey and Grey, he told her.

"I saw you with Missy today. I find it difficult to credit the change in her. She looked much like she used to, running with that puppy at her heels." His mouth quirked, and Brandy got ready to argue. This was his first mention of the dog, but she relaxed at his next words. "Panza I believe you've named him, a romantic name for such an odd little beast. Your taste in horse-flesh is commendable, but I cannot say the same for your choice of a dog. The kennels of King's Inland used to have quite a reputation, forever lost now, I fear."

Brandy laughed. "Mr. Cowperwaithe had the same opinion. Poor Panza, only Missy and I are able to see his finer points." She hesitated; it was presumptuous to give permission to the master of the house, but then she went on because she wanted desperately for Missy's progress to give Grey some direct gift. "I heard you had some fine dogs here, and I think if you wish you could have them again. I don't think Missy will be afraid of them now."

Grey always seemed to know her motives; to him she must be a pane of glass. "Thank you, I appreciate your thoughtfulness, Miss Claybourne, but I think it would be better to wait. Panza belongs to her as the cats belonged to Jasmine. Missy feared the hounds because they were mine. There is no assurance that she will not associate them with me again." No anger or bitterness, just resignation. Brandy swallowed hard.

To Mrs. Bailey at least, Grey's next words were as startling as a gun shot. "I regret that it will mean more work for you, Margaret, but in two weeks' time I plan to give a party here. I know it's short notice, but the Lord only knows when the first snow will come, which would make it difficult for Ruth and several others to come from Wiscasset. The weather should hold until then. Perhaps you can hire some extra help from Persia's family."

Mrs. Bailey's normal composure had fled. She stared

at him for a moment before she stuttered, "But I . . . we . . . there hasn't been a party here since. . ." Her voice trailed away.

Grey said steadily, "Yes, I know, since Jasmine died. But I think King's Inland has had a decent interval of mourning, don't you? I will leave a list of local people whom I would like you to invite. Use Rafe to deliver the invitations. And please make sure enough rooms are prepared to accommodate Ruth, the Coopers, the Robinsons, and several musicians."

Mrs. Bailey was recovering. Her eyes began to sparkle in anticipation. She accepted Brandy's offer of assistance gratefully and was already enumerating the things which Ivory, India, and Ben Cowperwaithe could do if they were willing. She went to her own quarters right after dinner to make a list of tasks to be done, saying that the orderly rows of words gave her a nice, if false, sense of competence.

For once Brandy did not feel at ease in Grey's presence, and she accepted his invitation to sit in the front parlor. She was, however, relieved that they were not in the music room under Jasmine's painted eyes.

Brandy settled on a wide sofa, and Tiger, who had followed them, jumped into her lap and settled herself with no apologies. Grey remained standing, and oddly for him, he seemed to be having difficulty with something he wanted to say. Brandy looked up at him inquiringly.

"I . . . well, that is, you are of course invited to the party."

Brandy giggled. "Thank you, I'm glad you're not one of those employers who locks the governess in the nursery when company comes."

He smiled briefly, but he still hadn't said everything, and he went on quickly. "What I wanted to ask, well, do you have a dress for the occasion? If not, I am sure Ruth would be quite willing to help."

She was touched that he had thought of it, but the last person in the world she would let choose for her was Ruth; she could imagine the miserable, pale-shaded, fussily fashioned creation she would foist on her. Mischief rose in her as she thought of what she would wear. "Thank you for the offer but honestly, I do have a dress which will suffice. Hugh liked it, so I shouldn't disgrace anyone. I promise I won't wear my trousers."

No smile answered her own. "Damn, I nearly forgot!" Grey exclaimed, pulling something from his coat pocket and handing it to her. "This came by my yard in Wiscasset."

It was a letter from Hugh. He had not received hers yet, and he was waiting anxiously to hear from her. The letter was full of love and bits of news about the family, his patients, and her students. He described the teacher who had taken her place as "a whey-faced gentlewoman of ninety years or so." Brandy laughed at that, but she felt sorry for her former pupils. The letter finished with a plea for her return. She felt a moment's lonesomeness for the uncomplicated household at Greenfield, and she sighed as she put the letter down.

Grey's question startled her. "Homesick?"

"Just for a moment," she admitted, "but I wouldn't leave Missy for the world." The finality of her voice left no room for argument. Grey shrugged and went to a cabinet and took out a decanter of brandy and two glasses.

When he handed her a glass, she was tempted to refuse it. It was not a lady's drink, and she suspected he was teasing her about her rowdiness by offering it. Then she was amused by her pique—with her name and her upbringing, she could hardly claim the right to delicate sensibilities. Defiantly she took a sip of the liquid fire and managed not to gasp.

"Thank you, it's very good, but isn't this against the law here?"

"Yes, it is, but surely you've seen enough of the people in the state of Maine to realize a little thing like that isn't going to stop us—it just makes procuring it more challenging."

She could well believe it. He looked like a prime candidate for a rumrunner himself.

Cynically Brandy suspected the liquor, but for whatever reason, she and Grey managed to chat amiably for quite some time. He told her about the high-hope horses he had at other farms, about things such as the first Maine pulp mill, which had been built the year before in Topham, about the state's desperate need for new industries and more people owing to the changes brought by the war. He spoke with disgust about the conditions in most factories throughout the country—the long hours which came with increased demand for a product and then the long days without job or pay when the demand lessened—and in the surrounding areas where people lived in squalor with too little light, air, and food. "It is not only inhumane," he said, his voice intense, his look no longer withdrawn, "it is impractical. If a man is tired, ill fed, ill clothed, and generally wretched, he cannot work efficiently, and he stands a much higher chance of coming to serious harm from one of the machines. And he's a danger to other workers. I have the ledgers to prove it from my own businesses—offer a man steady, reasonable hours and wages, add a decent place to live, and he will give you a better-made article and higher profits. It's such a simple balance, but you would be amazed by the number of factory owners who don't think they're getting their just due unless their employees are miserable."

Brandy asked about his family and saw them come alive with his tales. His ancestors had been gallant and stubborn, surviving the War for Independence, Indian raids, losses at sea, and violent deaths at home to build an empire based on far-flung trade—an empire Grey had inherited and expanded greatly, Brandy knew, though he did not say so. She found that Grey and Melissa were the only King family names which had no connection with the sea; the others—Amanda, Drake, Cabot, Isabella, Miranda, and Raleigh—all carried images of the tide. He and Missy's namesakes had been Grey's great-grandparents. The writing box in Brandy's room had belonged to the first Melissa. As far as Grey knew, he, Raleigh, and Missy were the only surviving members of the family; an uncle had gone West and had never been heard of since, so he was presumed dead.

"I wonder if perhaps he is somewhere in California. Maybe I even met him once," said Brandy.

"Not a chance! I only saw him a few times before he left, but young as I was, I could tell he didn't like people at all. If he's still alive, he's in the wilderness miles from anyone else. All right, I've done my part. Now it's your turn."

She told him stories about Pearl, about her father, about Chen Lee, who took the time to make kites of magic colors for the children in spite of the demands of his many ventures. She told of the marvelous madness which was so much a part of San Francisco; of the fire companies that raced each other to be first at a blaze; of the strange little man who had proclaimed himself Emperor Norton and who was given tickets not only for himself, but for his two dogs, Bummer and Lazarus, to every major event in the city; of the famous performers who came to sing or dance or act and were never again free of the city's enchantment.

They talked on, and though Brandy's head was full of memories of her past and new things learned about the Kings and Maine, she was not too oblivious to notice that Grey was drinking steadily, refilling his glass often while she still had more than half of her first glass left. His words began to stretch and drawl much more than usual. He really is getting drunk, she thought, fascinated because he was such a disciplined man; it seemed completely out of character. *Like killing your wife,* her mind added involuntarily. But she stayed where she was, her eyes narrowed and golden, gleaming like Tiger's. Pearl had taught her long ago not to be afraid.

He poured himself another drink and glanced at hers. His face became exaggeratedly sad. "What's a matter, won't you drink for your namesake's sake?" he asked, grinning at his pun, words sliding into each other.

Brandy laughed aloud; he was being so ridiculous, so boyish. She had never seen him so stripped of his cold arrogance, and the change was remarkable. She could imagine what he had been like when he had been young, wild, and foolish. He looked younger than Raleigh right now. Her laughter died abruptly as she watched the change—his smile vanishing, his face becoming a mask with midnight eyes. Tiger landed on the floor with an outraged yowl as Grey lunged for Brandy, and she stood and stepped aside in the same instant. But Grey's rage made him quick, and his reach was long. He spun and caught her before she could get out of range. His hands were hard and bruising on her arm, his face distorted as he spat out the words: "Little cat, judging me, always judging, killed one, he'll kill one more. Destroyed his child, killed her too, another way. Why not keep on?"

Brandy still wasn't frightened, but she was in trouble, and there was no way to reason with him. She brought her foot down as hard as she could on his foot, and as he lurched forward, she brought her knee up. His hands dropped away as he grunted in agony, but he was a strong man further enraged by pain, and she was only a few steps away before his hand was clamped around her left arm. She had gone far enough; her right hand found the heavy silver box on the side table. He didn't even see it coming as it crashed into the side of his head and he fell.

Brandy suppressed her start of panic; she was quite sure she hadn't killed him; it took a great deal of strength and good placement to do that. She found his pulse; it was rapid but strong. She sat back on her heels, thinking about what to do next. She was thankful Mrs. Bailey had not appeared; explaining why Grey was stretched out unconscious on the floor would be difficult.

She went quietly to the kitchen and brought back two bowls, one full of cold water, and some toweling.

She knelt beside him again and felt the lump which was already rising, blood oozing from a small cut where the corner of the box had struck.

She put a cold compress against it, using the edge to wipe Grey's face. He began to toss his head from side to side, mumbling unintelligibly. His eyes opened, wide and unseeing, narrowing as he brought her into focus.

"My head. I . . ." was as far as he got. She held his head and the empty bowl skillfully. She had done it many times before, helping her father and Pearl with their similar patients; it didn't bother her. When his retching had stopped, she settled his head back in her lap and sponged his face with cool water.

His voice was muffled. "I haven't had many occasions to be ashamed in front of a woman, but this will do for a lifetime." He was completely sober.

Brandy's response was sharp because she found to her surprise that Grey's being humble was something she could not bear. She remembered when she had fallen from Lady how she had dreaded losing her dignity in front of Grey. "Nonsense, you wouldn't have had any problem if I hadn't knocked you out. And you forget, my two best teachers were a doctor and a saloonkeeper; holding heads was part of the course. Now, do you think you can stand?"

His color was improving and he managed a wry grin. "I'm proof that Pearl taught you a deal more than holding heads," he said as she helped him up. He winced as he put weight on his injured foot. Brandy put an arm around him, tugged at his own until he put it around her shoulders; obviously the world was still spinning enough for him to be thankful for the support.

"Come on," she ordered, "no falling down again until you're in your own bed."

He swayed a little partway up the stairs, and she held on tighter, laughing softly. "Oh, no, you don't! If we both go crashing down, Mrs. Bailey will surely hear us, and my good name will be ruined forever." She got him to his own room, and she heard no sound to indicate that Missy had wakened.

He refused to lie down. His voice was firm as he stood looking down at her. "Miss Claybourne, there is no excuse for my behavior. Maybe I am as mad as some think I am. You must reconsider leaving now with full pay."

Brandy stared at him in open amazement. "I must have done more damage to your head than I thought, Grey King. What do you think I am, some missish ninny who goes to pieces because a man has a little too much to drink now and then? Do you think I would leave Missy just because you suffered a lapse in manners? No one can live as you do, strung tightly as a bow, without snapping sometimes. Besides, you came off much worse for it than I. Do as I tell you, lie down!"

"Yes, ma'am," he said with mock meekness, much more the Grey she knew.

He settled back on the bed, and she worked to get his shoes off in spite of his protests. "Too bad for you I'm such a large woman," she said, running her hands over the bruised arch of his foot, "but I don't think I broke anything. You stay put, and I'll get something cold to put on that." She headed for the door.

"Ruth would have had me thrown out," Grey commented sleepily.

"Well, I'm not Ruth!" Brandy snapped with more vehemence than she intended.

"You certainly aren't," she heard him say as she shut the door behind her.

Downstairs she carefully removed all traces of the battle. Then she added more wood to the embers of the fire in the stove and brewed a strong cup of tea. She worked quietly, and Mrs. Bailey did not emerge from her rooms. She carried the tea up to Grey. He was half asleep but roused as she came in. He grimaced at the teacup. "You may not want it, but your stomach needs it, so drink it all," she commanded as she deftly slipped the pillows behind him so that he could sit up.

She held a wet towel against his foot to help bring the bruises out. She felt him watching her and turned her head to look inquiringly at him. "Sorry, am I hurting you?"

"No," he said, the intensity of his expression unaltered. "I was just thinking that California lost a gold mine when you came East."

Mockery she could handle, but the compliment made her blush furiously. As though Grey sensed this, deviltry danced in his eyes, and he asked sweetly, "I have another injury. Aren't you going to take care of that, too?"

Brandy gave a snort of laughter. "No, I'll leave that to Ruth."

"I deserved that," said Grey ruefully, and Brandy saw the bleakness in his eyes.

As she made him lie flat again, pulling the coverlet up over him, she had a sudden revelation. He grumbled, "You make me feel just about Missy's age."

She stood looking down at him, hands on her hips. She nodded in agreement. "That's just about how old you were tonight. Drunk as you may have been, that was all deliberate, wasn't it? Though I think you let it get a bit out of hand. You were providing me with one more reason to leave King's Inland, weren't you? Good Lord, you are determined to have your own way!"

"Didn't work, you're even more stubborn . . ." His voice trailed off, and he was asleep.

She stared at him for a moment, thinking how changed faces were by sleep. Grey looked weary and sad, all traces of ruthlessness erased. She searched for the word—he looked vulnerable. She shook her head in disgust at herself for the late-night fantasies; no word was more unfitting than that for Grey King.

She checked on Missy and found her sleeping peacefully. Suddenly she was so tired it took an immense effort to get to her own bed, and she slept as soon as her head touched the pillow.

When she awakened in the morning light, she knew

Grey had gone again. Beside her pillow was a small box and a note. She opened the note slowly and read: "You win. I expect you always will. Please accept these with my compliments for a brave battle. They belonged to my great-grandmother, Melissa. G. K."

She stared at the bold handwriting for a long time before she opened the box. She thought of Grey coming in and leaving the offering while she slept; it gave her a strange feeling, fear or pleasure she couldn't tell. In the box lay a pair of earrings, the jade of each delicately carved into flower buds with golden leaves. The green was deep and pure, perfect for her coloring. She knew it was as improper for her to accept them as it was for him to give them, and she knew she was going to keep them anyway.

CHAPTER VII

The next two weeks were the busiest and happiest Brandy had known at King's Inland. Ben, India, and Ivory often came with Persia, and sometimes even Hank and Amos were allowed to accompany them. The little ones were very well behaved and would play together for hours, quiet, eyes full of wonder. Persia said it was because they thought they were in God's house so they'd better be good. Brandy suspected Persia had started that rumor.

The house rang with laughter and bustle as rooms were aired and every surface polished. Mrs. Bailey was in her element—as though returning King's Inland to its old splendor were her own responsibility, her own passion. For the first time Brandy saw the rooms on the third floor and found them equal in magnificence to those on the second. They moved the extra furniture into the storage room at the end and prepared the others for guests. It seemed as if there were space for an army to sleep comfortably. For what she hoped was casual asking, Brandy learned that most of the guests were to sleep on the upper floor while Miss Collins would, of course, have the room next to Mr. King's, the room which had been Jasmine's. Of course, thought Brandy, and wondered why she felt so vicious about it, but at least the room had not been locked up and left as a morbid shrine to Grey's wife.

Rafe helped in the house when he could, and when he did, Persia's face glowed so brightly that Brandy thought he must feel the light, but he gave no sign. Most of the time he was off with the wagon, going to deliver invitations to neighboring farms, bringing back extra foodstuffs for the party.

Brandy watched Missy carefully, fearing at first that all the added confusion would upset her, but quite the contrary, she seemed to be enjoying it, though without laughter or smiling, it was hard to tell. At least she did not grow tense or rock or try to build the wall again. Brandy wondered if perhaps the excitement stirred some joyful memories of when her mother had been alive, her world in order. She was touched by Missy's reaction to Hank and Amos, for after staring at them for a moment, she patted each one gently as she did Panza, as though she recognized all three as fragile young things. If the boys thought it odd that she touched them but did not speak or play, they made no point of it, accepting her on her own terms.

By the time Ruth and Grey arrived the day before the party everything was in order. The house gleamed; the kitchen and springhouse were full to overflowing with crocks of butter, freshly baked bread, slabs of meat, fowl, salted fish, relishes, jellies, and pies. And as soon as she was in the house Ruth behaved as if she were its mistress and responsible for the work which had been done. Though Mrs. Bailey did not seem at all offended and chatted amiably with her, Ruth's attitude annoyed Brandy so that she excused herself, saying that she had to take Lady out since the horse had had so little exercise lately. Beyond a brief greeting, Ruth had managed to ignore her presence but when Grey said pointedly, "Do be careful where you jump, Miss Claybourne," Ruth's dislike and suspicion flashed openly for an instant.

Brandy said demurely, "Thank you for your concern, Mr. King."

She changed into her trousers and left Missy in

Persia's care. She took Lady out, and they worked off their excess energies together. But when she got back, Persia met her, and Brandy knew something was dreadfully wrong. Persia's words tumbled over each other in her anxiety. "Oh, Brandy, I didn't want to, but what could I do? She told me to leave her alone with Missy, an' she's still there with her."

Brandy didn't have to ask who "she" was. She said, "All right, Persia, thank you, I'll attend to it." She was amazed that a calm voice was possible in the midst of so much anger.

The door to Missy's room was ajar, and Ruth did not hear Brandy approach; she was too busy scolding. "The idea, no discipline, that dog should not be in your room." Panza was on the floor, looking miserable and cowed. Missy was rocking, her fingers flickering furiously in front of her face. "Progress indeed! You are as mad, as empty as you ever were, aren't you, you blank-faced little idiot, destroying our lives. You can be sure I'll bear your father no brats; one fool is enough."

"Get out, get out right now, Ruth, before I throw you out!" Brandy muttered. She was afraid of what she would do to the woman if she got close to her.

Ruth spun around, her mouth hanging open in shock before she collected herself enough to speak. "How dare you! I shall tell Grey immediately."

"Please do. Then I can tell him how you treat his child."

"I've heard enough about you to know you aren't fit to be in this household. I am going to be mistress here soon, and you, Miss Claybourne, will be the first to leave."

"That may be, but it isn't so yet, and if you don't leave this room this instant, you are going to go to the party tomorrow with a very bruised face." Brandy's hands curved into claws.

Fear supplanted arrogance on Ruth's face. She gathered her skirts and sidled past Brandy, her voice reduced to a gasp. "You'll be sorry for this."

Brandy ignored her, caring for nothing but comforting Missy. She gathered the child into her arms rocking, soothing her. "My darling, don't mind her, she's a bad woman. She doesn't like you because you are so beautiful and because everyone loves you so. She's jealous of you." She didn't know how much Missy understood, but it was enough, for the child relaxed in her arms, burrowing against her warmth. Brandy lifted Panza up and Missy cradled him tightly.

She stayed with her all afternoon and into the evening until the child had eaten at least some of the supper Persia brought up and had finally fallen asleep. Brandy did not want to go down for dinner, but she felt her absence would be a victory for Ruth, so she changed into a dress and arrived late at the table.

Grey asked instantly, "Is something wrong with Missy?"

Brandy answered quietly, but her eyes never left Ruth's face. "No, she is all right. I think she was just a little upset by all the excitement." She could not say, "By that bitch, your mistress," but she knew Ruth heard the silent words, for she flushed an unbecoming red and chattered aimlessly.

Grey's eyebrows quirked as he looked from one woman to the other, but he made no comment, and Brandy knew he was attributing the tenseness to simple jealousy. For her it was a miserable meal, and she went upstairs as soon as it was over, wanting to be asleep before Grey and Ruth came up to bed.

Her last thought before she slept was of Ruth's claim that she had "heard" things about her. Who would wish or bother to spread lies about her, she wondered, then dismissed the words as the false claim of a jealous woman.

The next day dawned cold and clear. Brandy spent it with Missy, trying to explain to her that there would be many people in the house but that they wouldn't hurt her and she mustn't mind. Brandy didn't want to be downstairs where she would have to watch Ruth greeting people as if she were Grey's wife.

The guests from farthest away arrived first, and Brandy heard the traffic of footsteps on the staircase and overhead as they were shown their rooms. And late in the afternoon she answered the knock on Missy's door with no idea of who it might be. To her surprise, she found Raleigh standing there. She was so delighted to see him that she hugged him and received a kiss of greeting in return. Neither of them saw Grey at the end of the hall as they turned and went into the room.

Brandy had been afraid to ask whether or not Raleigh was invited, and so his coming was a special gift. He laughed about it. "Even Grey has to keep up some show of being civilized, so he had to invite his only brother. My, my, how he must hate it!"

He stayed with them for about an hour, holding Missy and telling outrageous stories about sidehill badgers which had short legs on one side for hill living, about a marvelous city of crystal and gold somewhere in Maine, about lumbermen, Indians, and pirates. Brandy was sure Missy was enjoying it; she looked so contented.

He left with admonitions to Brandy not to be late to the party because he wanted the first dance. But in spite of that, she did not leave until Missy had had her supper and was asleep. As she went to her room to get ready, the first strains of music drifted up the stairwell, but she resisted the impulse to hurry; tonight she wanted to look her best.

She pinned her hair up, letting the heavy curls fall in a cascade from the back. She needed no rouge; her honey skin was already glowing with excitement. And finally she was ready to put on her dress. She took it from the wardrobe, her fingers touching it lovingly, remembering the careful work Pearl had put into its making as a going-away gift. The amber velvet held the same rich light as the brandy of her name, and Pearl had made it to suit her with total disregard for what the fashion plates demanded. The bodice was cut in a low curve, and the material was molded to every line of her long, supple figure until it fell into soft fullness from her hip bones to the floor. The long sleeves with tiny buttons fitted her slender arms perfectly.

When she was dressed, she put on the pendant from Chen Lee. The exquisitely carved birds and flowers had all been done from one delicate piece of jade which hung from an intricately wrought gold chain—California gold; she touched it for luck. The last things she put on were the earrings from Grey.

She surveyed herself in the mirror. She knew Ruth would be scandalized, as she knew Grey would approve, and there was pleasure in the knowledge.

As she descended the stairs, however, her courage deserted her. The air hummed with many voices underlaid with music, and several people who were on their way to find refreshments in the dining room eyed her curiously. She could not quell the hot blood rising in her cheeks; she didn't think she could face so many strangers. As kind as it had been of Grey to include her, she felt the awkwardness of her position and had a sudden longing to be back upstairs where she belonged. But as she turned to go, Raleigh stopped her. He had been watching for her from the door of the music room.

"Oh, no, you don't," he called, coming down the hall in long strides. "Shame on you, Brandy, I wouldn't have taken you for a coward, but I was beginning to think I was going to have to come up and drag you down by your hair, which looks lovely by the way. You're beautiful head to toe, and I am claiming the privilege of showing you off."

Her confidence flooded back as he took her arm. He made everything seem so easy. He escorted her into the music room, introducing her to the people they passed. She received only admiring comments about her dress. She was delighted to see the Cowperwaithes and to meet others from the region's farms. Whatever his faults, Grey was not snobbish in his choice of guests. The farmers and their families were just as welcome as the modish people from town. She stopped to talk to Mr. and Mrs. Cowperwaithe, telling them of the great success Panza was with Missy. She saw Persia looking very pretty in a green dress which complemented her bright curls. One of the local boys asked Persia to dance, and she accepted, but Brandy saw her looking wistfully across the room. Rafe stood alone against one wall, obviously ill at ease and wishing to be gone. She also caught sight of Grey and Ruth dancing. One she could do something about; the other she could ignore.

Raleigh said there had been enough talking and swept her out onto the floor. He was a good dancer, and their steps matched well together. The musicians played a variety of dances from polkas to waltzes to the Scottish set dances—reels, and flings, and the lovely slow strathspeys. Brandy managed to smile politely at Grey and Ruth when the sets brought the couples in contact.

Grey left Ruth every now and then to dance with other ladies, and Brandy chided Raleigh for shirking his duty.

"Ah, but I have no duty. Luckily for me, I am not master here. I can dance with you. Another privilege of the second son." Brandy heard no bitterness in the words.

"Well, there's one duty you're going to perform, if only for a minute," she said, and explained her scheme.

Raleigh shook his head. "I never would have thought you were a matchmaker."

"This is special, and don't you dare tease them about it," she retorted.

Raleigh agreed, and at the next slow tune he was at Persia's side, asking her for the dance while Brandy headed for Rafe. "I know this is unladylike, but it's the only way I am going to get a chance to dance with you," she said, holding out her hand. "Please?"

Rafe stammered in his embarrassment. "I am . . . I do not dance well. Your feet, they will be in great danger."

"I'll take that risk. Come on, before it's finished." She pulled at him, laughing, giving him no choice.

He wasn't at all bad, just a bit stiff with unease, and her plan worked splendidly. Raleigh maneuvered himself and his partner close to them and said apologetically, "I know it's most ungentlemanly of me, especially since I am dancing with such a lovely girl, but I find it impossible to see Brandy in another man's arms without becoming extremely jealous. If you permit . . ." The change was smoothly made, and there was no way out for Rafe except by being rude to Persia, which Brandy was sure he would not be.

As she glided away with Raleigh, she looked back at the couple. There was an instant's pause, and then Rafe took Persia in his arms, and they joined the slow measure. Persia's face was radiant, and Rafe's body was no longer tense. Brandy knew her ruse had been transparent and Raleigh's excuse overdone, but Persia and Rafe were accepting it gladly because it brought them together without either of them having to take the initiative.

Brandy was standing beside Raleigh, who was talking to the Robinsons when the next waltz began. Grey's voice startled her; she had assumed he was with Ruth.

"May I have this dance, Miss Claybourne?" he asked formally. She wanted to make a caustic comment about duty dances not including governesses, but she found the words wouldn't come. She caught a glimpse of Raleigh's angry look as he turned and of Ruth glaring as Grey swept her away, and then she forgot everything save for being in his arms. He was a fine dancer, better even than Raleigh. He executed the steps with perfect grace, but Brandy was aware of the barely harnessed strength of him in every movement they shared. She gave herself up to the joy of it, wishing it would never end. But had it not been for his strong lead, she would have faltered toward the end of the dance when he said calmly, as if commenting on the weather, "Thank you for wearing the earrings. They suit you. You are the most beautiful woman here tonight." She looked up at him. All his attention was fixed on her; he meant exactly what he said.

Her mind was still whirling in confusion when the

dance ended. Grey signaled to the musicians that they could rest for a while. Brandy saw Raleigh coming toward her, his face still mutinous, and then she heard Ruth's voice, deliberately raised. "Yes, it is an odd dress, but then Miss Claybourne is a rather strange person. Her background is interesting, to say the least, but I really can't bring myself to discuss it."

The last thing Brandy wanted was a cat fight at Grey's party, but the sudden silence and the eyes turned curiously on her destroyed her good intentions. She made her voice loud enough to be heard clearly throughout the room but kept it sweet and even. "Why, Miss Collins, you mustn't suffer any shame on my account. I'll be happy to tell them about my dress." She pirouetted gracefully, causing the skirt to swirl and ripple with amber light. "It was given to me by Pearl Orient, the woman who raised me. She was a prostitute, you know, and many of her gentleman friends gave her gifts, they liked her so much. That's where this material came from. Pearl made the dress during the day, when she didn't work." She touched the jade at her throat. "The necklace was given to me by Chen Lee; he too was one of her friends and mine." She did not mention the earrings, not wishing to involve Grey.

She had the satisfaction of seeing several reactions: Ruth's face was alternating between chalk and hot red; Raleigh looked as if he were enjoying it; Mrs. Cowperwaithe was beaming, and Mr. Cowperwaithe's taciturn face was showing a gleam of humor in the eyes, the twitch of a smile in the mouth; Persia was glaring with open dislike at Ruth. There were a few shocked faces, but Brandy felt the overwhelming response of approval. Stupid Ruth to forget that the right to be different was one of the most closely guarded privileges in Maine.

Then she saw Grey, and her glow of triumph vanished. Even here, across the room from him, she could feel his anger. She knew what she would see in his eyes if she were close enough. She turned her back on him just as he signaled for them to resume. She began to chat mindlessly with an elderly woman who was smiling at her, and she could hear the dancers taking to the floor, but all she could think of was what she had done to Grey. *Brandy, you absolute fool, fine to revenge yourself on Ruth, she deserved it, but you embarrassed Grey, too.* It was one thing for him to have accepted her despite her upbringing; it was quite another for her to be bragging about it, casting doubt on Grey's choice of a governess for his child.

Brandy burned with shame, and she escaped as soon as she could. She did not think anyone had noticed as she slipped out into the hall and went up the stairs. She stopped short when she was within sight of the landing and then hurried on. There was Missy, huddled in the cold corridor, listening to the music with Panza beside her.

"Hello, little lamb, I bet you're lonesome all by yourself," she said as she sat on the floor and drew the child and the puppy into her arms. Panza slid halfway off her lap and went back to sleep. Missy had made no attempt to flee on being discovered and now she reached for the softness of Brandy's velvet dress timidly. Brandy experienced the same thrill she had every time the child made some new contact with the world. She gave her an extra hug. "Isn't that nice to touch? I'll make you a dress that feels the same."

Missy made her small nestling movement which signaled her contentment, and Brandy hadn't the heart to move her. In spite of the chill air, she felt very peaceful sitting there, cuddling the child, music drifting up around them. She began to hum and then to sing the soft, nursery rhyme words from her own childhood with Pearl:

> Rest, my sweetling, rest.
> The dove is in her nest.
> The dreaming way is best
> Rest, my sweetling, rest.

Sleep, my darling, sleep.
There is no cause to weep.
You have my love to keep.
Sleep, my darling, sleep.

Missy's eyes were closed, her breathing deep and even when Brandy finished.

The creak of a board gave him away, and Brandy stilled her start of terror as she turned her head and looked up at Grey. He put his finger to his lips, signifying he would keep the silence. Then he walked carefully until he stood above them. Panza woke up and thumped his little tail happily. Grey reached down to take Missy out of Brandy's arms, and her heart lurched. She couldn't deny the man his own child, but she didn't know what Missy would do if she awakened in his arms.

The absorption in Grey's face prevented her from stopping him. She made no protest as the child was lifted away from her. She got up, holding Panza, and followed Grey down the hall to Missy's room. She watched him as he put his daughter down on the bed; his face was completely open, full of love and yearning for the child. As he put her down, her tiny hand touched him for a moment before it dropped to her side, but she did not awake.

Brandy barely choked back her sob before she turned and fled the room, unable to witness any more of his pain.

Her eyes were still blurred, but she was in better control by the time he met her at the head of the stairs. Before she knew his intent, he leaned down and kissed her gently on the mouth. "Thank you for letting me carry her," he said.

His gratitude threatened to start her tears again, and her voice was brusque. "Good grief, she's your child!" She could not interpret the strange look on his face, and she rushed on before he could shut himself in again.

"I'm truly sorry about what I did down there. It was childish, and hurtful to you, besides."

He gazed at her in amazement. "What are you saying—that it was your fault? That you shouldn't have told the truth?"

"But I . . . the way you looked, I thought you were furious with me and for good reason."

His voice was very quiet. "You must think me a monster indeed. I expect I deserve it, but I don't quite see how. I haven't many virtues, but one of the few I possess is, I hope, a sense of justice. Ruth was deliberately trying to slander you with half-told tales, and I could have wrung her neck for it. She got exactly what she deserved. Most of the people down there have even more admiration for you than they would have, much to Ruth's sorrow."

Brandy's relief that he had not been angry with her was so great that she even felt generous toward Ruth. "Don't judge her too harshly. She loves you so much it's difficult for her to see that I'm no threat."

The dangerous light kindled in his eyes again. "Yes, I suppose it is," he said as he drew her hard against him. His mouth came down on hers, and this time it was not gentle.

It was Grey who ended the kiss. Brandy's mouth was bruised, she could taste blood where her teeth had cut into her lip, her whole body felt shaken and weak, and she had done nothing to stop him. She backed away, more astonished at her lack of resistance than his behavior. The sunlight eyes met the midnight without flinching. Grey's laugh was harsh. "That, my dear Brandy, was punishment for underestimating yourself. Now shall we go down? My guests will be wondering."

Her hand flew involuntarily to her mouth, and Grey said mockingly, "No, no one will notice. I didn't brand you. I only kissed you. Your mouth is just a shade fuller and redder now, very tempting."

He gestured to her impatiently to descend ahead of him, and she obeyed. She seemed to be doing everything he wanted without protest, and she couldn't even find the gumption to be disgusted with herself. "My dear Brandy" he had said, not "Miss Claybourne."

She watched him make his way across the room to Ruth and she jumped when Raleigh touched her arm and asked her to dance. She looked up at the soft copy of Grey's face. Raleigh grinned maliciously at her. "My, my, when the lord and master beckons and even when he doesn't, people do take notice, don't they? You had better be careful of your reputation, little Golden Eyes, my brother has a way of ruining them."

Brandy stamped her foot. "Do you or do you not want this dance?"

"Always forgetting the kitten has claws," he said as he swept her out onto the floor.

She followed her partner and answered when he spoke to her, but all she could see was Grey, all she could feel was his kiss. It meant nothing at all to him, she told herself ruthlessly, and still could not stop the strong singing of her heart.

It was stopped for her at midnight when Grey, with Ruth at his side, announced their engagement. The wedding would be sometime in the spring; the exact date would be announced later.

CHAPTER VIII

Brandy knew she had managed well. She had congratulated Ruth, countering her cat-with-the-cream expression with wishes for her happy marriage. And her voice had not faltered when she had moved on to offer her felicitations to Grey, though she could not meet his eyes. He had said what sounded like "It is for the best," as though it were a sentence of some kind, but Brandy could not be sure in the babble, and she had no thought for anything save maintaining her own control.

She danced the last dance with Raleigh, laughing and talking as they whirled around the room. "Why, you really don't care, do you?" he asked in amazement.

She did not pretend to misunderstand. She widened her eyes deliberately and said, "Care, why should I care? I am only here to work with Missy, and that is going very well. Grey needs a wife, and I hope the child will be ready for a new mother by spring. Then my job will be done." In her highly sensitive state, she had the feeling that this did not please Raleigh, that he would have liked it better had she wanted Grey, but that made no sense at all, and Brandy dismissed the idea.

By the time she retired to her room she had herself in hand. Her first impulse, to throw herself on the bed and weep, was checked. She was ashamed of herself for being such a green girl, for thinking herself in love with

Grey because of a kiss—a kiss most likely initiated by the hard liquor the men had been drinking in the back. Grey most certainly had had his share, and a taste of Brandy was just one more, she thought ruefully.

What really mattered was that before too long, Ruth would have charge of Missy. That was horrifying, and Brandy was newly resolved to equip Missy with all the weapons of normality so she could hold her own against the woman.

She was lying with weariness edging her closer to sleep when a new thought struck her, and she sat up suddenly, sure it was true. Missy had known she was in Grey's arms, and she had touched him on purpose when he put her down. It had to be, because Missy, even with her great progress, did not touch involuntarily, not even in sleep. Each time she reached out it was to make contact deliberately.

Brandy shook her head with the effort to understand. It was as though Missy were playing an elaborate game in which she was not responsible for things she did while others thought her asleep. So what did that mean? What sort of self-defeating act was it to accept her father only while feigning sleep? Even with all of the child's problems, Brandy had refused to think her mad—a sickness of the mind and true madness were very different things to Brandy. But now she felt her first chill doubt, her first realization that there might be two very separate children in Missy, a day and a night child living under completely different rules. Before she had accepted the night prowlings as part of one problem; now she was unsure.

She settled down to sleep exhaustedly, knowing she must speak to Grey before he left again. She was dozing fretfully when the door creaked open. She lay frozen, heart thundering in her ears, as she watched the small, barely discernible shape of the child pause at the doorway and then come partway into the room. Brandy was lost; she didn't know whether to call out or keep silent, and to her horror, she found she was afraid,

afraid of a tiny child. She had a sudden vision of Missy in her room not to seek comfort but to glare malevolently from the darkness or to prowl close to suffocate her. She remembered the torment of waking with face covered by pillow or bedclothes, something which had never been self-inflicted before, something which she doubted was self-inflicted now. An ineffectual way to kill someone, but would a child know that? She lay still and made her breathing deep and even. With a little sigh, Missy turned and left the room, carefully closing the door behind her.

Brandy rolled over and clenched the pillow, moaning audibly. "Dear God, it can't be! She can't mean me any harm. She's got to be the same frightened, lost little girl all the way through. She's just checking to make sure I haven't left her in the night as her mother did." The words echoed hollowly in her ears as she lay waiting for the safety of the sun.

She dressed in the first pallid light and made herself sit at the desk writing letters until she heard Grey open his door and go downstairs. She had counted on his usual early rising so much that she felt as if she had been holding her breath since dawn.

She went down and knocked on the door of his study. His voice was brusque as he bid her enter, obviously annoyed at being interrupted at this early hour, but it changed to surprise when he saw her.

"Up with the dawn, Miss Claybourne, and after such a late night! Something on your conscience?" The memory of the kiss gleamed wickedly in his eyes.

His sarcasm made her own voice cool. "No, sir. But there is something about Missy which I think you ought to know." His eyebrows lifted in question, and she forgot her reserve. "Missy knew who picked her up last night. She touched your hand on purpose!"

His response was controlled, but his face was tense and the telltale vein throbbed at his temple. "And how did you come to that conclusion?"

Brandy tried to make her answer coherent, explaining

what had led her to the knowledge, but Missy's mode of expression was so subtle that it was difficult, and in the pause that followed her disjointed words, she thought she had failed.

But then Grey said, "All right, in case you are correct, what do you suggest I do about it?"

Brandy frowned in bewilderment; she hadn't thought that far. She supposed they ought to test it, but not with Ruth around, and Ruth and Grey were due to return to town today. She was still mulling it over when Grey solved the problem.

"I'll remain here for another twenty-four hours. Ruth can go back with the Coopers."

Brandy's words were choked as she thanked him and left. Honestly, it wasn't fair, the way he could see straight into her head. She blushed at the thought of what else he might have seen.

The morning was hectic with the guests' departures, and one in particular Brandy wished she'd never witnessed. She had gone to Missy's room with the child's breakfast, and her first sight of the slight golden girl made all her imaginings of the late hours seem not only impossible, but insane on her part. Missy reached out to her immediately and ate her breakfast docilely. There simply couldn't be room in Missy for an evil twin.

Brandy was crossing the hall to her own room when she heard Ruth's voice coming from Grey's room. She stopped, wondering if Missy could hear it too, deciding she could not through the closed door. She knew she should close her own door on the sound, but she stood where she was, eavesdropping shamelessly, transfixed by the rising venom of the words.

"I'll not go back with the Coopers! What will everyone think? We've just become engaged; they know you and I were to go back together, and now you are sending me back like some ship's cargo. I won't have it! Either you take me back, or I'll stay here until you're ready to go."

Grey's voice was harder to hear in its quiet, precise anger. Brandy shivered involuntarily at its quality. "You will go back with the Coopers. And you will learn to do as I say while you are in my house. I don't give a damn what people think, and if you are going to marry me, you had better learn not to care either. Perhaps you've made a mistake."

Brandy expected Ruth to become placating at that, but her anger had carried her too far. "Oh, no, I haven't made any mistake at all. I want you and I want King's Inland. I think the regret is yours; you know I won't let you keep that woman once I'm mistress here."

Brandy's reaction was simple—she wanted to go scratch out Ruth's eyes. She expected Grey's reaction to be similar, but with a mixture of chagrin and acceptance of her just deserts, she heard him laugh. "My God, Ruth, I know what you are thinking, but you might as well accuse me of having an affair with Margaret Bailey— she's years older than I am, and Miss Claybourne is years younger. Between them there is a wasteland with me in the dead center. Now run along like a good girl with the Coopers. I'll be in town by tomorrow night."

Brandy hurried to get into her room, but she needn't have bothered; it was quite a few minutes before Ruth, accompanied by Grey, passed her door and went downstairs.

She was consoling herself with the thought that Grey's dismissal of her as a woman was just too glib—after all, if he trusted her with Missy, he could hardly consider her a child; unless, of course, he thought of her on the level of an informative playmate for his daughter. "Enough, Brandy," she said angrily to herself, "you can't have him, he belongs to her. Don't want him anyway," she added defiantly, "he's a dangerous piece of work."

She jumped when someone knocked at her door, fearing for a moment that Grey in his omniscience knew of her eavesdropping, but it was only Raleigh coming to say good-bye. His smile lit up the morning, and he gave her a casual kiss of farewell, but he was as preoccupied as she and in a hurry to be off so that he could catch up with the Coopers and Ruth. The disquieting idea she had been trying to ignore rose again; she was beginning to think that Raleigh, for all his charm, operated from one desire—to take the greater part of what Grey possessed, to take Missy's and Mrs. Bailey's affection, her own, and, now that the pact was sealed, Ruth's. All perhaps because he could not have King's Inland. As she had suspected before, it seemed that the bitterness of being second son ran deep, probably deeper than even Raleigh knew. She shook her head wearily to brush away the thought; the Kings' problems were her concern only when they affected Missy.

The next knock on her door was Grey's. He had come to ask what she wished him to do about testing her new theory. He was twisting his hat in his hands, seemingly unaware he carried such an odd thing for indoor use, and Brandy felt his fear of failure as if it were her own. Her voice was gentle and pleading. "I know it may not work, but we've got to keep trying. I think the best plan would be for me to take her for a walk down the woods trail. You wait and then come riding down it. The woods are neutral territory and maybe she will feel easier there than if you walked into her room."

He agreed, but his voice was so hopeless that pity welled in Brandy's throat, making her voice uneven. "I know how hard it is for you, but I swear she's not nearly as afraid of you as she seems. Maybe someday she will be able to tell us why she acts the way she does with you."

Brandy couldn't help thinking of the appalling possibility that Missy's first words might be: "I'm afraid because you killed my mother."

"Even that would be better than silence," said Grey as he turned and left. Brandy was certain she had not said the words aloud.

She dressed Missy warmly for their walk, thinking as she did that this was another area where the child must achieve some independence. But even for a normal child of five, dressing oneself wasn't easy with sashes to be tied and gaiter boots to be pulled on. And as finely made and pretty as Missy's clothes were, Brandy considered them too fussy for a good romp and felt remiss that she had not thought of making some simpler things before this. No one had thought to provide the child with playclothes—why should they when she never played?

They set off at a brisk pace to ward off the cold. Panza ran in glad circles, and Missy seemed very eager. Brandy hoped it was not because she knew her father was still at home and wanted to be well away from him. The trees were quite bare now, spiny against the still-luxuriant evergreens. The thick carpet of leaves crackled beneath their feet and gave off a faint, spicy dust.

When Brandy judged the time to be right, she turned the little party for home. She had to take Missy's hand for a moment because the child seemed bent on continuing onward, and Brandy suspected she wanted to go to the pond. "No, Missy, we must go back. We didn't bring any lunch with us today, and we'd be awfully hungry if we stayed out all day." Her voice sounded calm and reasonable, but she hoped her inner tension wasn't communicating itself to Missy, who had so little need of words to tell her what was happening.

Missy and Panza were walking ahead of her when the hoofbeats became audible. The dog sat down and cocked his head. Missy stopped, but nothing happened; obviously she assumed it was going to be another meeting with her uncle. But when Orpheus was visible, Missy swung around and stared at Brandy for an instant before she sat on the ground abruptly and began to rock, flicking her fingers in front of her eyes.

Brandy's cry was a wail of despair. Missy's brief look had told her she knew she had been tricked. "Missy, oh, Missy, don't, please don't! He loves you, and I know from last night you love him."

A shudder passed through Missy, but the rocking

continued jaggedly, as though the slight body were being pulled two ways. Brandy, cradling the child against her on the ground, wasn't aware of Grey's nearness until he spoke. He towered above them on the black horse. "Don't fret, child. I won't bother you. You're safe with Brandy." The kindness in his voice made Brandy want to weep; she would have preferred it had he yelled at both of them. She didn't watch him as he rode off.

Missy's hand stopped fluttering, her body stopped rocking as soon as the sound had died away. Brandy heard a strange noise, and her heart jumped. She looked around for Panza; he was sitting a little ways off, looking puzzled by the strange behavior of the humans. Brandy was sure he had not made the sound, sure that Missy had made that one small, strangled sob of grief. A sound of grief, not anger or fear, from a child who neither laughed nor cried. Tears were too much to expect, but she saw the suspicious brightness in the dark eyes. The full horror of Missy's world washed over her anew—not to speak, to laugh, to cry, not by any outward means to acknowledge the emotional turmoil inside.

She continued to hold Missy until the cold forced them to start back. She knew she was at the stage where she took comfort from any crumb, but still the fact that Missy had been moved enough by Grey to let that sound escape had to be of major importance. Her mind started on another of its endless spirals of wondering about Missy's motives—was she grieved because her father had committed an unforgivable crime or because she loved him and shared his sorrow but could not overcome some barrier of her own making?

Grey was not home by nightfall, and Brandy wondered if he had ridden on to Wiscasset; she wouldn't have blamed him. But even without knowledge of the day's disaster, Mrs. Bailey thought he was probably off on one of his hard rides. "He'll come in mud-splattered and tired, but at least he'll be at peace for a while," she said sadly. "I can hardly wait until he's married. Ruth is such a nice woman. She'll be able to make him happy."

Brandy had difficulty keeping her savage disbelief to herself—happy with a woman who hated his child and would give him no others? It amazed her that Mrs. Bailey was taken in by Ruth, but she realized that could easily stem from a readier acceptance of things as they were and would be than she herself possessed. After all, Grey loved Ruth.

The house was very quiet after Mrs. Bailey had retired. Missy was long asleep, and Brandy hoped she would stay that way. Persia had left early after seeing to much of the disorder created by the guests. It was strange to Brandy that one party had made her so aware of how empty the house was, as if it still craved the numbers it had been built to contain. She went to the music room, and though the furniture was neatly back in place, it did nothing to dispel the memory of waltzing in Grey's arms.

She knew why she wanted to play the piano. It wasn't just to fill the silence with music; it was to pass the time waiting to see if Grey was coming home, to be sure he was safe.

She started with the clean precision of Bach, but for once it did not satisfy her, so she began to play and sing the songs Pearl had taught her and the many she had learned since. She could not brood much when she was both playing and singing. Her voice rose clearly, rich and well trained. She took the same impersonal pleasure in it as she did in the piano which played the proper notes on command; in her mind its quality was just one more gift from Pearl.

She was singing the last lines of "Shenandoah," seeing the rhythmic hoisting of the countless anchors for which the song had been used, when Grey came in. She heard him and stopped, but he protested, "No, please, if you're not too tired, continue."

Tired! she thought. *I am many things when you are near, but never tired.* Her hands wandered aimlessly over the keys while she caught her breath. Grey was the weary one; her brief glance had taken in his stained clothing and lined face the color of his name. Outriding the devil was work indeed.

When she began to sing again, she did so with fierce energy; if it gave her solace, so might it give him. She sang "Oh, Susanna" which had been so much a part of the early gold seekers in California; she sang silly songs such as "The Girl That Keeps the Peanut Stand" and drew appreciative laughter from Grey; she sang ballads and lullabies and anything that occurred to her, not wanting the gift to end. The lyrics did not seem overly important to her, but apparently they did to him, for when she had sung the lines "Oh, that I was where I would be, Then should I be where I am not; Here I am where I must be, Where I would be, I cannot," from "Katy Cruel," he stopped her. "And where would you be, Brandy?" he asked very softly.

"Exactly where I am," she replied firmly, and she chose as her final piece the Shaker song "Simple Gifts," enunciating every word clearly:

'Tis the gift to be simple, 'tis the gift to be free,
'Tis the gift to come down where we ought to be.
And when we find ourselves in the place just right,
'Twill be in the valley of love and delight.

When true simplicity is gain'd
To bow and to bend we shan't be asham'd,
To turn, turn will be our delight
'Til by turning, turning, we come round right.

"Love and delight at King's Inland? I hardly think that's what you've found." But there was no mockery in his voice, only rueful disbelief.

"Missy is my love and delight," she said, but she avoided his eyes. She was on the verge of telling him that Missy had sobbed for him, but she realized she couldn't explain why that was a good sign; Grey had been too badly bruised by the whole situation to think that crying was any better than a scream of terror. So instead, she mumbled something about Missy's having accepted the meeting much better than her outward actions showed.

Grey looked at her in silence for a long moment before he spoke. "Well, as long as you go on believing in her, I suppose there is hope." There was none in his voice. "Thank you for the music. Good night." He went down the hall and into his study. Not once had Brandy seen him look at Jasmine's portrait; he had not even glanced at it as he left the room.

When Brandy went upstairs, there was no sound of Missy scampering, and when she checked on her both child and puppy were asleep, only their heads showing from the heavy coverings. Brandy sighed; here was another problem. Winter's first snow would come soon, and already the rooms were cold unless a fire was kept burning. But Missy would not allow a fire in her room. The flame for light in the lamp she tolerated because of her fear of the dark, but she seemed indifferent to the cold, and Persia had told Brandy that the minute a fire was lighted in Missy's hearth, the child would retreat across the room and rock blindly until it was extinguished. Brandy wanted to change this, too, but she felt her ground was less firm here than in other areas; since her mother had died by fire, Missy certainly had a right to fear it.

She resisted the impulse to lock her door against Missy's night wandering; it would show a lack of trust and would undoubtedly frighten Missy if she found it bolted against her. And she was sure the child did not have the strength to suffocate her. Even if those episodes had been Missy's doing, she had only covered Brandy's face and departed before Brandy awoke. Certainly her hands did not have the power to hold the wrappings firmly enough to kill while Brandy struggled.

She heard Grey come up as she climbed into bed, hoping the events of the last twenty-four hours and her lack of sleep the night before would give her instant oblivion. And she did doze peacefully until the dreaming began and her sleep became a restless confusion of people and places, her dream eyes seeing first New England, then California, then both together. There was a fire in San Francisco, and she was going with her father to help, but it was Aunt Beatrice's Boston house which was burning. And the smell was getting stronger.

Brandy's terror awakened her. It was no nightmare. The flames were licking at the floor under one of the windows and beginning to run up the heavy draperies. She was at the desk without knowing she had moved. She hitched up her night rail and clambered up on the desk. Reaching as high as she could, she could just manage it; her hand found the protruding end of the heavy rod holding the curtains. She tried to push it up and out of its metal cradle; it moved but did not fall. In desperation she gave a little jump and hit the rod as hard as she could with the palm of her hand. It crashed to the floor, breaking a pane of glass on the way, and landed in a crumpled heap of heavy cloth. She jumped from the desk and began to use the material to smother the flames.

She screamed when rough hands grabbed her and shoved, and Grey's voice yelled, "Stay out of my way!"

She stood tight-lipped, watching him put out the fire. When he was done, he turned to her, his face grim, but she spoke first. "I was doing very well, thank you. You didn't have to push me!"

He stared at her for a stunned second, and then he burst out laughing. "Sweet Christ, Brandy, you are the only woman I know who would demand the right to fight her own fire!"

As suddenly as it had come, the humor drained from his face. "All right, how did it start?"

"How in the hell should I know!" she snapped. "Things have been rather busy since I woke up."

He examined the scene closely and found what he was looking for. The desk lamp lay on its side on the floor, its chimney blackened by the trail of oil fire it had bled. "That was very careless; you could have burned the house down." Implacable anger sounded in each word.

Brandy felt very strange. She sat down with a thump. "But I didn't leave the lamp burning. I never do when I go to bed. Even the one in Missy's room makes me nervous. Spending any time at all in San Francisco teaches one to be careful. And isn't it peculiar that it fell off without me hearing it and that it didn't break? Was the door open when you came bursting in?"

He nodded slowly.

"It was closed, though not locked, when I went to bed. And how did you know to come anyway?"

"I heard the crash, and then the smell . . ." His voice trailed off as he met her eyes. "My God," he said incredulously, "you don't think I did this? What do you think I came in here for, to see you burn?"

The world blurred, and Brandy could not bear the look on Grey's face. She hid her own face in her hands, and her voice was barely audible. "I don't know, I really don't. But someone started the fire, and whoever it was must be quite mad."

"Missy?" he asked, very quietly.

"How dare you suggest such a thing?" hissed Brandy, shooting out of the chair. "Your own child! She's terrified of fire; even if she did wish to harm me, which she doesn't, she would never do it that way." She believed what she said, but she could not quell a sudden doubt. Missy was brave enough to creep out of her room sometimes at night, even to go as far as entering Brandy's room; perhaps brave enough to have attempted smothering. The night child at work? What a choice, the child or the father.

"I will have a lock put on the outside of Missy's door, and I want it to be locked every night, Miss Claybourne."

The return to formality added an extra spur to her fury. "I'll see you with the devil first, Mr. King," she snarled, trying to keep her voice steady. "If anyone locks that door, I will unlock it. Missy is in enough of a prison without adding bolts and keys. If you knew your own child at all, you would know she is not capable of causing what happened tonight."

He watched her, the demonic light which unnerved her so beginning to show in his eyes. "As a matter of fact," he said very deliberately, "I have no idea what Missy is capable of. Perhaps the sins of the fathers are visited on the daughters when no sons are available."

She was blind to his leaving. It was as though he had admitted killing Jasmine. She did not check to see if Missy was awake. She climbed into bed and lay staring at the canopy above her. Even if Grey had started the fire, he had had enough remorse to come to her aid—unless he had thought the noise of the falling rod sufficient to alert Missy and maybe Margaret. He had been dressed in trousers but no shirt, still enough to cover him if he had had to leave the house quickly. It made no difference; she was too weary. She sobbed out her grief for him and did not know when the tears ended and sleep began.

When she awakened and looked at herself in the mirror, she wished she had done neither. She looked awful. She bathed her eyes to ease the swelling and pinched her cheeks to add some color, but the results weren't encouraging. For once she would have liked to possess some of Pearl's beauty potions. Then she chastised herself for being idiotic; what did it matter, everyone would know about it anyway.

As she went down the stairs, her assumption was confirmed. Persia and Mrs. Bailey met her, their faces full of shock and concern. "Oh, Brandy, how terrible for you!" cried Persia, hugging her tightly.

Brandy drew away and said firmly, "It's all right, though I am sorry about the draperies; you can be sure I won't do it again."

She watched them closely, but neither gave any sign that they doubted it was an accident. At least Grey hadn't told them he suspected Missy.

She went to brew a cup of tea and found Grey finishing his breakfast in the kitchen. Neither of them said anything until Mrs. Bailey had assured herself that Brandy had all she wanted to hand and had bustled out. Grey's face was pale in spite of his weathered skin. He regarded her intently, but said nothing, and Brandy spoke quickly out of nervousness.

"Thank you. I know you didn't tell them that you thought Missy started the fire or that she ought to be locked up."

"I still believe both," he said flatly, "but I am leaving the decision up to you. For all I care, this whole place can burn down, but since it is a most unpleasant way to die, much worse than a quick fall from a horse, perhaps you will reconsider. I am leaving, so one of your worries at least will be absent."

She should have been relieved that he was going, but instead, she was desolate and barely restrained herself from running to ask when he would return. She heard the faraway thud of the front door.

When she went to Missy, she paused in shock on the threshold of the room. The child was sitting on her bed, rocking furiously. Brandy had never seen her rock so hard. She felt all the ground they had gained together slipping away. She sat on the bed and gathered Missy into her arms, joining the motion of her own body with the child's, crooning to her as she rocked. "Missy, Missy love, I know you are upset; I know you know something about what happened last night. Don't worry, it was an accident, nobody did it, and nobody was hurt."

A shiver passed through the child as Brandy said that, but the rocking went on. Why? Had Missy started the fire, after all, or did she know who had? Or had she heard what Grey had said about her? All the possibilities were terrible, and the only comfort Brandy could find was that Missy's reaction was one more sign that the child was aware of what went on.

It took much longer than it had before, but it worked.

Brandy continued to rock, and Missy stopped. Brandy laid her back on the bed when her eyes closed and waited until she was sure sleep had come. She was sure Missy had not slept much of the night.

She knew why she didn't want to do it; she was afraid of what she might learn. But she steeled herself and went to find Rafe. He was in the stables, and one look into his eyes was enough to tell her that he knew about the fire.

"Please, Rafe, I need to talk to you."

"It is better for me not," he mumbled, not looking at her.

"You are the only one who can tell me. It was no accident, someone tried to kill me last night and I suspect on several other nights, and it was undoubtedly the same person who cut the girth. I don't want to be part of a pattern which was started long ago."

The silence between them thickened like a dangerous fog until Rafe began to speak, his words coming slowly with great effort. "You think he began the fire with the purpose to kill you. For why would he do that thing when the other has brought only sorrow? You have given life again to the house and a new beginning for his child, for why would he finish it?"

Brandy shook her head in despair. "I don't know, I don't! He says he thinks Missy did it, but I can't believe that. And Jasmine died by fire. You testified for him; you said he wasn't responsible. Is that true?"

His scarred face was wrenched with pain. "God, I should not say it, but you are in danger, you have the right to know. I did not tell the truth of that night as I saw it but as I knew it to be. You know my house; it is in the woods, away from the view of the stables. That night I was outside of it to listen to the dark things singing, to think dreams under the stars. The smell of the burning came to me strongly, and then I saw a light in the sky which was not of the night. I ran, hearing the distress of the horses as I was nearer. I saw Grey's horse tied away from the danger. Yes, he was there before my coming, and I do not know for how long before it.

"The fire was very bad; many of the fine horses died in it. Grey was wanting to go in to help them, most especially the young one, Orpheus, who was chosen for his own. I could not prevent him and so I went with him. It was such terror, I do not remember all that happened, but we reached the black colt, and near we found Jasmine. I led Orpheus away; Grey carried the burned body of his woman."

"Then it is true; he could have killed her himself."

"No!" He sounded furious with his effort to make her understand. "Because I did not see him come does not make it that he did something he would not do. In the war it is sure he killed other men as they tried to kill him. But not this thing, not this killing of a woman he loved. Some men, yes, not Grey." Brandy stared at him, ice beginning in her bones. His eyes were dead, and without their light, his face was truly ugly, menacing. She knew without doubt that he included himself in the phrase "some men." Had he killed Jasmine? No, she believed his harsh admission—Grey had been there before him. Then his own woman, had he killed her? And the fire in her room, had he set it? She knew two things at once: She knew that he would have no hesitation in committing such an act if he thought it was necessary to protect Grey, and she knew that she was no threat to Grey. She could still not see any way in which Rafe could judge her so. The frantic beating of her heart slowed. She sensed there was no use in asking him what his own crime had been, no use in admitting she knew there must have been one. If he wanted to tell her, he would have done so. Instead, she asked him how he had come to work for Grey.

As he spoke, she watched the light rekindle in his eyes. "From my life in the north country, I came south. I drank the whiskey and fought and did not care. I wanted to die, but I had not the courage to do it. Then one day I was by the docks. There was much going on, many ships being unloaded. Close to me was a wagon, very heavy, and hitched to it were a pair of horses, very big, very beautiful ones. While the men were taking things from the ship and putting them on the wagon, one of the horses, he fell. The stones under his feet were wet from the morning and the sea. He fell against his mate, and both went down, tangled with the wagon going over too. They were screaming in fear and hurt, but only one man went to them, all others were as stone. I was there helping him before I knew. Together we made them quiet and got them to their feet. They were cut and had swellings, but not of a serious nature. The horses, they were Pete and Polly, and they were my friends starting then. They are kind, for they judge a man only by what they know of him in the instant.

"For me, it was enough to have given succor. It was the first thing of value I had done in a year's time. But not for the man, not for Grey. He said he had need of a man to work with horses, and to me he gave the work. I told him I had not much knowledge of them except for the ones I had known on a farm as a boy. I remember, he laughed and said the knowledge was easy to teach if the love was there in the first. I told him of all the evil things of myself; it made not a difference. I have worked for him since that day."

He had explained more than he meant to, Brandy guessed. She remembered the bleak look he had had when once before he had mentioned the north. He had committed some unspeakable crime there and fled his home and his first language. And in his solitary way, he was still fleeing most people. Most people except for Grey. She was certain that Grey knew what he had done and that it made no difference; Rafe was too loyal to him not to have made his confession complete in every detail. It explained the strange bond between them. But there was no comfort in knowing that Rafe maintained Grey's innocence so vehemently, not because he had proof of it, but because he worshiped Grey and believed him to be superior to himself. *Oh,*

Rafe, she thought, *don't you see, in spite of whatever you did, you are basically kind and gentle, and you love him enough to damn yourself that he may appear to better advantage. He is more ruthless than you have ever been, much more likely to have committed a savage act and with less reason.*

She voiced none of this to him. His expression stilled her doubts. He stood patiently, as though waiting for her to turn from him in disgust at the picture of a wharfside drunkard and brawler. She touched his marked face lightly and said, "Rafe, whatever is in your past is past, and you've paid for it. You mustn't spend the rest of your life in a prison like Missy's. It isn't fair to you or to the people who love you; it isn't fair to Persia." She believed it as she said it; Grey and Persia were two people he would never harm.

The scar was white against the sudden ruddiness of his face. "How do you know of this?" he demanded harshly.

"I know because of the way the two of you look at each other and the way you try not to. I know because of the things you say to each other and more because of all the things you don't say. And I know because Persia is happy or sad according to whether or not she's seen you. She doesn't hide things very well."

"I have done nothing to give her sorrow, nothing," he said in despair.

"That's exactly what you've done—nothing. It's the hardest thing for her to bear, loving you the way she does."

"She must not love me then. It is not right. She is too young, with too much of life, with too much innocence. I have not anything to give her."

"You are a coward, Raphael Joly, and you're wrong about her. Persia's deep and true and as stubborn as this land. She can handle whatever you have to tell her. Why do you think she looked so bored with all those country boys at the dance? She doesn't want someone young and green. She wants you, seasoned by years, gentle and strong. And she'll go on wanting you even after you tell her about your past. Nothing will change her mind or her heart."

His face was still, but his beautiful eyes had the light of hope beginning. Brandy wished she did not feel compelled to ask her last question.

"Rafe, can you tell me anything about Jasmine?"

He shook his head. "I cannot speak badly of another's dead, of Grey's dead. But I will say because he is my friend that he was deserving of a better woman than he had, and in his brother also he deserves more than such a one who takes much and gives little."

"Well, perhaps Grey will be happy with Ruth."

"No, she and Raleigh, they are both the same nature. Not dangerous, but like little winds having no bodies and no hearts, blowing to make small noises and small mischiefs."

Poor things, not even full of sound and fury, she thought. She felt disloyal to Raleigh, but she could see the truth in Rafe's judgment. His unconscious raising of Raleigh's name with Jasmine's told a great deal.

"Thank you, my friend, for trusting me with so much of yourself," she said, hugging him briefly and pretending not to see the sudden brightness in his eyes.

When she got back to the house, she found Mrs. Bailey busy as usual dusting one of the cabinets in the hall, even doing the inside, handling each object with loving care. "You make me ashamed, Mrs. Bailey, don't you ever rest?"

As the housekeeper turned to smile, she lost her grip on the slippery piece of jade she was holding. There was a moment of midair gasping before she got hold of it again and set it back in the cabinet with trembling hands. Her face was so white that Brandy was alarmed and put a steadying arm around her. "That's quite enough cleaning for today," she admonished her gently. "Let's go make a cup of tea."

Mrs. Bailey closed her eyes for a moment and

gasped, "I've never broken anything in this house, never! That was so dreadfully careless of me."

"I think it was very agile of you to catch it, and you didn't break it, so come along," Brandy soothed her as she led her toward the kitchen, but privately she was a little taken aback by the housekeeper's distress. She was quite sure Grey wouldn't make any fuss over an accidental breakage. She realized anew how deeply Mrs. Bailey was dedicated to preserving every small part of King's Inland.

She made the tea strong and sweet and watched the color come back into the older woman's face. Mrs. Bailey smiled and nodded at her. "My, that does taste good! An old lady should know when to stop for a moment."

"Old lady, she says," snorted Brandy.

They were chatting about inconsequential things when Brandy heard herself ask abruptly, "Do you know what it was Rafe did that caused him to leave the north?" She was appalled to have asked. She hadn't meant to. It was as though the question had grown swiftly of its own accord to ask itself at the earliest opportunity. "I'm so sorry! Forget I ever asked. It's none of my business," she apologized.

Mrs. Bailey's face had grown very still and thoughtful, but then she shrugged. "No, my dear, you have a right to know since we live in such close quarters here. I think Rafe is a changed man, but at one time he must have been a very jealous, very violent one." She drew a deep breath before she continued. "He was married to a woman much younger than himself, and that is often bad business and cause for distrust. I think her name was Marianne. He only told the story once, to Grey and then to me when he first came here. He killed his wife because she had been unfaithful. He got the scar on his face in the struggle. That's all I know, but I don't think he is dangerous. That was, after all, a special case. And I'm happy to see you don't look too shocked."

"No, I'm not. That sort of thing happens in any part

of the country, and out West my father treated many cases where jealousy didn't have a very good aim with a gun or a knife. If you are capable of great love, then you must also be capable of great hate, or so it seems to me."

"Yes, that is very true," Mrs. Bailey said slowly. "I've lived long enough to see it proved time and again." Brandy excused herself and went slowly up the stairs to check on Missy. It was true, she wasn't shocked. She had suspected as much. But she did have a curious double feeling about what she'd learned. She could understand the impulse to kill for infidelity, but the actual picture of Rafe murdering his wife was gruesome and chilling. She did not want it to taint her friendship with him, and so she would just have to believe that her faith in him was justified, that what he had done had been necessary for him, and that one impulsive act in the past did not predict the future.

CHAPTER IX

For the next few days Brandy wondered if her mind would ever function properly again; every time she thought about the fire it went blank, refusing to consider the possibilities.

She could easily have moved to another room, but the one she occupied was the only part of the house that was particularly hers. She did not want to leave the solitary owl, Melissa King's writing box, the figured chair, or any of the other things which had become so familiar. Mrs. Bailey and Persia understood and helped her to put up new draperies borrowed from one of the third-floor rooms. The soft blue complemented the yellows of the room, but it was a constant reminder of what had happened to the original hangings. Rafe replaced the pane of glass from a store kept for repairs; windows did, after all, get broken now and then. But not many were broken under such circumstances, thought Brandy when she saw the clearer piece, which did not match the older, heavier panes.

Seeing Rafe with her new knowledge of him gave her an instant's pause, but she was relieved to find it was no more than that. She simply could not believe that his gentle eyes were the eyes of a habitual murderer. It was no hardship at all to smile at him and thank him for repairing the window.

Her numbness was broken by the arrival of a package

brought by special messenger from Grey. It contained a velvet dress for Missy, made in the same style as Brandy's, though the bodice was higher to fit the childish figure. It was sapphire blue, perfect for Missy's coloring. It said so many things that Brandy could hardly take them all in. It meant that Grey had witnessed the whole scene of Brandy holding Missy and singing to her at the top of the stairwell; that he had watched until the creaking board had given him away. It meant that he knew Missy well enough to describe her size exactly; Brandy was sure the dress would be a good fit. It meant that he had noticed every detail of Brandy's dress and that he cared about what his daughter wanted, cared enough to have done some very fast work in getting the fabric and having the dress made.

Every time she looked at the gift she thought of Grey and of the fire. She was faced again with the choice of the same five people: Rafe, Persia, Mrs. Bailey, Missy, and Grey. Only they had been around both when the girth had given way and when the fire had started. Persia, Rafe, Mrs. Bailey? They all accepted her, or at least they seemed to, and they had nothing to gain and everything to lose by a catastrophe at King's Inland.

Missy or Grey? She loved them both; it was agonizing to suspect either. And if either had done it, the action must have arisen out of madness. If it were Grey, then the gift to Missy was a weak protestation of innocence or a manifestation of a good side, one which loved and built rather than a side which hated and destroyed. She knew her love for him was clouding her judgment, and it was no easier to transfer the guilt to Missy. But in spite of herself, Brandy could see that the child might have a very good motive. Perhaps she did not wish to come back into the regular scheme of things; perhaps the night child was the stronger of the two and resented the intrusions Brandy had made.

She was still not convinced that the covering of her face had been intentional, and she willed herself not to believe it had been, for Missy was the one with the most opportunity to have done it. If true, it would seem the final proof of the night child's work.

In addition, she had to consider Raleigh, for if he was as jealous of Grey's position as she suspected, then his was the best motive of all. The house was easy to enter; there were many windows, and the front door was never bolted as far as she knew—why bother in the middle of nowhere? But Raleigh had gone back to Wiscasset, as had Ruth, long before the fire broke out. And even taking him at his worst, accepting the possibility that he operated out of sly greed, Brandy did not think it was in character for him to attempt murder. She agreed with Rafe's judgment, that Raleigh was a "little wind making small noises and small mischiefs."

Her jealousy and dislike interfered with her judgment of Ruth. She wondered if the woman was cruel enough to bribe someone, for she surmised she was too cowardly to soil her own hands with murder. But who at King's Inland would do such bidding, even for a price? Brandy couldn't believe it anyway; Ruth was too petty surely to be involved in any killing passion. Full, useless circle again.

She wished she could believe all the incidents had been accidental, but that was impossible. She had to face the fact that someone had made at least two outright attempts on her life. And accepting that meant she had two choices—to flee or to stay at King's Inland. She saw Hugh welcoming her home. But it was small temptation; her decision had been made with her first sight of Missy. She would go on with her work, and she would be very careful. But she would not abandon the child, not even if she found her to be guilty.

Though Missy still wandered at night, by no sign did she show hatred of Brandy or a wish to harm her, and Brandy did not awaken again to find anything pressed over her face. And while the nocturnal visits unnerved Brandy when she woke and lay silently watching Missy, she did not lock the door, and she took comfort from the fact that Missy never carried anything—no weapons at all. Her decision made for good or ill, she took up the task of expanding Missy's world again.

From Mrs. Bailey Brandy acquired some lengths of muslin, calico, and wool to make playclothes for Missy. It was possible now to order patterns by mail and even to acquire garments which only needed to be stitched together, but Brandy was a good seamstress, thanks to Pearl, and she had her own ideas about what she wanted to make. Everything was to be very simple so that Missy might be taught to dress herself. The lighter materials would do for indoor wear, and Brandy made dresses which buttoned down the front. From the wool she made Missy a pair of fitted trousers for the expeditions outside. She worked in Missy's room, and the child watched the movement of the needle with apparent fascination. Brandy guessed that wonder about how things were made and where they came from had not been part of Missy's shuttered existence until now, and she was delighted with her first interest.

When the first dress was completed, Brandy tried to explain to Missy how to put it on. She took the small hands in her own and showed them how a button went through a buttonhole, but it seemed to make no impression at all. Missy was quite content to wear the dress hanging open if Brandy didn't button it for her, even though they went through the learning exercise every day. And to her wry amusement, Brandy discovered that Missy didn't mind wearing no clothes at all if no one dressed her.

The child did take particular interest in the trousers, touching the material often and anxiously as Brandy worked on them, and Brandy was sure that was because she understood they were for going outdoors, something Missy was growing very fond of, even on the coldest days.

Brandy did not show Missy the dress from Grey until she judged the child to be, she hoped, happy and relaxed enough to accept it. Missy was sitting on the floor with Panza in her lap. Brandy had brought the

parcel with her that morning. Missy had shown no
curiosity about it then, but Brandy saw the sudden
tenseness as she unwrapped it, explaining where it had
come from.

"Isn't it beautiful? Your father sent it to you. He cares
so much for you he had it specially made."

Brandy held the dress out to her, and she watched
the conflict which was becoming so familiar. She was
willing to swear Missy wanted desperately to touch the
soft luxury of the velvet; her hand reached out tentatively, but then the fingers curved into rigid claws as
though inner strings were pulling them back puppet-
fashion. The dress was from her father; therefore, she
would not touch it. The strength of her control was
awesome. Brandy sighed and hung the dress in Missy's
wardrobe; if the child wanted it, she could reach it. No
one else would put it on for her; the decision had to be
her own.

Brandy went back to her sewing, and out of scraps of
material, yarn, and buttons, she made something else
for Missy—a rag doll with floppy hair and a happy
mouth. Missy had more dolls than any child Brandy
had ever known, and to Brandy they constituted a sad
mockery of Missy's inability to play. The dolls were the
finest from several decades, but they were all of wax,
wood, or china, and even those with cloth or leather
bodies had an unyielding formality to them which made
them seem more like showpieces than toys. Missy now
picked them up once in a while, but she obviously did
not see them as characters in imaginary situations, only
as objects to touch. She seemed to take everything at
its face value, not as a representation of anything else,
so a doll to her was simply a collection of materials put
together in a certain way.

When the rag doll was finished, Brandy presented it
to her and struggled to give it new meaning. "You saw
me make this, so you know it's just bits of things sewn
together. But now we are going to pretend it's a little
girl like you. Let's call her Molly. You can make believe

that Molly goes for walks, or rides, or anything you wish. Missy, do you remember, a long time ago, when you used to pretend things?"

Playing was so natural for normal children that Brandy felt there was no adequate explanation for it; she could explain what to do, could set up mechanical games, but that had nothing to do with the essence of playing or why it was done. She watched Missy anxiously. The hands reached out and took the doll, holding it limply for a moment, but then a strange cast came into her eyes. They shifted beyond Brandy, narrowed as though with the effort to see something very elusive and far away, and then came back to Brandy and finally to the doll. With a convulsive movement, Missy clutched the soft thing to her chest. Her body jerked a little, and Brandy knew what she was doing—she was remembering holding and rocking a doll in her arms.

"I'm very proud of you, darling," Brandy said unevenly. "Remembering how to do things is hard sometimes, but you've done it." Inwardly she hoped she was doing the right thing; too much remembering might be very damaging.

It was close to Thanksgiving before Brandy tested her next line of attack. The velvet dress still had not been touched as far as she could see, but at least Molly had been fully accepted and went everywhere with Missy. Brandy wanted to believe it was because she provided an imaginary playmate, but she was too realistic not to suspect it was much more likely that the doll represented a security link between herself and the child.

Grey had not been home since the day after the fire, and Margaret had received word that he would be spending the holiday in town with Ruth. Though Brandy missed his disturbing presence more than she liked to admit, this fitted in perfectly with her plans. She wondered fleetingly about Grey's reaction to Thanksgiving. Considering that President Lincoln had made it an official holiday after Gettysburg, she didn't think it would hold many happy memories for Grey. Then she

made herself quit thinking about it; the less concern
she had for his welfare, the better off she would be.

Missy could go down the stairs quite gracefully now,
and she went willingly because it meant going outdoors. But she still shivered while going through the
interior. Brandy wanted her to go into the rooms on the
first floor, but she knew how big a step it would be, and
she had put it off. Finally, she decided she had to risk it
on account of the weather; already rainy days kept them
inside, and once the snow came, outdoor activity would
be much more limited. She couldn't bear the thought of
Missy spending most of the winter in one room.

Brandy warned Mrs. Bailey and Persia of her plan,
and though they were both skeptical, they promised to
act as if nothing out of the ordinary were occurring.
And so after breakfast one morning, Brandy announced
to Missy that they were going downstairs. Missy was
wearing a calico dress, and she pulled it fretfully.
Brandy never ceased to be amazed at how clearly the
child could communicate when she wanted to, without
uttering a single word. Missy was plainly pointing out
that something was wrong because she wasn't dressed
for going outdoors.

"We're not going outside, sweetheart. We're just
going downstairs for a while." Softly spoken but a
definite command.

Missy sat down abruptly and began to rock and flick
her fingers. Panza whined worriedly and licked her face
and cried louder because of the lack of response. Brandy's temper rose, and she had a sudden terrible urge to
slap her, something she had never done to any child.
Instead, she reached down and picked the child up,
heavier now with more food and exercise, awkward
again because of muscles so rigidly held.

She made her way downstairs carefully, carrying her
burden and talking quietly. "You can't live in that room
forever. There are all sorts of rooms in the house, rooms
full of lovely things which belong to you because you
are part of the family."

She put her down at the foot of the stairs, expecting her to sit and rock, but after a moment's hesitation and one quick look down the hall toward Grey's study, Missy put her arms around Brandy, hiding her face in her skirt. Brandy knew she was terrified of being tricked into another confrontation with Grey. "No, don't worry, he isn't here now," she assured her, thinking how miserable it was that that should always be good news to the child.

Missy pulled away and stood looking around. Brandy took her by the hand, and she walked willingly. They did not meet Mrs. Bailey, but Persia was dusting in the front parlor when they walked in. Her eyes grew wide in astonishment, but she managed to say quite calmly, "Good morning to you, Missy," before she hurried out on the pretext of another chore to do.

Missy surveyed the room and suddenly grew tense again. Brandy followed her gaze and saw the fire burning in the grate. She cradled the child against her. "I know you don't like it, love, but fire is only bad when it burns the wrong things." *Oh, no,* she thought wildly, *how else could I have said it, but that's ghastly, the wrong things—such as your mother, such as me.* She went on steadily. "It is a very good thing in your lamp, where it gives you light, or in a fireplace, where it gives you warmth. You really must get used to it. Soon your room will be so cold that even Panza's fur coat won't keep him warm enough."

Missy understood; she reached down and patted Panza as though to reassure him. Brandy breathed a sigh of relief and settled herself in a large chair with Missy in her lap, not holding her too tightly, letting her decide what she wanted to do. After a little while Missy got down and began wandering around the room, touching everything within reach. Brandy was so happy about it that she wouldn't have minded having to explain a few broken treasures to Grey (though telling Mrs. Bailey would be like bringing news of a death), but Missy was being very careful. Brandy took her upstairs again as soon as she showed signs of becoming restless. One room at a time was enough.

But she pressed her advantage about the fire, and she lighted a small one in the fireplace of Missy's room. She picked up a storybook and settled herself in a chair by the fire, pretending to be engrossed in the book, but aware of Missy's every move. At first the child shied away to the far side of the room, holding herself tautly but at least not rocking. But then Panza flopped down on the hearth with a wheeze of contentment, and that was too much for Missy. She came over and crawled into Brandy's lap.

Brandy began to read the story aloud as though nothing unusual had happened. She often read to Missy, but she doubted that Missy understood the words as anything other than separate units which she recognized. If she didn't play, what sense could a story make about others playing or doing a host of things she did not do? Brandy tried to choose stories about dogs, horses, and other things which were familiar to Missy, but she really didn't think the connection between fact and fiction was very clear. Streams of words couldn't make much sense in Missy's silent world, or so Brandy had reasoned. This time she wasn't so sure, for as she read, she became aware of a small but continuous motion of Missy's head against her breast. At first she wondered if it were some new means of shutting things out, but then a startling possibility struck her. She increased and then decreased the speed of her reading; the head followed the changes, followed them because Brandy was sure the eyes were reading the words.

She stopped reading abruptly, mumbling an excuse about resting her voice for a moment. The golden head stopped moving. Brandy's mind whirled; mixed with her elation was a good deal of apprehension. Missy could read, so God only knew what other hidden talents she possessed. It gave her an eerie sense of not knowing the child at all, despite all the time they'd spent together. She wondered if reading was a remembered skill of a precocious three-year-old or if Missy had somehow picked it up in the last two years. And she wondered if Missy had followed the words before while she sat on her lap. She didn't think so; the motion of the head was so noticeable. So why had she betrayed herself? Had the day been so full of rediscoveries that some of her self-control had slipped, or had she done it on purpose, letting Brandy know? Brandy thought in despair that she would never understand all the complexities of Missy's character.

As soon as she had the opportunity, she asked Mrs. Bailey if Missy had known how to read in the time before. The housekeeper looked thoughtful for a moment before she spoke. "Well, as I've told you, because of Jasmine, I never had much to do with Missy's upbringing, so I don't really know. But I do remember that Grey would hold Missy on his lap and read to her, pointing out words they had not read together before. She was very bright in those days, so maybe she learned a bit then. Why do you ask?"

When she had explained, Mrs. Bailey said sadly, "I still fear you see too much progress in Missy because you want it so badly, but I must admit there have been remarkable changes in the child since you came. None of the others managed to do a thing with her; they came and went like the tide, and I don't think she ever really saw any of them. Though I must admit some of them reported strange things." Her voice trailed away, and she looked apologetic.

"What kind of things, Mrs. Bailey?" Brandy asked, wishing her voice didn't sound so sharp.

"Oh, nothing much, little things left on the top of the stairs where one might trip over them, and other things disappearing, never to be found. Why, one poor lady lost a very precious—to her anyway—packet of letters from a particular gentleman friend. But there, child," Mrs. Bailey said, patting Brandy's hand, "I don't think they had anything to do with Missy, just careless women blaming others for their own foolishness."

The housekeeper's reassurances rang hollow comfort in Brandy's ears until she convinced herself that whatever those other women had done or had had done to them had nothing to do with her. She only wished she hadn't had to do so much self-convincing lately.

The changes in Missy were not the only ones at King's Inland, Brandy noticed. Rafe had taken to whistling happily as he worked, and Persia beamed all day long. Brandy guessed their new relationship was a delicate thing, and she didn't want to damage it with clumsy questions. She was flattered when Persia herself offered an explanation.

It was the day before Thanksgiving, and Brandy had Missy downstairs again. Each day they explored, and they had seen every room except for the music room, Grey's study, and Mrs. Bailey's apartment. The housekeeper had said they could come visiting anytime, but Brandy didn't know how she could explain to Missy; she wanted the child to develop the freedom to wander around the house, and it would be confusing to show her the housekeeper's place and then to tell her she could not go there at will. Brandy knew Mrs. Bailey would give up her privacy for the child's sake, but she thought she deserved a place of her own just as Grey's father had intended. As for Grey's study, it was certainly not a room Missy would enjoy. The music room, with Jasmine's picture dominating it, they would tackle when Brandy thought Missy ready.

They were in the dining room, and Persia was there, too, polishing everything in preparation for the morrow's festivities. They could hear Mrs. Bailey busily at work in the kitchen. Missy wandered around looking at the marvelous wall hangings and touching chair coverings shyly, glancing back often to make sure Brandy was still there.

Brandy asked Persia what she would be doing for the feast and was startled by the sudden flood of color in the girl's cheeks. "Well, I'll help here in the mornin', an' then I'll hurry home to be with my family. But, oh,

Brandy, this year's special, Rafe's comin' home with me!"

"Why, that's wonderful!" exclaimed Brandy.

"Ayuh, 'tis all round wonderful 'tween Rafe an' me now. He's still holdin' back somethin', I can feel it, but at least we know we care for each other, an' I reckon he'll get round to tellin' me what's so heavy on him when he has a mind to. I can wait. I was beginnin' to think I was goin' to have to wait my whole life, be an old maid before anythin's happened." She glanced shyly at Brandy. "I don't know quite how, but I know you had something to do with bringin' us together, startin' with the night o' the dance, an' I thank you for it."

Brandy laughed guiltily. "I'm glad it's working out. I don't fancy playing the meddling old maid myself."

"You'll never be an old maid! It isn't my business, but I know Mr. Raleigh is fond o' you, an' you seem so o' him. Even if he is a bit o' a will-o'-the-wisp, I wish the two o' you could get together. Accordin' to Mrs. Bailey, he ought to be comin' in tomorrow."

Brandy said gently, "Thank you, Persia, but we're just good friends." She knew Persia wanted everyone to be as happy as she was. She tried to shut down an inner voice wailing, "I want Grey, not Raleigh!" She looked around for Missy and saw her staring at them. Brandy suspected she had heard and understood everything they had said, and to her amazement, Missy's reaction looked like relief, eyes and face quiet. The only thing Brandy could make of it was that the child was glad she did not love Raleigh, another hard-to-fathom response. She dismissed it, thinking that Missy was probably jealous of her loving anyone except herself.

She was seldom away from the child for long now, but when she was she usually found on her return that Missy was very anxious, sometimes shivering in what could only be acute fear. Brandy worried about it but felt helpless to change it. It was so important for Missy to love another human being that her dependence on Brandy was certainly healthier than her former withdrawn state, but the day would come when Brandy would be leaving, Ruth arriving to take over the house. Brandy hoped she would be equal to the task of making it acceptable to the child. Then she thought ruefully: *Acceptable to the child? How will I ever accept it myself, I love her so.*

She had taken Missy to the dining room several times for a specific purpose; she wanted the child to eat Thanksgiving dinner with the rest of them. In houses of the size and richness of King's Inland, it was not unusual for the children to eat at different hours from their parents or in the nursery for quite some years, but Brandy thought it important that Missy share the feast and learn to carry on normal tasks in the presence of others, one more weapon against Ruth. She did not think Missy could be any more nervous than she was about the experiment.

Raleigh was a big help. He had ridden hard to arrive on time for the midday meal. Even with her new opinion of his character, Brandy could not resist his high spirits and teasing ways, and apparently neither could Missy.

Raleigh came to her room, picked her up, and swung her around. "Well, pet, I hear you're going to eat with us today just like a young lady. I know you can walk there by yourself too, but Uncle Raleigh is claiming the pleasure of carrying you." And so it was easily accomplished.

But the meal was not a success. Missy was ill at ease, not looking at anyone, eating little, shivering occasionally but trying her best to behave properly. Brandy sat beside her, hugging her now and then, whispering words of encouragement to her, thankful for Raleigh's banter, which eased the strain.

After it was over, she told Missy how proud of her she was, and as a reward she brought up some extra food which Missy ate hungrily. At least it was another step forward.

Raleigh stayed for a few days, and they rode and

walked during the day, Brandy making sure Missy went with them. She did not want a repetition of Raleigh's kiss; even the memory of it made the comparison of Grey's harder to bear. In the evenings, when she played the piano and they sang, Mrs. Bailey was with them, and so she was safe then, too.

Raleigh wasn't blind, but all he said was: "Running away or to, Golden Eyes?" And when she pretended not to understand, he shrugged and let it go.

On Sunday he left early because the sky had a new look, low and shrouded in heavy gray-white clouds, and the air had the unmistakable clean, sharp fragrance of coming snow. Brandy gave him some letters to post and asked him an additional favor, apologizing for putting him to so much trouble. Though Rafe served as messenger and supplier for King's Inland, she knew this task would be easier for Raleigh. She gave him a list of purchases to make for her and the money for them, asking that they be sent out with the next delivery, if he could find out when that would be. She laughed, looking at the sky, and said she would understand if the articles didn't arrive until spring.

He didn't want to accept the money, but she overrode him, thinking cynically that it would more likely be Grey than Raleigh who paid if she didn't. He brushed aside her misgivings about the delivery. "Don't worry, I'll get them to you in a few days. There are always ways; we don't get frozen in here as solidly as they do in the north. But, Brandy, you haven't been away from King's Inland since the day you arrived. I could at least arrange to take you to Union, if not to Wiscasset."

She answered him truthfully. "I haven't really thought about it, and the only reason I need anything now is for making Christmas presents. I always start much later than I should. I'm perfectly happy here, and I don't want to leave Missy too long."

He looked at her searchingly for a moment, nodded,

gave her a light good-bye kiss on the cheek and was gone.

The snow began at twilight, and later Brandy sat by the window holding Missy. She felt as excited as she always had by the first snowfall in the high mountain country of California. Memories flooded back, and she was strangely close to her father, to Pearl, and to all the varied characters she had known in her old life. For a moment she was so homesick for the West that her throat knotted and her vision blurred, but then Missy stirred, curling her body into a more comfortable position as she fell asleep, and the old images vanished, leaving nothing but the weight of love for the child she held. She did not think she could feel more than a mother to Missy even had she given birth to her; they had come so far from infant blankness together. She tried to banish Ruth from her mind; surely even so selfish a woman would be charmed by Missy once she really knew her. She put Missy and Panza to bed and sat for a long time watching, drawing peace from them.

It snowed all night, and morning saw a new world. The sun shone fitfully, offering moments of flashing brilliance as an extra gift. Brandy could hardly wait to be out, and after breakfast she hurriedly bundled herself and Missy into warm clothes.

Snow was no new thing to Missy, but she hadn't been out in it for a long time. She touched and tasted it and delighted Brandy with her explorations. But Panza was best of all to watch. He had never seen it before, and his antics were hysterical. He put his nose in it and gave a startled yelp. He tried to pick up his feet up and walk on top to no avail. Finally he sat down, his fat rump sinking into the snow, and yowled his outrage. Brandy was laughing so hard she hardly had the strength to pick him up, but when she did, he gave her face a grateful swipe with his tongue. She heard another sound and looked around at Missy.

Missy was smiling, not a tentative movement of the mouth, but a true smile, and the sound had been the rusty beginning of a laugh. As Brandy had guessed, Missy's face was unbelievably beautiful when she smiled. Her black eyes danced; her whole face curved into new planes of joy.

Brandy went to her and kissed her as Panza snuggled between them. She thought that laughing and crying after so long a time of denial must be similar to trying out a leg which had been broken and immobile for months. The sob in the woods and now this—they were fine beginnings.

They plowed through to the barn and found Rafe busily at work putting special shoes on the horses. The shoes had sharp cleats on them so the animals would not slip on the ice. A big old sleigh had been pulled out and stood in the middle of the floor, gleaming with evidence of Rafe's hard work.

He greeted them with the happy look he so often wore these days. "Yes, you see, the horse too must change his clothes for the winter." Missy smiled again and Rafe saw it. His eyes flew to Brandy, who nodded, but he went on as though nothing extraordinary had happened. "When the ice is on the top of the snow, then we will go on the sleigh."

Missy wandered around the barn while Brandy talked to Rafe. Brandy didn't want to pry, but she couldn't stand it anymore, so she asked, "Rafe, did all go well at the Cowperwaithes? Did you have a good time?"

His eyes held the same softness they had for Missy. "They are a good people, and it was good sharing such a feast with them. I think even they like me and do not mind that Persia and I may be together," he added with wonder.

"Of course they don't mind, you fool," Brandy admonished him. "You are a fine man and the only one who will make Persia happy, so why shouldn't they like you?"

"I do not think I yet believe it, but little by little it seems true. And the bad things of myself, these too I will tell her," he assured her anxiously.

"That's up to you, Rafe, but surely you know Persia well enough by now to know that whatever you have to tell her will make no difference in her love." She met his eyes steadily, not wanting to betray how much she knew. He nodded as though not trusting himself to speak, and Brandy headed Missy and Panza back to the house.

Raleigh was true to his word, and the things Brandy had ordered arrived by the end of the week. She was glad to start on the gifts, and she let Missy watch all the work except that on the child's own present, a wardrobe of clothes for the rag doll. For the Cowperwaithes she had got a bag of hard candies for the toddlers, bottles of scent for the girls and their mother, and hunting knives for Ben and his father; they were all so self-reliant that she couldn't think of anything to make that they hadn't made already. For Mrs. Bailey and for Dorothea Adams she planned ruffled aprons, and for Rafe a pair of mittens. Raleigh would receive handkerchiefs with finely rolled edges and his initials embroidered on them—a nice gift but not too personal. She decided on the same for the Adams men. She would knit a shawl for Pearl, though she thought ruefully that it would probably arrive in California quite a time after Christmas. Only with the choice of Grey's gift was she at a loss. She thought of making him a pair of mittens like Rafe's, a scarf, a shirt, but nothing seemed right, nothing seemed adequate. Then she made her decision and was satisfied, though she reflected sadly that he probably wouldn't even be at King's Inland for Christmas; he would probably be with Ruth.

She and Missy were outside at every opportunity, and when the snow crusted over, Rafe took them out in the sleigh. Brandy loved it all: the merry sound of the harness bells; the smooth slip of the runners carrying them through an enchanted kingdom of trees transformed into white castles, of distances changed in lost perspective, of bare patches on the evergreens making eerie black silhouettes against the snow. And Missy's cheeks were always bright from the cold air and her pleasure by the time they got home.

It kept snowing on and off, and by the week before Christmas there had been no word from Grey, and Brandy resigned herself to the fact that he would not be coming for the holiday; even if he wished to, the drifts would discourage him, and there was no reason for him to want to anyway, not with Ruth in town.

She couldn't help feeling a little lonesome with everyone's plans that Saturday, for Rafe was leaving early to spend the day at the Cowperwaithes, dropping Mrs. Bailey off at a neighborhood farm on the way, but she had never minded their absence before and knew she did now only because she was missing Grey. Outwardly she gave no sign of it, ordering everyone to scat because she had Christmas secrets to work on, and finally they were gone.

Brandy took Missy outside for a while, but it started to snow again as it had been threatening to do since early morning, so they were forced back indoors. They had lunch from the lavish spread Mrs. Bailey had left for them, and then they went up to Missy's room, and Brandy put some more logs on the fire, something Missy now accepted without fear.

The child fell asleep at once, exhausted by the romp in the cold. Brandy tried to work on Rafe's mittens, but her own eyes were intolerably heavy, and soon she was sleeping soundly in the chair by the fire.

A log breaking with a rumble in the fireplace and Panza's worried cry woke her. She sat up rubbing her eyes and looking around dazedly, feeling very muddleheaded. But then her pulse quickened. Missy wasn't in the room. Panza was, and Molly lay on the bed where Missy had been sleeping, but the child was gone.

Brandy stood frozen for a moment, trying to still panic with reasons for Missy's absence—perhaps she had gone to a room downstairs on her own. But no, she wouldn't go without Molly and Panza. Brandy didn't think she would go without her either.

She raced out of the room, checking her own room and the others on the second floor, calling Missy's name all the while, before she ran downstairs. The draft hit her immediately, frigid air sweeping in through the open front door, snow blowing in to melt in the hall.

She stared at the opening, trying to take it in. Missy outdoors, by herself in the falling snow, in a dress as light as the one Brandy herself was wearing. She grabbed her cloak from the rack in the hall; there was no time to change into sensible clothes and boots; a child would freeze to death so quickly.

The snow was deep and hampering, and Brandy cursed in desperation. It blinded her and was coming down hard enough to cover tracks as soon as they were made. She reached the barn, calling as loudly as she could, finding no one.

Brandy didn't pray often, but she did now, repeating over and over, "God, don't let her be dead, please, please keep her safe until I find her!"

She tried desperately to think of where Missy might have gone—Missy who did not seem to feel the cold but who would die of it anyway. She had a sudden image of the first happy day at the pond. It had remained Missy's favorite place. Brandy tried to run, struggling and falling in the deep drifts, sobbing in fear. If only someone else had been home today, if only, if only.

She was already tiring, and she forced herself to go more slowly down the trail, peering through the muffling curtain for any sign of the slight form. She lost track of time and distance as she plodded on. The world was becoming a bright mass of pain starting in her hands—gloves or at the very least mittens for a lady, she thought crazily—her feet, her uncovered face, and moving through her whole body.

She swayed dizzily as she caught sight of a dark spot at the side of the trail. But when she reached it, it was no more than a fir branch which had dropped its burden of snow. She sank down, deciding to rest for a while.

She knew it was dangerous, this peaceful sleepy feeling, but it was so much better than the earlier pain of the cold. She would rest just a little longer. Nothing mattered anymore anyway; Missy must be dead by now. *Missy, I love you, and there was so much hope, someday you would have left your private darkness and joined us in the sun. Ruth, damn her soul, will be glad. But Grey, your father, no, I don't think so, I think he loves you much more than I do.*

She curled herself tighter in her cloak. The shivering had stopped. She felt a comforting warmth spreading through her. No, she wouldn't move now; it was so nice here. The snow went on about its gentle business of covering her.

Someone was pulling at her, shaking her, picking her up. Her blood poured like fire, searing its way back into her frozen limbs. She screamed in protest.

"I know, I know, but it can't be helped. I've got to get you back." Grey's face was close to hers.

She remembered, and the shivering started again, adding agony. "Missy, Missy's dead, she's out here. I couldn't find her. Oh, Grey, I couldn't find her. My fault, my fault, I went to sleep." She thought she was shouting, but the words came out in a broken whisper. Grey had to bend closer to hear them.

"Brandy, Missy's fine, she's warm and safe at home. Can you hear me? Nothing's wrong with her."

She slipped from the jarring pain of being carried into darkness. She did not feel Grey's strong hands holding her fiercely against his own warmth; she did not hear him repeating her name over and over.

Icy fire brought her back. They were robbing her with it. Everything hurt, and she struggled to get away from the relentless hands.

"There, Brandy, the snow will start your blood again, then we'll make you warm." Grey's voice, then something held against her mouth, her head lifted. "Drink it slowly, Brandy." She gasped as the heat of the liquor cut her breathing for a moment. "There are two kinds of brandy in Maine," she said, and tried to smile, but the shivering had started again. "Missy?" came out through her chattering teeth.

Grey lifted her head again so that she could see her in the corner hugging herself and rocking. "Don't do that, Missy, I'll rock you," she said, and slipped back into the shadows.

She was watching her father gamble at the Belle Union. It was much too hot there. She tried to tell him she was going outside for air, but he didn't seem to hear her. Then she was with Pearl, who asked her if she was all right, but a customer called her, and she left. She was back in the high country. Winter had come early, and she was freezing. Again she tried to tell her father. He was setting Jed Mitchel's broken arm. He didn't look up; he just said, "Brandy doesn't freeze." Why were they out in the snow in the middle of nowhere? No one would explain. And then Missy was beside her, saying her name over and over. "Oh, Missy, that's wonderful. We've got to tell your father. He'll be so happy." But Missy disappeared, and so did her father and Jed. She ran through the snow calling their names. She ran into the sun's blazing heat and back into winter again and again, finding no one.

CHAPTER X

She felt flat and light as though her body weighed nothing at all, but she was awake; the West had gone back to where it belonged, and she knew where she was. Then, as she took in the scene in her bedroom, she wasn't sure she was as conscious as she thought. Grey was sitting beside the bed, watching her anxiously. Obviously she'd had her eyes open before in delirium and hadn't recognized him. Across from him, separated only by the bed, was Missy, curled up in a chair, fast asleep with Molly clasped against her. Brandy's eyes widened; Missy had on the dress Grey had sent, and it had been buttoned so crookedly that she must have put it on herself.

Brandy looked at Grey again and saw the relief dawn on his face as he realized she was back with the living. His smile answered her own, and the rhythm of her heart beat a curious tattoo.

He spoke softly so as not to wake Missy. "How are you feeling? May I get you anything?"

"No, thank you. I'm fine, really, just tired." She didn't have to make any effort to keep her voice low; her best effort was weak and faraway-sounding. "How long has it been?"

"Today is Monday, or rather tonight is. Who is Jed Mitchel?"

Brandy stared at him blankly for a moment, trying to

follow, finding her mind was working very slowly. He sounded jealous. She had an instant's temptation to make up a wild story to tease him, but she had more important things to talk about. "Jed Mitchel was a prospector my father and I knew. He must be at least eighty by now, but I bet he's still roaming the mother lode looking for his next fortune. He's made and lost several." She glanced at Missy again; the child was still sleeping soundly. "The dress, Grey, and her being in the same room with you, I don't understand."

"Neither do I. Persia's been staying with her, but even so she's been rather neglected the past few days, and she put the dress on herself and came in here, in spite of my presence. I'm not concerned about why she did so; both acts were so positive that nothing else matters. But I think it's because she was worried about you and wanted to please you. She ignores me completely, but I prefer that to screaming terror." His tone was matter-of-fact, but his face betrayed his intense love for his child as clearly as it had on the night he had carried her to her room. Knowing as she did now that, despite outward control, Grey's emotional reactions were fierce, she wondered how he could love so cold a woman as Ruth Collins. But then she chided herself wryly; for all she knew, Ruth was anything but cold when she was alone with Grey.

Though he still spoke quietly, there was an underlying note of urgency. "Brandy, I'm not sure you're strong enough to talk about it yet, but I want to know what happened, why you were out there, why you thought Missy was in danger. God, you nearly froze to death!" He covered his face with his hands for a moment, hiding his expression.

Brandy relived the wild panic which had sent her out into the snow. She fought for control so that she could make the story sound reasonable, but before she could begin, a movement from the chair drew her attention. Missy was staring at her, her small face drawn with worry.

Brandy held out her arms. "See, darling, I'm fine, just sleepy. Come here so I can hug you."

The beautiful smile appeared, and in the next instant, Brandy was cradling Missy in her arms. Missy burrowed against her warmth, sighing in contentment, a strange new sound for her, not once looking at Grey. The slight jostling against the bed and sharp squeaks told of Panza's attempts to join them. Grey went around and picked the puppy up and deposited him on the bed. "I'll talk to you later, but right now I'm going to go tell Margaret and Persia the good news and have them bring you something to eat." *And if I leave, Missy's joy will be complete*, rang in Brandy's mind as if Grey had said it aloud.

Missy's vigil must have been even more tiring than Grey's, for once assured that Brandy was safe, she relaxed again into sleep. When Persia came in, Brandy put a finger to her lips in warning against waking the child.

"Mrs. Bailey's bringin' your supper. She wouldn't let me do it, wanted to see for herself that you're all right. I'll just put Missy to bed. She's been terrible worried, poor mite." Persia's whisper sounded awfully loud to Brandy, but Missy didn't wake, not even when Persia picked her up, and Brandy was thankful that her anxiety had lessened enough to allow her to sleep so deeply.

Mrs. Bailey arrived next, bearing a heavily laden tray. "Well, my dear, you really are back with us. What a fright you gave us! This room has been a meeting hall, what with Grey and Missy insisting on staying and Persia and I in and out."

"There isn't any adequate way to thank you all for your care of me, Mrs. Bailey. I just hope you know how grateful I am. But I'm completely in the dark. How did Grey find me?"

"You were very lucky. Since it was snowing so hard, I had Burt Thomas bring me back from the farm a little earlier than I'd planned. I didn't want to be stuck there. When I arrived, the front door was wide open which seemed odd, though I thought a gust of wind might have pushed it if it hadn't been properly shut. But when I couldn't find you, I started to worry. Then I found Missy asleep in the music room all by herself, but of course, she couldn't tell me where you were."

"The music room! She's never gone in there." Brandy shut her eyes, remembering that she hadn't even checked it. What grief she could have spared herself!

"Well, that's where she was. And I had taken her back upstairs and was still looking for you when Grey came in. I told him about the open door, and he seemed to know instantly what had happened. He went out to find you. Lucky for you he did! Now you eat what you want and leave the rest. And then you go right back to sleep; you've had a difficult time."

After Mrs. Bailey left, Brandy picked at the food, but she wasn't hungry. A very disturbing question was forming in her mind. Why had Missy let her go out in the storm? The only reasonable answer seemed to be that Missy had opened the door and tricked her into going out on purpose. She must have heard her calling, yet she had given no sign of her whereabouts, had stayed in a room which, if she were as clever as Brandy thought she was, she had known would not be checked. Further evidence of the demon side?

Brandy clung to her knowledge that Missy had been truly worried about her recovery, so at least the good side was still operative. She turned restlessly, shutting her eyes tightly, wanting to sleep so that she would not have to think. But her mind refused to stop working. Missy had put on the velvet dress, and she had betrayed her ability to read, both actions connected with Grey. What was she trying to say? Maybe nothing at all, maybe just the good side trying to please Brandy or maybe a statement about her father, that he was guilty, innocent? What if Missy herself had lured her mother out to the barn? She moaned aloud in confusion, not hearing Grey come in.

He was beside the bed, asking urgently, "What's wrong? Are you in pain? Shall I get Margaret or Persia?"

She managed to smile weakly at him, touched by his concern. "No, I don't need anyone, but thank you. I'm just disgusted by my own stupidity. I could have saved myself and the rest of you a great deal of distress had I searched for Missy more thoroughly before I ran out of the house in panic." She wished she sounded more convincing; Grey was a hard man to fool.

"Tell me exactly what happened, Brandy." No room for refusal.

She related the events, hoping that even if they made her seem foolish, they would provide a logical explanation for the whole thing. But Grey's capacity for detail extended to everything, even to the behavior of his daughter. Brandy realized that someone must have given him even better reports of Missy's activities than she had.

His eyes never left her face; his voice was slow and deliberate. "But Missy doesn't go anywhere without you and you've never taken her into the music room, have you?"

Brandy shook her head and closed her eyes again so that she wouldn't have to look at him anymore. His voice went on inexorably. "Then she must have done it on purpose. She must have opened the door and hidden so that you would go out in the storm."

Her eyes flew open, and she met his, bird and snake. Her throat worked convulsively, but when she spoke, she had herself in mind. "I would like to believe she went to the music room because she wanted to do it on her own and that she fell asleep there—we were both very sleepy; we played out in the cold that morning. But I admit that sounds pretty farfetched, and I'm prepared to accept the idea that she did it on purpose, or at least part of her did.

"Grey, sometimes it seems as if Missy might be two different people, one good, one bad, and the more progress the real child, the good child, makes, the more the bad one tries to disrupt things."

She didn't have to wait long for his reaction. "So where in the hell does that leave you?" He was making an unsuccessful effort not to shout. "Apparently she has tried to kill you by a fall, by fire, by cold. What do you think she'll try next, so clever and inventive a child?"

"Stop it! She'll hear you! All those accidents or whatever they were . . . . well, I still have no proof Missy caused them. You are still just as likely a suspect save perhaps for this last episode." She watched him as she said the brutal words, but he did not flinch. "But if she did, then just the fact that I'm aware it's a possibility will help. Trouble is always easier to handle if you know where it's coming from.

"Can't you see, if it's true, it must be a good sign? It must mean that the sick part of Missy feels so threatened by the progress she's making that it feels moved to do something about it. My job is to make the good part stronger and stronger until it can take over completely."

Grey shook his head wearily. "I think you would judge it a good omen if Satan himself appeared." He stared blindly at a shadowed corner of the canopy above Brandy's head. "I want her to get well more than anything else. But I do not want anyone dying in the process. Yet, if you leave now, everything will go back to the way it was; she will cease to exist again. Perhaps you are right about being able to avoid further danger, but I can't give you any more chances. It is hard enough to let you stay now. If anything else happens, you will leave immediately. If you are still capable of leaving, if you are still alive," he added grimly, his ebony eyes once more focused on her.

She knew it was an ultimatum without recourse, and ultimatums usually made her angry, but this one was just. She reached out and took his hand. He looked startled; then he smiled ruefully and shook her hand firmly as if sealing a gentleman's agreement. Inwardly Brandy cursed her weakness; even touching his hands made her giddy. The controlled strength, the hard ridges of muscle or sinew, the calluses from reins and work, the long fingers with blunt nails—for a moment Brandy was lost in the sculptured beauty of them. She saw them younger, finer, carving the little boat for Mrs. Bailey; she saw them controlling Orpheus with ease, she saw them touching Ruth, and she dropped the one she had been holding for such an embarrassing length of time.

The hot blood rose in her face, and she forced herself to look at Grey, expecting him to be sardonically knowing and amused. But strangely he looked as if he had been caught out, too, stunned and unsure of what to do next.

Brandy took a deep breath and brought them back from the dangerous place. "I am certainly grateful for it, but I'm curious, how did you happen along at just the right moment to find me? How did you know where to look?"

This brought the reaction her earlier comment had failed to provoke; all the harsh lines were back in an instant, and she realized he had mistaken the reason for her question. "No, Grey, no. I'm not blaming you. Had you not come, I would be long dead. I'm just curious because your timing was so perfect for my need."

His defensiveness was replaced by a wry smile. "For once I was trying to do the right thing. Ruth wants me to spend Christmas with her, and she won't come here." Brandy knew she was the reason for that, but there was no rancor in Grey's statement. "I came out to deliver gifts and early wishes for a happy Christmas. And I knew of your walks with Missy into the woods and to the pond. It used to be my favorite place when I was a child. I suppose some instinct told me you had gone that way."

How ironic, Brandy thought, to owe thanks to Ruth for her life. "Then, please, don't delay because of me. I'm fine, and I'm sure Ruth must be anxious to have you back." She was satisfied with the cool reasonableness of her voice.

But Grey's eyes glinted and bored into hers as he asked with false sweetness, "Trying to get rid of me? Ruth will just have to celebrate Christmas a little later this year if she wants to be with me. Christmas Day will be soon enough to leave. Any objections? Will that interfere with your plans?"

Mutely she shook her head, ignoring his sarcasm, made much too happy by the prospect of having him at King's Inland for the holiday.

He was suddenly contrite. "You're tired, go to sleep now. I won't tease you further."

He turned back to look at her when he reached the door. "How very glad I am that you are safe."

She felt as if she had been given a special benediction, and she lay at peace, letting the unanswerable questions slip away at last. Her last thought as sleep found her was of the days ahead, with Grey.

Persia's entrance with a breakfast tray the next morning reminded Brandy of her first day at King's Inland; how long ago that seemed! "I'm not an invalid, you know," she protested. "I feel quite well this morning and can't wait to get out of bed." But to please Persia, she did as she was told and ate the meal ravenously, finding her appetite had returned with a vengeance.

Persia perched on the edge of the bed, and the absence of her normal chatter was very noticeable. Brandy glanced at her curiously and smiled to herself. Wherever Persia was, it wasn't in this room. Her eyes were soft with faraway dreaming, her mouth curved happily, and her skin glowed with a new radiance. She felt Brandy's gaze and turned. She hesitated, and then her smile widened, and she burst out: "Oh, we were goin' to keep it secret awhile longer, but I can't keep it from you a minute more. Rafe an' I are goin' to get married come spring! I'd like to have done with waitin' right now, but Rafe, my poor man, he had such a bad time afore, he's skittish 'bout takin' another wife."

Persia's eyes grew round, and she cried in dismay, "Jus' look what I've done, gone an' blathered half o' Rafe's shame." Her voice took on a firm, defiant note. "Only 'twasn't shame, 'twas only what any man would have to do. He was married to this Marianne woman, an' a right piece o' sin she was. She cheated poor Rafe, but he killed her more for th' child than for that."

Brandy had thought it would be difficult to appear sufficiently surprised at the retelling of the tale, but her gasp of "The child!" would have convinced anyone that she had never heard the story before.

Persia nodded. "They had a little boy. Rafe wanted to give him lots o' things, so he spent a good lot o' time in th' woods, huntin' an' trappin'. An' while he was gone, that woman took another man, a man who was supposed to be a friend to Rafe. But my man is a good man, an' I think he could have put up with that. It was comin' back to find his child ailin' an' left in the hands o' neighbors that pushed him too far. Th' child died in his arms, an' Rafe went lookin' for Marianne. He found her with her lover, an' he killed 'em both, an' I can't fault him for it."

"I can't either," murmured Brandy softly. Her faith in Persia had been justified; Rafe's confession had made no difference to the girl, save to make her love him more compassionately. A new thought struck her—how typical of human nature; the crime remained the same as when Mrs. Bailey had told it, but seen through Persia's lovingly prejudiced eyes and with all the details, all the venom was gone.

She congratulated Persia wholeheartedly and tried to ignore a sad pang of envy; Maine people seemed to take spring very seriously as a season for new beginnings—Persia and Rafe, Ruth and Grey, marriages to come at a time when she would be leaving King's Inland, Missy, Grey.

When she had finished her breakfast and Persia had left with the tray, Brandy got up. Her legs felt as if they belonged to the rag doll Molly, and she fumed impatiently over the time it took her to dress. She was appalled at the changes the short but violent illness had made in her appearance. Her face was pale, her eyes ringed by bruised shadows, and she had lost enough weight to make her dress hang loosely.

"No wonder everyone is making such a fuss," she said to her reflection. "You look quite horrid; not even the cats would associate with you."

There was a knock at her door, and Persia brought Missy and Panza in and then went off to do her chores. Brandy was content to rest in her favorite chair by the fire with Missy on her lap. Missy held Molly tightly against her, and Brandy still found it difficult to believe that there was a part of her so separate that it could abandon the treasured doll.

That afternoon Persia came to take Missy and Panza for a walk. Missy tugged at Brandy's hand, but then she went willingly with Persia after Brandy had explained it would be a few days before she could go out.

Brandy decided she had been upstairs long enough. She pinched her cheeks to give them some color and headed for the stairs. But she wasn't halfway down before she had to stop. "Damn!" she swore in vexation as she hung on to the banister. The stairs seemed to be moving of their own accord while the whole world rocked gently as if at sea. Perspiration stood out on her face and ran down her neck. She wondered giddily if this was how Missy had felt when she had first walked down the stairs. She shut her eyes and shook her head to clear it and yelped when Grey swung her up into his arms.

He gave her a little shake. "Do you have some overwhelming desire to break your neck? You looked as if you were going to finish your descent with one plunge from the top."

She was so thankful that he'd caught her before she'd done just that that she answered meekly, "I guess I overestimated my strength, but I got so bored up there!"

"Please, next time yell for assistance. Now, where to, miss?" he asked, causing her to giggle because he sounded just like a polite hansom driver. Her laughter helped her to ignore the disconcertingly intimate feeling of his heart beating against her.

He was carrying her when Mrs. Bailey met them. Her eyes went wide with surprise behind her spectacles. "Gracious!" she exclaimed, shocked by the impropriety of the scene.

"Just found an early Christmas present," explained Grey, wickedly straight-faced. "We'll be in the front parlor. Please bring Brandy some tea and something good to eat. We'll have to feed her up for a while. I know from firsthand experience, she's pretty bony right now." Brandy, for fear of being dropped, restrained herself from finding his ribs with her elbow.

When she was comfortably ensconced in the parlor, she apologized for troubling him further but asked if he had any books or sheets of Christmas music, and she was surprised by the wide selection he brought to her. But the inscription in *Christmas Carols New and Old* reminded her of why it should be so: "To my wife and my daughter, the music of my days, with all my love, Grey." The book had been printed in sixty-five, a time when Jasmine, Grey, and Missy were still a family, two years before the fire.

She looked up at Grey, suddenly aware that Christmas might be a bad time for him. Though she said nothing, he answered the expression on her face. He spoke gently, as though explaining something to a child. "Life is difficult enough without being haunted by the dead, particularly by someone else's dead. And Jasmine, for all her faults, would not have relished the role of a ghost. She was far too vital for that."

He left to work in his study as Mrs. Bailey brought in the tea tray. She glanced at the music. "Oh, it will be nice to have carols again! I do think Christmas music is the most fun of all." They chatted amiably until Mrs. Bailey said she had to get back to work, and Brandy was relieved when she left because she could not take her mind from Grey and Jasmine. In spite of what he had said, the music had ended for Grey when Jasmine died. Brandy was stunned by the emotions she felt; she was ragingly jealous of the love Jasmine had had from him and afraid that by her death she had killed his capacity to love anyone else. "But it's Ruth's problem, not mine," she said to the empty room, and forced herself to study the lines and notes until she began to hear the melodies in her mind.

By the time Persia came in with a pink-cheeked Missy and a slightly damp Panza, Brandy was feeling much more in spirit with the season. She hugged them both and chattered about festive plans.

She felt stronger each day, and by the time Friday brought Christmas Eve there was no denying that King's Inland was in tune with the season, ghosts or not. Grey and Rafe had brought in armloads of greenery, which, tied with red ribbons, filled the house with the clean fragrance of pine. They had cut a beautifully symmetrical tree, which stood in the music room bedecked with candles waiting to give light. Packages had been appearing as if by magic at its base, and Brandy had to restrain herself from behaving like a child and prowling through them to shake, weigh, and to guess their contents. Enticing smells drifted out of the kitchen, and Brandy worked frantically to lend a hand and to finish the gifts she was making. As she set the last stitches in Raleigh's handkerchiefs, she couldn't help breathing a sigh of relief that he was not there; she hoped he wasn't lonesome, but his presence would bring the awful tension between the brothers, would break the fragile peace of King's Inland.

Brandy donned her velvet dress for the festivities. She was ready well ahead of time and went to prepare Missy. The child had not dressed herself again since the episode of the blue dress, but when she saw Brandy, she ran to the wardrobe and pulled out her own velvet gown. Brandy was so pleased with this performance that her hands were unsteady as she helped Missy with the buttons, and she buttoned one wrong on a sleeve. Missy's hand immediately touched hers, and the child shook her head. Brandy laughed. "How right you are, and what a clumsy buttoner I am!" *And how observant you are*, she added silently.

She explained the plans for the evening as thoroughly as she could, hoping that knowing what was to come would make her less fearful. And at least Missy did not protest going downstairs, though she clutched Molly tightly and looked around every time Panza lagged.

Before supper they met in the parlor for holiday toasts from a bowl of hot spiced cider which Grey had laced liberally with spirits. A milder brew had been set aside for Missy, and Brandy thought she ought to share it with her since she already felt drunk with the excitement of the evening. But then she decided to hell with caution and drank the stronger punch, feeling the warmth explode and flow through her. She watched Missy carefully and had the absurd thought that she was the only adult in the room; the rest of them, even Grey, were acting as silly as five-year-olds at a first party. Missy was solemn and self-contained, valiantly holding her body still, only fixing her eyes on Brandy, ignoring the others completely.

Persia and Rafe were with them, dividing their time between what they called their two families. Christmas Day they would spend at the Cowperwaithe farm. The first toast was to the couple, for Persia had gone on spreading the news of their engagement.

"That one, my Persia, she is not to be trusted with the secret," Rafe complained in mock disgust, but the melodious way he said her name betrayed him. Brandy knew he must be relieved that Persia was so open; Marianne had had far too many secrets.

Grey raised his glass. "To Rafe, my most trusted friend, and to his lovely bride to be, may your years together be long, happy ones." If there was a double meaning in "most trusted," Brandy didn't care; Grey's wish for their happiness was sincere, and the toast made her want to weep for the couple's joy and Grey's lack of it.

But Mrs. Bailey's tart comment made her laugh instead. "I declare," she said, "I am getting old and blind—I didn't know. It's a sure sign of being in your dotage when you miss the signs of a couple courting. Grey, I may have to retire to my rocking chair for the rest of my days."

"Not on your life!" he exclaimed. "If you gave up, I am sure King's Inland would fall into ruin in no time at all."

Mrs. Bailey scolded him for being a flatterer, but her cheeks were bright with the compliment.

They toasted crops yet to be planted and colts yet to be born in the spring yet to come, and Brandy watched Missy lifting her glass to drink at each signal. At first she thought the child was just aping her elders, but the final toast convinced her that Missy was listening to every word and knew what was going on.

The solemnity of Grey's voice brought stillness to the room. "To my beautiful daughter, Missy, who has traveled so far in so short a time, and to Brandy, who made the journey possible and who, thank God, is still with us."

Tears blurred Brandy's vision, and in spite of herself, she could not stop the few that left warm, wet traces on her cheeks. Grey's eyes looked into hers as if no one else were in the room, and she turned away, meeting the same black intensity in Missy's. The young eyes were narrowed, aware, and focused on her as the child raised her glass with the others and gravely sipped her sweet cider. The good side was thankful for her safety.

Supper was lavish and gay, and even Missy ate well, though still she looked at no one but Brandy. Brandy was glad that the custom of keeping Christmas Eve rather than Christmas Day prevailed at King's Inland; she and her father had done likewise, finding the night a better harbor for miracles than full sun. As they left the table, she drew a deep breath and hoped her next plan would work as a small miracle and not a disaster.

The tree had been set up in the music room at her request. Grey had been doubtful but had complied. Brandy reasoned that Missy had made the first decision about the room by going there to cause harm; therefore, she must be shown that the room was a place for joy. One point more for the good side.

Rafe and Grey went ahead and shut the door behind them, leaving the ladies to wait outside, Missy pressed closer to Brandy, and Brandy could feel her trembling—from fear, anticipation, guilt, or old memories? Who ever knew what Missy was truly feeling?

When the men opened the door, there was a collective gasp of astonishment. The room was in darkness save for the pyramid of radiance from the many-candled tree. For an instant it seemed to Brandy the essence of the season, the sudden splendid light, but then Missy shattered the moment by sinking to the floor and beginning to rock and flick her fingers.

Ignoring the stiff agony in Grey's face, Brandy motioned everyone to go in as she sank to the floor beside Missy and drew her into her arms.

"It isn't the same, darling, it isn't. It's like the fire in your room, in the lamps, the good fires I've told you about. There are many flames, but they are for happiness, not sadness. If you'll just look at them, you'll see how beautiful they are." The rocking stopped; the fingers ceased to dance. Missy looked up at her and then slowly turned her gaze to the tree. A small sigh escaped, and she stood, waiting quietly for Brandy to get up. It was as if she had said, "If you say it is so, I will believe it." Brandy felt that no gift could exceed that of Missy's trust.

She smiled at the others to reassure them, but as Rafe lit the lamps in the room, her attention was on Missy. As incredible as it seemed, she was sure that the child did not remember her recent visit to the room. Her eyes were exploring everything with the peculiar

intentness she only showed when seeing something for
the first time. A barely perceptible jerk of the golden
head told Brandy she had recognized the portrait of her
mother and had been startled by it, conclusive and
comforting proof that the good side shared nothing
knowingly with the bad. It followed logically that the
Missy she loved had no wish to harm her. The last
miserable knot of doubt eased and disappeared.

Gay with the relief of it, she drew Missy against her,
telling her of the music to come, of the rainbow packages to be opened. The others, who had been chattering
with false brightness to cover Missy's reaction, relaxed—
all save Grey, who looked withdrawn and thoughtful.
He never missed anything; he had seen Missy's response to the room as clearly as she had, but the
difference was that he did not see it as a cause for
rejoicing.

She didn't want him to think about it anymore. She
went to the piano, settling Missy at her side on the
bench. She stroked the keys softly at first, wandering
from one tune to another, watching Missy. Missy concentrated on the hands touching the keys, and Brandy,
noting the absorption in her face, saw another way to
teach her to communicate. She wondered what kind of
ecstasy and terror Missy would ask from the piano if she
knew how to play.

Mrs. Bailey, Rafe, Persia, and Grey gathered around
to sing, but Missy's only acknowledgment of their
presence was to press closer to Brandy. Brandy struck
the chords for "Joy to the World!" and started to sing
while the others joined in. The women had sweet
hymn-trained voices, and even shy Rafe sang, his accent softening the words, but the biggest surprise was
Grey's voice, deep and true on every note. Brandy
pushed away the thought of all the music he and
Jasmine must have made together.

They sang "Hark! The Herald Angels Sing," "It Came
Upon the Midnight Clear," and many traditional English tunes. And when they sang, "O, Come, All Ye

Faithful," Grey sang the Latin words in perfect harmony. Brandy finished with "O Little Town of Bethlehem," a song which had been written the year before, but she faltered when no one else joined in, realizing that new music had not come to King's Inland after Jasmine's death. Grey said, "Please, go on," and so she finished the song, knowing she was singing not to praise the Lord, but to please Grey.

After the caroling, Grey read from the Gospel, according to St. Luke, and Brandy felt closer to the miracle than she ever had. She was thankful King's Inland was not a rigidly churchgoing household; she and her father had rarely had contact with organized churches, and warnings of doom and lists of rules made her feel embarrassed and uneasy rather than pious.

When the reading was finished, Grey smiled briefly. "Now I trust the Lord will forgive a secular ceremony," he said, gesturing toward the packages.

Brandy led Missy toward the tree, and after one hesitant pulling back and a long look at the tiny flames, the child went without resistance. Brandy settled down on the floor, the velvet circle of her dress rippling out around her, and drew Missy into her lap.

Grey read the names on the packages and handed them out. Brandy discovered that one of the nice things about being older was the pleasure she got from watching other people's joy. Rafe donned the mittens to show what a perfect fit they were, and Persia dabbed scent on her wrist and held it out to ask Rafe if he liked it. Even the redoubtable Mrs. Bailey was so pleased with her apron that she put it on. Brandy saw with amusement that the bright wrappings and ribbons fascinated Missy as much as the contents of the packages, but when she had finally got to the clothes for Molly, she knew immediately what they were, and dressed the doll in a new dress before she went to her next gift. Surely that was playing.

The one thing Brandy decided not to watch was Grey opening her gift to him. She was suddenly and uncom-

fortably aware that the gift was much too intimate. She
didn't look at him as he handed her her packages. One
was small and bore Hugh's unmistakable script. She felt
guilty because Hugh must have gone to much trouble
to get the gift to her on time while her presents for the
Adamses would be late. One of the other boxes was
large and heavy, and it was from Grey. These two she
saved for last.

She was touched by the gifts she received from the
household. Persia and the other Cowperwaithe girls
had made a many-colored quilt for her. It reflected the
same passionate love for brightness that she had seen in
the little touches such as the knots of colored yarn in
the oil wells of the lamps and the brilliant hooked rugs
on the polished wood floors in the Cowperwaithe home.
Mrs. Bailey gave her an intricately embroidered work
bag, and from Rafe she received finely braided leather
reins which she knew he had made.

She crowed aloud when she opened a package she
had not even noticed at first. The book was newly
published, and Pearl must have taken great pains to
send it to her. It was entitled *Eminent Women of the
Age* and contained, in addition to thick pages of text,
marvelous steel etchings of its heroines. On the flyleaf
was written: "To Brandy, to her unquenchable and
independent spirit, with love, Pearl." How like Pearl to
use a sly pun to send her such a book.

Brandy looked up to see Grey regarding her quizzically.
She handed him the book. He smiled and said, "I think
I would like to meet her; then I would have some idea
of what you'll be like in fifty years or so."

Brandy turned her attention to the box from Hugh;
Grey's remark had been so odd and personal that she
didn't know what to make of it. Tears stung her eyes as
she saw what Hugh had sent her. On a bed of purple
velvet lay a heart-shaped locket. Tiny blue forget-me-
nots enameled one side and on the other was engraved:
"To Brandy, my love, Hugh." It was a precious gift, but
it made her feel miserable and treacherous. *Oh, Hugh,*

she pleaded silently, as if he could hear and heed from so far away, *stop loving me, please, please, stop!* She kept her head bowed, not wanting Grey to see.

Her hands fumbled for the solid weight of the box from Grey. There was no use putting it off, and its bulk suggested something safe such as a set of books. She had noticed what he had given the others—puzzles, books, and a dress for Missy, and for his employees small personal gifts and bonus wages. Brandy thought she would not be able to bear it if her gift included money from him.

The first thing she saw when she opened the box was the candlelight reflecting on a glistening sea of heavy silk. She had never seen such a variety of ambers, browns, and golds; the material might have been woven into a shawl just for her. She picked it up and buried her face in it, loving the sensuous touch of it against her skin. "Oh, Grey, I . . ." Her voice trailed off as she caught sight of what had given the box such weight.

She knew what it was only because Chen Lee had one like it, and among all his possessions, it was his most treasured, the one inanimate object he vowed he would risk his life to save from destruction. It was a thousand or more years old, yet still patches of the original finish remained as evidence of the blues, reds, and greens which had decorated the pottery tomb horse. And the beast himself had lost none of his arrogant power to the ages. His muscular haunches held him as one foreleg forward, one up curved, he prepared to leap skyward.

Brandy touched it timidly but did not pick it up. "Grey, it's beautiful. It's the most beautiful thing I've ever seen. But I can't accept it—it's much too . . ." She looked up and saw her father's watch chain with the gold nugget in his hand.

She and Grey were alone. Even Missy ceased to exist. Grey watched her with amused tenderness, swinging the gift she had given him gently back and forth. "Too precious? Too valuable?" he asked softly.

She felt as she had that day on the steps before he had saved her, as if she were going to fall a great distance. But now she wanted to fall, she wanted to say, "Grey, don't marry Ruth. She'll never love you as I do." Instead, she felt the sudden urgent weight of Missy pressing against her, and the room slipped back into focus. Persia, Rafe, and Mrs. Bailey were staring in dazed silence.

Never had Brandy wished so much for the affectations of a gentlewoman, for a dishonest face. She managed to say, "Thank you. I shall take it with me when I leave King's Inland," quietly and with only the slightest tremor in her voice, not looking at Grey.

Grey said something in reply, but Brandy lost the words in the uneasy chatter which rose in the room and in Missy's need. At first she could not understand what had caused the shivering which gripped Missy like a chill, but then she realized how stupid she had been to speak of leaving. She held Missy close and crooned to her, ignoring everyone else. "Darling, I'm sorry to have said such a silly thing. I won't be leaving for a long while and not until you don't need me anymore. I promise." *Forgive the lie when the time comes*, she begged silently. Missy nestled against her, still and trusting. Brandy had to wait a moment before she could speak. "Missy and I are tired. We'll go upstairs now. Thank you all for the lovely Christmas, and Persia, please wish your family a Merry Christmas for me.

"Come, Missy, we'll collect our presents tomorrow; they're quite safe here now." Missy waited docilely to go up, insisting only on bringing Molly with her as usual. Brandy felt sneaky as she picked up the locket from Hugh, but she did not want anyone to read the inscription.

Grey watched them leave but did not protest their going.

As Brandy readied Missy for bed, she glanced out the window and saw that it was beginning to snow, and she was glad of it. Perhaps Grey would not be able to leave in the morning.

She was very tired by the time Missy was asleep, and she was in her own room, but her emotions were wide awake. "All right, wise one," she said, staring at the owl, "what does it all mean? He is marrying Ruth, yet he gives me gifts fit for a queen. Is it only gratitude for Missy's improvement? Is it only that?"

The owl stared back, solitary, silent.

CHAPTER XI

Christmas Day dawned with mocking brightness, and by late morning the snow proved to be neither refuge nor barricade. Grey was preparing to depart, and disaster arrived.

In Persia's absence Brandy was helping Mrs. Bailey in the kitchen when the front door slammed. Thinking Grey was leaving without saying good-bye, she flew into the hall only to stop short. Raleigh was there beaming at her, his smile quickly changing to a frown as he got a better look at her, and Ruth Collins stood beside him, her face distorted with hate she made no attempt to conceal.

"Why, Golden Eyes, what have they done to you? You look like a haunt!" Raleigh crossed to her swiftly, taking her in his arms, and she did not resist. She forgot her nasty suspicions of his character, taking comfort in his warm care of her, in the barrier he provided against the vengeance of Ruth.

She did not hear Grey come out of his study, but she suspected uneasily that Raleigh had, for when the icy voice cut the air and made her flinch, Raleigh did not start or put her out of his arms. It was she who stepped away.

"No wonder you did not wish to delay me, Brandy. You did indeed have other plans." Grey's eyes raked her insolently. He did not even notice that Ruth was there until he heard her gasp of outrage. He gave her one cold look which damned her for coming uninvited and froze her into silence for a moment. Brandy shared her silence, staring at Grey, helpless with anger, afraid of what she might say. Not so Raleigh; his carefree tone told that he was enjoying the situation.

"Shame on you, big brother, for jumping to such an unjust conclusion. Actually Ruth and I made the long cold journey, even to spending Christmas Eve in a strange farmhouse, on your account. Ruth threatened to make the trip alone if I was not willing to escort her. Such love this fair lady has for you to be so inconvenienced. You were, I believe, supposed to spend these days with her, and you are to be the honored guest at her New Year's Eve party. She couldn't help fearing some harm had befallen you."

Grey's voice lost none of its chill; if he felt guilty about his treatment of Ruth, he did not show it. "I would not have suspected you of such consideration for me, little brother." The emphasis was on "little." "I was going back today, but since you are both here, I will delay my departure for a few days, and we can go back together."

"That will not be necessary." Ruth had found her voice. "I will return with you today. I know what's been going on, and I will not spend one minute more than I must in this house with your whore. If you want me to stay, send her packing this instant!"

Brandy did not know whether or not Grey would have defended her; her anger rose so quickly that her own voice seemed separate from her, the words spoken by someone else. She moved to stand glaring down at Ruth. "You have a foul tongue, Miss Collins. I'm thankful that I can't see the muck in your mind. I too know what's been going on. Though I expect you use a more delicate word for yourself, you've been Grey's whore for years. Keep the title—there is no contest."

Ruth raised her hand to strike, and Brandy grabbed it fiercely, hissing, "I wouldn't do that if I were you. I'm much stronger than you are, and right now I'd welcome an excuse to teach you some manners."

Brandy released the hand, and Ruth shrank back. Grey's voice lashed out, "Enough!" as he stepped between them, pushing them roughly to get them out of each other's range. His breath came quickly as though he had been running, and his terrible anger seemed to include everyone, even himself. For an instant he looked blind with it, and Brandy stepped back and felt the renewed comfort of Raleigh's arms, just as Grey turned to say something to her. The sudden and queerly gentle expression was gone so quickly from his face that Brandy thought she must have imagined it. His eyes ignored her as he spoke to Raleigh. "We'll leave shortly. Will you be accompanying us?" It was a thinly veiled command, but Raleigh stood his ground with surprising firmness.

"No, you go right ahead. The only thing I have waiting for me in town is an empty house, and the only family I have is here. I think I'll just spend a few days at King's Inland for the sake of holiday cheer."

"All right. Do as you please," Grey said, his voice flat and empty. Though Brandy thought Raleigh's victory was deserved, she hated the idea of Grey losing any battle. She was, she decided, just as bad as all the lovesick, simpering misses for whom she had always had such disdain. How could she feel compassion for him when he was preparing to leave with the woman of his choice? She was a complete fool.

Grey barely gave Ruth time to freshen up and accept a cup of tea from Mrs. Bailey before they left. Brandy suspected that the housekeeper must have heard the whole disgraceful scene, but in no way did the older woman betray it. And Brandy, in the music room with Raleigh, was shocked at the jealousy that rose in her at the thought of Mrs. Bailey soothing Ruth's ruffled feathers, of Ruth preening. The housekeeper seemed so genuinely fond of Ruth, Ruth so deferential to Mrs. Bailey—Brandy had a hard time understanding it. She suppressed the cynical thought that perhaps the two didn't truly like each other at all but had simply made an early truce regarding which shares each would own of Grey and his possessions.

Raleigh and Ruth had come by sleigh, and Grey tied Orpheus in place of Casco to the back. As soon as Ruth left the house, Brandy went to the door to watch them depart. It made further shambles of her pride, but she couldn't help it. If Grey saw her, he made no sign.

"Poor Golden Eyes, you do have a bad case of it, don't you?" said Raleigh as he came up beside her. His voice was pleasant, but for an instant his eyes had a strange glitter which made him look disconcertingly like Grey. Brandy had the fleeting thought that perhaps all three members of the King family were mad—light and dark. "I asked you some time ago, before the recent war, why you are so thin and pale."

She watched the sleigh disappear before she spoke. Ignoring his remark about her feelings for Grey, she told him what had happened, emphasizing how much the fault lay with her for losing her head, but he was not taken in. "He is a very clever man, my brother, when it comes to getting his own way. And the second time must be easier."

Brandy was so overcome with fury and revulsion that she didn't know what she was doing until she felt the sting of her hand on Raleigh's cheek. She backed away, stunned to have done such a thing. "I'm sorry! I am no better than Ruth, and that is bad indeed. But Grey saved my life. Don't flaunt your disloyalty to him around me. I don't want to hear it." She turned on her heel and left him rubbing his jaw and staring after her.

When she brought Missy down with her for the midday Christmas dinner, she felt as if Grey had taken the holiday with him, leaving the house with nothing more than echoes of his presence. She had difficulty swallowing any of the tasty meal she had helped to prepare. Seeing Raleigh sitting at Grey's place in pale imitation made it worse. She was glad he and Mrs. Bailey had so much to talk about since it saved her the effort, and she was glad neither of them mentioned Ruth; it would please her mightily if she never heard that name again. Her misery was compounded because Missy was obviously aware of her tension; her smile had vanished, her body shook with slight, periodic tremors, her hands clenched now and then as if to prevent the forbidden finger flicking, and she reached out with jerky motions to touch Brandy every now and then as though to reassure herself. It was a heroic attempt at self-control, and Brandy had to fight the same battle to keep from breaking down and weeping.

She felt a little better when she took Missy and Panza out for a brief tramp in the snow before the early dark came down. It was the first time out since her illness, and she drew in the crisp air thankfully. Raleigh insisted on going with them, but he said little, being careful not to make her angry or to distress Missy, and so it was easy to ignore him. Seeing the barn made her wish Rafe was there to visit; disfigured and gnarled as he was, he seemed a gentle, protective force at King's Inland. She shivered suddenly as she remembered his Marianne, and she told Missy it was time to go in.

She excused herself early in the evening but remained awake long after Missy had been put to bed. Her life was becoming unbearably complicated. Raleigh had found his package from her, had opened it and thanked her, but then he had made a cryptic remark about waiting until the right moment to give her his gift. It gave her the uneasy certainty that she was going to have another problem on her hands fairly soon. Meanwhile, the locket from Hugh and an unfinished letter to him waited accusingly in Melissa King's writing box. She sat at the desk, took the letter out, and struggled with the words once more. How do you tell a fine man who has offered you the best of himself that you aren't interested, are in fact distressed by his persistence? She gave up, put the letter back in the box, and got up to pace impatiently around her room. She almost wished for one of Missy's eerie visits, but that wasn't even a possibility; the child had an uncanny knowledge of when it was safest to prowl.

No matter where she looked in her room, her eyes always came back to the pottery on her bureau. She felt as if through the carved and painted eyes, Grey watched her. If she were not such a weak fool, she would hide the figure. Then she snorted in disgust at herself; trying to banish Grey from her mind was like trying to lock the wind in a closet.

In desperation she settled down to read from the book Pearl had sent her, quickly deciding that by comparison with the courageous ladies of the text, she was absolutely spineless. "Olympia Brown, I hate you," she declared grimly as she closed the book.

For the next few days she played a child's game of hide-and-seek with Raleigh. In spite of his persistent efforts to see her alone, she managed to be chaperoned by Persia, Rafe, Mrs. Bailey, or, absurd thought, Missy. But she suspected he knew what she was doing and that for him it added just that much more spice to the chase.

He finally trapped her one night, and Mrs. Bailey served as his willing, though unwitting, ally. Missy was asleep, and Brandy was playing the piano for Raleigh and Mrs. Bailey when the older woman yawned and said, "It's rude of me, I'm sorry, it's all the Christmas excitement catching up with me. I can hardly keep my eyes open." She left the room swiftly, telling Raleigh to have a good time.

Brandy stood up abruptly, fully intending to follow Mrs. Bailey, but Raleigh's lazy insolence stopped her. "Running away again, Golden Eyes? You've been very busy avoiding me all week. Aren't you weary of it?"

Brandy planted her feet, and her chin went a shade higher. "What did you expect me to do, set the stage for whatever scene you plan to play?"

She expected him to be angry, but instead, he spoke gently. "No, of course not. I just prefer to make my proposal in private." He was at her side, holding a small open box out to her. In the box was a ring. "Will you marry me, Brandy Claybourne?"

She stared at the thing. She saw Raleigh's hand tremble a little, and all she felt was a rush of pity for him. He truly wanted the marriage, but for all the wrong reasons. She spoke to him in the same careful way she used with Missy. "Raleigh, you hardly know me, and maybe you know yourself even less. You don't love me; you just want me because you think I'm one of Grey's possessions. You're wrong; he's marrying Ruth of his own free will. He chose her, not me. You mustn't base your life on hurting him." She wondered again how much truth there was in the rumor that he had had an affair with Jasmine; that would certainly have been a pretty piece of vengeance.

Raleigh had a right to be angry for her blunt speaking, but he only looked thoughtful and his voice was mild. "Perhaps you're right. I always have liked getting the best of Grey, though I haven't done it very often," he added with a disarming grin. "But I think you're underestimating Grey's interest in you. I'll try not to slander him anymore, not in your hearing at least, but I warn you, he is not a gentleman. Be wary of him, Brandy. You're wrong about us, too; I think we would suit admirably. Just consider all the improvements you could make in my character," he teased. "Will you accept the ring, anyway, as a Christmas gift of friendship and for being kind to Missy? I got it for you. I would not give it to anyone else, so it will be a great waste if you don't take it."

Brandy was at a loss. She had braced herself for an angry battle, but now she felt as if she had purposely kicked Panza. She had to suppress a laugh; Raleigh would hate to be compared to a puppy. She looked at the ring, three flawless amethysts set in an ornately scrolled band of gold. It was beautiful, and she wanted to accept it for the reason given, but she still felt uneasy. Lavish gifts from both brothers. What would she say if she had to explain? Raleigh saw her hesitation and took her right hand gently, placing the ring on her third finger. It fit perfectly, and defiance rose in Brandy—it was no one's business but hers.

It burned with purple fire as she turned it on her finger. "It looks quite old. Wherever did you get it?"

Raleigh laughed easily. "I would make a fine pirate, and I know several fellows who would make a good crew. The ring came from an old salt who managed to collect a fair store of plunder during his sailing days. His chief delight is trading his treasures for someone else's and making a profit besides. We both had a good time dickering."

She was afraid to ask what he had traded for it. Instead, she reached up and gave him a light kiss of thanks and a firm good-night. As she fell asleep, she thought of how odd it was that when Grey was in the house she was always conscious of his movements, of when he retired to his room, yet she never heard Raleigh come or go from the one he used. She did not care whether he slept or not, and perhaps in time she would not care about Grey either.

Raleigh left the next morning, and Brandy saw him off with relief and cynical amusement. She was quite sure that having failed in his object at King's Inland, he would find ample consolation in town. Despite what he had said to Grey, she doubted very much that Raleigh's house was ever empty for long.

His leaving did raise one unpleasant thought—tomorrow night in town, Ruth and Grey would see the new year in together, while she would probably see it in alone or, at the very best, in the company of a bored Mrs. Bailey—so open and welcoming with Raleigh and Ruth Collins, so distant with her—and a sleeping child. An overwhelming pang of homesickness hit her as she recalled the riotous celebrations she had enjoyed in San Francisco. She lectured herself sternly for self-pity. Nothing would be the same, even if by magic she could spend the night there. Her father was dead, the city was more straightlaced now, and Pearl would probably be sleeping just as soundly as Missy by midnight.

By afternoon she was happy and at peace again as she bundled Missy and herself into warm clothes. Rafe saw them and insisted he had enough time to take them for a sleigh ride. The world seemed very empty and still save for the jingle of the harness and the muffled beat of hooves, but then Brandy caught sight of the rusty stealth of a fox moving in and out of cover and pointed him out. Missy squirmed in delight as the fox stopped in mid-trot to glare haughtily at them before he melted into the shadows of a snow-laden tree. Panza barked and tried to jump out of the sleigh, and Rafe took his hat off in salute. "That one is very sure of his cleverness. To him we are slow and stupid beasts."

When they got home, Brandy jumped down and Rafe handed Missy to her. She put the little girl down and then reached for Panza, turning to hand him to Missy, but Missy's eyes were focused far down the lane, and she paid no attention to the puppy. Rafe let out a hiss of surprise. Brandy saw the horseman and thought it was Raleigh returning until the sun turned Orpheus' coat to black satin.

She felt the blood pour out of her head, leaving her brain dry and dizzy, and she clutched the edge of the sleigh for support. Grey back, now, why, what about Ruth and the party? She looked around wildly for Missy and found her in the same spot regarding first her, then her father with no apparent signs of panic but rather with a calculating expression which unnerved Brandy even further.

"Aren't you trying to do too much too soon?" he asked, looking down at her, enjoying her discomfiture.

She was weary of allowing herself to be played with,

cat and mouse. She forgot anyone else was there, and her voice was waspish. "Why are you here? What about your darling Ruth and her party? Don't you belong somewhere else?" She stressed "belong" but Grey did not rise to the bait; her anger pleased him just as much as her first shocked reaction had.

His voice was easy, pleasant. "Surely you know by now I come and go as I please?" No explanation about Ruth. "Is my brother still here?"

"No. He left this morning. I'm surprised you didn't cross trails." An even more satisfied glint appeared in his eyes. Brandy turned away in disgust and took Missy into the house while the men went to stable the horses.

Mrs. Bailey met them in the hall, and her inquiry about the ride died as she saw Brandy's stormy face. Brandy forestalled any questions by snapping, "Grey's back," and continuing her march with Missy up the stairs.

It took Brandy several incredulous moments to recognize the child's reaction—Missy was gleeful, not indifferent or fearful about her father's return. Her movements were quick and light as she danced around her room picking things up at random, hugging Panza now and then, flitting as Rafe had once described it, "as a butterfly flower to flower," making Brandy's confusion absolute. The only reason for the child's joy might be that Grey's return represented a blow to Ruth, clearly an enemy in Missy's eyes. But as clever as Brandy thought her, she did not think her capable of such inverted thinking. She left her as soon as she could and took refuge in her own room, trying to bring order to the chaos in her mind, trying to slow the frantic beating of her heart. Grey's influence on her emotions was something she had never encountered before, diametrically different from the effects of Hugh and Raleigh. And never had she resented another human being as much.

She wanted to have supper with Missy or take her downstairs as a shield. But then she was so chagrined to have thought that way, her defiance flooded back. With so little effort, Grey had her completely cowed. "Not anymore, Grey King, not anymore," she muttered to herself.

There was a soft knock on her door, and Persia came in timidly in response to her harsh permission. "Mrs. Bailey said you seemed upset, an' I see she was right. She wanted me to check on you. Do you need anythin'?"

Brandy felt like saying, "Yes, Grey's head on a platter, please," but instead, she relaxed and smiled at Persia, whose concern for her was genuine. "No, really, I just had a bad temper tantrum. I seemed to have had quite a few since my silly illness." She patted the bed. "Come, sit down and talk to me if you have time. I've hardly seen you all this week."

The ready warmth colored Persia's cheeks. "I'm like to be sent packin' if I don't behave myself. I keep findin' th' best reasons in th' world for goin' out to check on things to th' barn."

Brandy laughed and hugged her, her own tension easing. "Seems to me the best reason in the world spends most of his time in the barn. I'm surprised you can make yourself spend a minute in the house. I'm so happy for both of you!"

Persia's smile died abruptly. She looked away as though afraid of meeting Brandy's eyes, and she spoke in a rush, words tumbling over each other. "Oh, I want you to be happy, too, an' I know you haven't been lately. Mr. Raleigh, he had somethin' to do with it, didn't he? He was walkin' around with love in his eye, an' you were runnin' an' hidin'. But it's Mr. King—*funny,* thought Brandy, *it shows even in the way people speak of him; Raleigh is the diminutive, "Mr. Raleigh," Grey is the only "Mr. King"*—who frets you, isn't it? Do you love him?" Her eyes went wide with surprise at her own audacity.

But Brandy wasn't offended. It was a relief to tell someone. She nodded slowly. "Yes, I guess I do, if that's what this awful, helpless, churning feeling is."

The worst thing of all was that Persia, try as she might, could provide no comfort. She loved Brandy and loathed Ruth, but Grey had, after all, chosen Ruth, and Brandy knew another though unspoken factor bothered her—Ruth and Grey were of equal station. In Persia's mind for Grey to marry one of his employees would be odd indeed. Brandy realized how differently the West had set her mind. When she had been growing up, society had had few levels beyond honest and dishonest, and sometimes it had been difficult to tell which was which. When high society had begun in San Francisco, Brandy, her father, Pearl, and others like them had dismissed it as artificial. The East, she reflected grimly, had had much more time to put things in order.

When she went down to supper, her pride surfaced over everything else. Her head was up, chin out, her back was straight, and she was ready to take on anyone who thought that mere social position made one superior. Mrs. Bailey blinked in surprise, and Grey grinned to himself—obviously they both noticed her new demeanor. But before the meal had progressed very far, she was suffering new doubts. Grey was openly making an effort to charm her, speaking gently, smiling often, questioning her with what seemed like genuine interest about Missy, about music, books, teaching, and a myriad range of subjects. Brandy felt herself thawing and couldn't do anything about it.

Grey excused himself and returned with a bottle of wine and three glasses. Brandy was awed by the idea that the precious liquor had come all the way from France to this isolated spot in Maine and wondered why Grey thought the occasion special enough to warrant it. Her pride dissolved under his smile, and the world seemed to explode into the bright colored sparks of Chen Lee's fireworks.

Grey handed Brandy her glass, and as she reached out to take it, the amethyst ring caught the candlelight. Had she not taken it quickly, Grey would have dropped the glass. As it was, some of the ruby liquid sloshed over the edge. She knew it was the ring. She looked up at him, wanting to know why it had disturbed him so, willing to explain why Raleigh had given it to her. But his expression stopped her. The black eyes bored into her ruthlessly, saying they found her beneath contempt. She feared him at that moment more than she ever had before. She gathered the tattered vestiges of her pride and rose unsteadily.

"You will have to forgive me. I am suddenly very tired." She kept herself from running to the door, and she didn't care what Mrs. Bailey thought. Let Grey explain in his own devious way.

She lay awake with her heart pounding until she thought she would suffocate in the sound. Then fear gave way to anger. If Grey wanted to know about the ring, let him ask. Damn him for his arrogant judging, for doing as he pleased and denying her the same right. She slept peacefully after that.

The next day brought an overcast sky and air rich with the snow scent. Brandy heard Grey leave his room, and she cherished the hope that he had decided to go back to Wiscasset and had started early to avoid the storm. She did not inquire about his whereabouts, and no information was volunteered by Mrs. Bailey or Persia, who were both behaving with nerve-racking caution, tiptoeing about and not mentioning Grey. Finally, she stole out to the barn and noted with satisfaction that Orpheus was gone. Rafe was nowhere in sight either, and that was a relief because he usually saw her thoughts far too clearly.

She spent the day happily with Missy and found that the prospect of a quiet New Year's Eve no longer dismayed her after the past twenty-four hours of tension.

The first snow did not fall until dusk. She was standing idly by her window watching it when she caught sight of him—a moving shadow at first in the dim curtain of snow, then starkly defined—Orpheus stumbling with weariness, Grey still arrogantly upright. She saw the movement of his head and knew he was seeing her silhouetted by the light from her room. She jerked back out of sight and then suffered the rushing blood, bitterly aware of how much her childish action must have amused him. But there was at least some satisfaction in the conviction that she was the demon he had spent the day outriding.

She dressed carefully for the evening, choosing a simply cut brown dress with a soft full skirt and cream lace trimming on the bodice and sleeves. She pulled her hair into a tight chignon, hoping the total effect would make her appear severely proper. But looking in the mirror, she wasn't so sure; already tendrils of hair were escaping, curling willfully, destroying any semblance of neatness. She sighed and made a face at her image.

She heard Grey going to and from his room, and she waited until he was gone before she ventured across the hall to Missy's room. And then she was late going down because of Missy's behavior. The child was so restless and twitchy, so impish, that Brandy thought she would never go to sleep.

When she finally arrived at the table, her faint hope that Grey's temper of the night before might have eased was lost in one quick glance at him. The harshness in his face added years to his age. He made no attempt to carry on a conversation, and Brandy heard herself and Mrs. Bailey go from nervous chatter to a silence that matched his. It frightened her further to realize that Mrs. Bailey, the formidable Mrs. Bailey, was just as apprehensive as she was. And they seemed to have no wills of their own, for though she knew they would both like nothing better than to escape to their respective quarters, neither of them protested when Grey announced after dinner that they would go to the music room, and Brandy did not refuse his command that she play; she hoped it would save her from thinking.

But only Pearl's training made it possible for her to find the right notes, for Grey's unblinking stare never left her, and she could feel it as strongly as if he were running his hands over her. As she played, the ring winked like a malevolent eye, and she wished she had not been so defiant as to wear it.

She strove fiercely to lose herself in the sound, and she felt the first wave of success, the beginning of the ascent into a universe created entirely by music.

He did not even have to raise his voice; low and even, without effort it shattered her refuge. "Jasmine used to do that, too, hide in her music. Especially after I came home from Gettysburg. I think it made her feel pure again. Is that what it does for you, Brandy?"

Her hands came off the keys curved rigidly as she swung around to face him. She gasped when she saw Mrs. Bailey was gone. He smiled pleasantly and nodded. The glitter in his eyes made Brandy shiver. "Poor old woman, she was too tired to see the new year in. But you're not too tired, are you?"

She was shaking so hard it was difficult to stand. "I don't know what you're talking about, but I've heard enough." She started for the door, but Grey moved in long strides to bar her way. "It's much much too early to end the last night of eighteen hundred and sixtynine, my dear." "My dear" was a threat.

Scorching anger rose in Brandy. "Get out of my way!"

His answer was to reach out and grab her so suddenly that she had no time to evade him. There was no gentleness in him, his hands were biting into her shoulders, her face was pressed so hard against the weave of his coat that she could feel a button digging into her cheek, and it was difficult to breath. It was hard to get any space, but she managed to kick him in the shins, and she tried to bring her knee up, but this was nothing like the other time. He was not drunk. He simply stepped back easily, holding her away from him. She had never seen a face so devoid of pity, so filled with grim intent. Terror exploded in her, and she fought frantically, kicking, biting, trying to get her hands up to claw his face, screaming for Mrs. Bailey. He seemed to feel none of it. He captured her flailing arms, pinioning her two wrists easily with one hand. He lifted her, and she jerked her body desperately to no avail. Her strength drained as quickly as it had come. The world was spinning crazily, and she shut her eyes.

She lay passively in his arms as he carried her. "Grey, no, please, no," she pleaded, and was disgusted by her whimpering. She opened her eyes to look at him; he gave no sign he heard her. His face was so savage that she closed her eyes again and felt a merciful numbness beginning.

She knew only vaguely when he no longer carried her, when he put her down, when she felt the pins being pulled from her hair, his hands on her clothing. Beneath the canopy of her own bed his face was contorted with lust and fury. He snarled something about Raleigh, Jasmine, Missy; none of it made sense except that when she started to struggle again, he said very clearly, "Lie still or I will kill you." She believed him; she thought he might kill her anyway. Nothing mattered anymore; this was the man she loved, this insane, evil man. *Oh, Missy, poor Missy, what things have you seen?*

She lay motionless, hearing the cloth rip as if it were someone else's body which was being stripped. The numbness spread, putting a barrier between her body and Grey's rough hands. The words ran over her, harmless as drops of rain—"bitch, whore, you too, just like her, the same, the same"—they had nothing to do with her. She lay unresisting when the weight of his body covered her own. But then her senses came alive, and she screamed before the darkness.

She hurt; she was bruised and torn but the unbearable pain had ceased. Someone was holding her, cradling, rocking her gently. He was crying. Why? The broken words dropped into strange patterns.

"Oh, my God, Brandy, my darling. I am mad! I didn't know. I was told you'd been with Raleigh, like Jasmine. His ring, my great-grandmother's ring. I couldn't bear it. It was worse than knowing about her, worse than knowing Raleigh is probably Missy's father." The sobs tore at his throat, making the rest of his words unintelligible.

"The devil doesn't cry," she said flatly. She turned her head away and tried to ease her body out of his hold. His arms tightened compulsively; then he let her go.

"Brandy, I think I ought to go for Margaret or someone." The desperate note in his voice grated.

"No. I am all right. There is nothing anyone can do, nothing that needs doing. You've done it all." Her voice rose frantically at the end. Hugh, gentle Hugh, why did I leave you?

She started to shiver, and it was worse than the time in the snow. Now there was no comfort in Grey's presence. He covered her with blankets, but when he took her hands and tried to warm them in her own, she pulled away, screaming, "Get out! Get out!"

He backed away, old, hunched, nothing like Grey. Pity stirred briefly in Brandy, and she strangled it with her will. Her shivering stopped; the numbness began to creep through her again. She lay staring with empty eyes at the shadows beyond Grey.

"Brandy, don't do that, don't go away like Missy! I love you. What I did tonight is unforgivable. There will never be enough I can do for you to make up for it. But I love you! Can you hear me? Ruth was no answer, and that's finished. I wanted to strangle her for calling you a whore, for saying such vile things to you. I had to take her back to town. I owed her at least that much. But I wanted to marry you. I know it isn't possible now, but I'll do whatever you want. I'll take you back to Hugh Adams. I'll explain. He won't love you any less for what I've done. Brandy, goddamn it, answer me!"

In contrast with his painful rush of words, her speech was slow and slurred, as if she had been drugged. "You love me? As you loved Jasmine and Missy? No, thank you, your love is a very destructive thing from what

I've seen of it. Explain, give me back to Hugh? And what choice would he have? He is too kind. I will stay here until you find someone else for Missy. I won't leave her to your tender mercies. Then I will make my own plans. Now, get out!"

She saw his face clearly again. If it was revenge she wanted, it was hers. Yet she felt no joy in her victory or in her sudden knowledge that of the grief this night, the greater share was Grey's. She closed her eyes against his image. She heard him blow out the lamp and leave the room. She drifted in the emptiness, wanting sleep, filling the void with anger when oblivion would not come.

Her bed was an intolerable place to be. The room was in darkness save for the ember glow from the hearth. She pulled her body out of bed as though it were a heavy, aged thing. She put more wood on the fire, fighting unreasoning terror of what might happen if it went out completely. The added wood caught, and she sighed with relief.

She curled up in the patterned chair, and before she wrapped the blanket around herself, she saw by the firelight the dark places on her body which were not shadows. Grey was a strong man.

Think about it, Brandy, face it and be free. Things hidden in the mind fester and cannot be healed. Would you have me face this too, Father? Could you face it yourself? Yes, Brandy, yes.

She let the thoughts come, dealing with them one by one. Where to go? Aunt Beatrice? No, never there. Somehow the old woman would know, would glory in it. To Pearl, back to California? Perhaps, but even as she considered it, she realized that of everyone, Pearl would be the most hurt by what had happened. Pearl's dealings with men were honest and businesslike. Grey's behavior would shock her deeply. She believed in a woman's ability to choose her own destiny and manage her own life. She had instilled this in Brandy, and she would never feel free of blame because she would sense how violent the death of dreaming had been. To the Adamses then, as Grey had suggested, to the home they offered her? That was more difficult. Hugh would take her back, that she knew, but she would never know how much pity would corrupt his love because he would have to be told; she could not bear to live with a lie hovering over her like some dark bird. Though she longed for his healing gentleness, she admitted to herself that what had happened would not make her love him any more than she did. And worse yet, how could he avoid thinking it was at least partially her fault? Desperate for order in the chaos, she decided she would go back to the Adamses and stay there only until, with their help, she could find another job. She could simply say that her task at King's Inland had been as hopeless as everyone had said.

Indeed, it was like touching a wound. Brandy was now convinced Grey had murdered his wife—his admission that he had taken her because he thought she, as Jasmine, had been Raleigh's mistress added to the evidence against him. She shuddered; she knew only too well the cruelty of which he was capable. She faced the act squarely. Nothing could erase the revulsion she felt. Nothing could be more physically demeaning than rape. But there was something apart from her body which was essentially herself, inviolate as long as she kept it so. Her greatest danger had been in being so ready to give that essence into Grey's keeping. She had been so wrong; the bleakness stretched into infinity.

But Missy, Missy still needed her, more now than ever for protection as much as for teaching. She had no right and no place to take the child, but she would stay until she was in safe hands. She knew Grey would accept her verdict on Missy's new companion; she would not allow any woman to come unless she was older and stronger than she was.

She was too exhausted to think anymore and too uncomfortable to sleep in the chair, but she had achieved a small corner of quiet in her mind. As she got up to go back to bed, she saw that it was snowing heavily, renewing the white purity of the landscape. "Much, much too late and only the first day of the new year," she moaned bitterly.

CHAPTER XII

She woke and remembered. She lay with fists clenched at her sides, heart pounding, sweat clammy on her skin. She knew what had wakened her; Grey was outside her door. If he came in, she would scream the house down. But he did not try the door, and she heard a scratchy sound, then his footsteps fading toward the staircase. The snow had stopped. Dim light filtered through the windows; it could not be much after dawn.

She got up and saw the envelope he had pushed under the door. Her hands shook as she opened it:

DEAREST BRANDY,

I will be well on my way by the time you read this. [How little he knew of her consciousness of his movements in the house.] I will do my best to find a replacement for you, though such a person does not exist, for there is only one Brandy. An adequate substitute is the only possibility. I will send word to Margaret regarding my return. In any case, if I cannot accomplish this in a fortnight, I will make arrangements for your passage to wherever you wish to go. Persia and Margaret can surely take care of Missy until a new teacher is hired. You are as important as Missy.

After last night, I know it is impossible for you to believe that I had nothing to do with the strange "accidents" which have befallen you at King's Inland.

*But I swear to you that I had no knowledge of them and
beg you to take care while I am gone. I have never used
another human being as cruelly as I have you, nor have
I ever loved another as I love you.*

                                        GREY

As she stared at the words, she remembered her
dream. In it, Missy had come and stood beside her bed
and whispered softly, "Don't go away, Brandy, Papa
needs you. Don't go away." For a moment she hated
them both for demanding so much, for taking so much.
But then she felt only pity for the tragedy which
continued to ruin their lives.

The full import of things which Grey had said the
night before began to hit her. He believed Missy was
Raleigh's child! It couldn't be, it just couldn't; Missy's
eyes were her father's. Yes, they were, and Raleigh's
eyes were Grey's. Raleigh, did you betray him so? And,
Jasmine, you started this and left the child to suffer.
No, whatever you did, you did not deserve to die by
fire.

The ring, what had Grey said? Brandy fought to
make her mind recall in spite of the terror of the
memory. Grey had recognized it; it had been his great-
grandmother's. Something Raleigh had inherited to give
to the woman of his choice? Then he had lied about its
origin on purpose, leaving it with her like his brand,
taunting Grey with it. She pulled it off of her finger
frantically. But Grey should have asked her about it. "I
was told you had been with Raleigh, like Jasmine." The
words came back with chilling clarity. Told? Who had
told him? Raleigh himself? No, the change in Grey had
come after he had seen the ring, so someone must have
added to his anger by telling tales after that. Rafe,
Persia—such dear friends? It was more likely that something had been innocently said by one of them and
wrongly taken by Grey.

She tried to quit thinking about any of it because she
was still too stunned by Grey's attack to see anything

very clearly, but one thing she saw very well—Grey
doubted he was Missy's father, and yet he had spared
no expense in his care of her. Of course, there were
many reasons which might explain that, among them a
way to torture Raleigh, who could never claim his
child, or perhaps an apology for killing Missy's mother.
But Brandy didn't believe it; she believed he loved
Missy, and she was appalled at the treachery of her
mind which, despite what Grey had done to her, made
her think kindly of him.

Missy still slept, and it was still early when Brandy
went down to the kitchen. Persia had the day off, and
Mrs. Bailey was not yet in evidence, and Brandy was
doubly thankful for that when she saw the note addressed
to Mrs. Bailey in Grey's script. She opened it with no
guilt:

DEAR MARGARET,
   *Please allow Brandy to sleep as late as possible. She
suffered a chill last night and needs rest. She is not
fully recovered from her illness, but you know how
stubborn she is, so please do not be obvious in your
cosseting.*

                                              GREY

Damn his attention to details, thought Brandy, struggling against tears as she shredded the letter. And then
the phrase "suffered a chill last night" swung her mood
around like the wind, and she had to fight against
hysterical laughter.

She was still taking deep breaths and clutching a cup
of tea as though it were a lifeline when Mrs. Bailey
came in, stopping in surprise when she saw her. "I
thought you would sleep late today." She peered closer
and snorted, "And it looks as if you ought to have done.
But happy eighteen seventy anyway, and may it be a
good year for King's Inland."

Brandy toasted her with her cup and managed to
keep the bitterness out of her voice as she returned the

good wishes. She had the sudden horrible suspicion that the housekeeper's concern for her well-being came from having heard some noise of the struggle with Grey. But then she thrust the thought away; even though she had been intimidated somewhat by Grey's behavior, Mrs. Bailey, a woman, for all that would have had to have come to her defense had she heard her screaming. Brandy's smile relaxed into a more natural line. If the older woman noticed the absence of the ring, she made no mention of it. They had a quiet breakfast together, and then Brandy took a tray up to Missy.

It was the final blow of too many. Missy knew what had happened. She sat rocking furiously, flicking her fingers with mad rhythm. The tray crashed to the floor, and Brandy buried her face in her hands, unable to check the choking sobs.

There was not even the prelude of a tentative touch, only the hurtling weight of Missy's body and the desperate tugging of her hands. Brandy sank down on the floor amid the ruins of the breakfast and submitted in awe to the tiny hands patting her, smoothing her hair, touching her tear wet cheeks, comforting her as if she were the frightened child. She gathered Missy into her arms.

"Little love, it's all right. I'm safe; I'm with you. Forget whatever you heard, whatever you saw." Missy stiffened in her arms, and Brandy saw her blunder— apparently trying to forget what she had seen and heard had caused Missy's illness. "No, you're right, and I'm wrong. We can never really forget things, can we? But we have to learn to live with the bad things we've seen and still be happy." Missy relaxed enough so that Brandy knew she was somewhat comforted, though obviously her burden was still too great for any child to bear.

When she went to get another meal for Missy, she met Mrs. Bailey and offered her own clumsiness as an excuse. The housekeeper nodded. "You might not believe it, but I can still remember when I was young enough to feel a little shaky on New Year's Day." Brandy smiled dutifully, doubting that Mrs. Bailey had any New Year's Eve memories quite like hers.

Though she was happy to see Persia the next day, she found it galling to hear tales of the fun she and Rafe had had at the Cowperwaithes' farm. She felt like snapping, "Oh, I had a fine time, too. I was raped," but Persia's glowing face killed the notion. She avoided Rafe because she was terrified that he would see that something was terribly wrong.

But she could not avoid Missy, and that was hardest of all. The constant, though subtle, expressions of love from the child made her imminent desertion seem indefensible on any grounds, and her guilt was constant. She considered countless ways to break the news and discarded each in turn as too cruel.

And Hugh was as unavoidable as Missy because Brandy knew that if she were going back to the Adamses' house, she must write to Hugh first, and winter mails were slow enough without adding her own delay. She decided to finish her letter about the locket, add her homecoming, and trust Rafe to find a way to get it sent. But she let a week pass with no word of Grey's return before she sat herself down to complete the letter.

Missy had been fed, and Brandy had time enough to write before supper. She opened the writing box, thinking how soon the glories and, she hoped, the terrors of King's Inland would be nothing more than memories. She took out the partially finished letter, and the locket gleamed from the corner of the back of the box. She picked it up and found that the chain had slipped under the back panel. Annoyed, she tugged, not caring if the chain broke. There was a click, and the chain was free and unbroken, but Brandy didn't notice. The locket slipped forgotten from her hand.

The sound had come from the panel swinging open to expose a drawer which ran the length of the box. Brandy pulled the little gold nob, and the drawer opened easily, revealing a stack of thin sheets of paper covered in fine script. She took them out thinking they were some old record of events kept by Melissa King, too long removed to harm anyone. But she froze when she deciphered the date on the top sheet. It was August 2, 1867. The last words on the page were: "I've got to get Melissa away from here. I hear her now c..." Trailing away, not finished, hastily thrust back in the secret drawer.

Brandy knew it was the date of Jasmine's death. She closed her eyes, denying the words, wishing she had never found the writing, knowing the pages might provide the final proof of Grey's guilt, still, after all, wanting him to be innocent. And she knew her only, frail right to read them came from having loved him. It was enough.

She rearranged the pages chronologically; the earliest date, October 10, 1862, was on the bottom of the stack, and she made that the first page, continuing to 1867. There were long spaces of time when nothing had been recorded; Jasmine had used these pages as a confessional, not as a journal of daily life. From the first entry onward, Brandy knew why Jasmine had hidden them— such a tale of infidelity was not the sort of record one shares. She read grimly, feeling ill as the story unfolded:

October 10, 1862
I married the wrong brother. I know that now. Raleigh is charming, young, and carefree. Grey is a great brooding devil in comparison. I don't even miss him. I would not weep if he was killed in the war. So many men are dying, why can't he be one of them? How dare he go off to fight my people, leaving me trapped up here with these sour-faced Yankees. Raleigh was right not to go; I respect his principles and love his company.

November 15, 1862
Raleigh and I went for a long ride today. I am never

frightened with him. I am a good horsewoman, but with Grey not even that is enough.

December 27, 1862
Raleigh brought me some beautiful violet silk for a new dress. I wonder how he got it; such things are hard to come by with this Godforsaken war on. I am going to have it made up specially to please him. I am still as slender as I was when I was seventeen, and Raleigh notices it. His hands are so gentle. If Grey comes home, I will not be able to bear him touching me.

March 3, 1863
I have not heard from Grey for some time now, and I have not written to him. Maybe news will come soon in my favor.

June 18, 1863
I wish there was some marvelous ball to go to. How I would love to dress up and dance with Raleigh. But at least he came in time for supper tonight. I think the old witch knows we are lovers. How I hate her! She loves Raleigh and fears I'll harm him.

September 7, 1863
No, no! Grey is coming home. He was wounded at Gettysburg and contracted a fever afterward. Oh, God, what shall I do? Raleigh will not take me away. He says we'll manage. How?

September 15, 1863
Grey came home today. He was sent by ship to Wiscasset and brought by cart here. He is too much of a wreck to even ride a horse. I should feel sorry for him, but I don't. He repulses me. His shoulder is still a great oozing wound, and he is yellow and shrunken with fever. Maybe he will die anyway. But his eyes are just the same, black and mocking and something else now. I think he suspects. If he knew, I think he would kill me.

October 13, 1863
Raleigh comes often to get me out of the house. I would go mad without him.

October 29, 1863
Grey is going to live. He is too arrogant to die. I wish I had the courage to poison him. Mrs. Bailey fusses over him. She has no more courage than I. I know she'd like to see him dead, too. Then Raleigh would inherit. I love my Raleigh. I desire him every minute of my day.

November 20, 1863
I feel sick, unclean. I did not think he was strong enough yet, but he was. He came into my bedroom tonight and took me brutally. He never treated me this way before, as though I were a slave, nothing, something to be used. I hate him. Raleigh, my love, please take me away.

January 25, 1864
I have prayed it wasn't so, but it is no use, it is true. I am with child. Grey's or Raleigh's, I don't know. But I will tell Raleigh it is his, and he will take me away.

February 3, 1864
There is no hope. Raleigh can do nothing. He is too dependent on Grey, for his job, for his money. And he says Grey would hunt us down and kill us both no matter where we go. I believe it. Maybe I will die in childbirth, and it will be finished.

April 17, 1864
I will not die. I have discovered the ultimate power over Grey. He is mad about the idea of being a father. He is being so kind and attentive, I want to laugh in his face. The fool. Mrs. Bailey is in a rage of jealousy, one more to come between the fortune and her favorite.

August 14, 1864
The child was born a week ago, a girl named Melissa
for Grey's, and Raleigh's, great-grandmother. Grey is
wild with joy. He doesn't even care that it is not a boy.
He looks young again; almost I remember why I
married him. I will never have another child. It is not
true that you forget the pain. I remember every horrible hour of it.

April 20, 1865
The war is over. If it had gone on a little longer, I know
Grey would have been well enough to rejoin his regi-
ment. He has not had an attack of the fever for months
now, and his shoulder is no longer as stiff. My God,
even Mrs. Lincoln has lost her husband, but I have no
more chance of losing mine. I wonder what has happened
to my family, but I don't care. Even though they were
right about my marriage, I will never forgive them for
the spiteful way they behaved. Days pass so swiftly with
the baby to look after, it is hard to spend much time
with Raleigh, but Melissa is my joy, so I do not mind.

August 7, 1865
Melissa is a year old today, a beautiful and clever child.
Every day she learns something new. She crawls all
over the place and hoists herself up and stands for a
minute. If I hold her by the hands, she walks quite
well. She is Raleigh's gift of love to me; I must go on
believing that. Grey plays the proud father until it
sickens me. Sometimes I am tempted to tell him. After
the birth of the child, I forbade him my bed, and he has
not troubled me. The child is enough. But I know he
goes to other women. They can have him. I still have
Raleigh, if only for stolen hours.

March 10, 1866
Melissa (I will not call her Missy as Grey does) walks
with great ease now and picks up new words every day.
She adores Grey and that makes me jealous except that

she has enough love for everyone. And Grey has the
means to give her a good life.

August 7, 1866
To think that Melissa is two years old today! She knows
more than four hundred words, and I am sure that
must be a record for such an infant. Raleigh gave her a
rocking horse. It must be hateful for him to see us as a
family and to know the child is his. I am sure he
believes she is.

January 5, 1867
We gave a New Year's Eve ball. People came from miles
away with sleigh bells announcing their arrival. Five
couples stayed the night, and the house was alive with
music and people. I know why Grey agreed—to show
off Melissa—but I don't care. It had been so long since
I had been to a party. I danced and danced and hardly
at all with Grey, thank God. Everyone said how beautiful I looked, even that spiteful Ruth Collins. Raleigh
danced with her twice, and I hated her, but I know he
didn't whisper the same things to her that he did to
me. Melissa was seen by all before she went to bed. She
was wonderful, chattering away and smiling her lovely
smile. Everyone was enchanted by her.

April 9, 1867
Grey hates leaving Melissa even for a day, but he is
involved in so many new ventures that he is gone for
longer periods now. What delight, more time with
Raleigh! If only that old hag wasn't here, watching
every move I make. She has been in this house for so
long, it seems impossible to get rid of her. But I will
keep trying. It helps that she isn't very nice to Melissa.
Perhaps Grey will notice.

June 24, 1867
The weather is unseasonably hot. Everyone is short-
tempered. I don't pay much heed to servants, but Grey

*has a new stableman, and he frightens me. His name is
Raphael Joly. The last name doesn't fit at all. His face is
horribly scarred, hard, and leathery, with eyes which
seem to look right through me. Grey found him at the
docks. What a way to pick a groom! Our dislike is
mutual. But Melissa took to him right off, and he has
already taken her out on several rides, holding her
before him. She has no fears and loves it, so I must
bear the awful man for her sake.*

August 2, 1867
*God forgive me, I've ruined everything for Melissa. I
told Grey, I didn't mean to, but I did. Back tonight,
drunk, started talking about making love to me again.
He grabbed at me, ripped my dress, I ran for my room,
but he got there before I could lock the door. Said he
wanted me, wanted another child. I couldn't credit I
was the one screaming the words, but I was. I told him
he couldn't have me and he didn't have a child at all,
Melissa is Raleigh's. I thought he would kill me, but he
just went dead still. I know where he's gone, gone to kill
Raleigh first. I've got to get Melissa away from here. I
hear her c . . .*

Brandy's eyes ached from reading the furtively small
script. She willed her stunned mind to impose some
rational order on the jumble of impressions. The out-
standing revelation was of Jasmine's character, and for
the first time, Brandy had a true picture of her: beautiful, willful, vain, educated enough to write well, totally
lacking in compassion for her husband and capable of
feeling justified in her infidelity, fearful of people who
saw through her too clearly, and yet with all this,
capable of deep love for her child and wild passion for
Raleigh. And now Brandy knew that Grey had not just
accepted vile rumors about his wife and brother but
had been told in the cruelest terms that he had been
betrayed and that the child he loved so much was not
his. Oh, Grey, it was enough to drive a man to murder!

In her mind, Brandy saw Grey coming home, his great strong frame diminished by pain and fever. The image closed her throat. And then she saw him fighting fiercely to live, growing stronger and then joyful with the birth of the child, bearing his wife's coldness, still loving her for a long time because Missy was his delight and Jasmine was her mother. And she saw his world destroyed again and his harsh right to revenge. She forced herself to picture him murdering Jasmine but could not, and she realized with a surge of joy that she could not because the picture was false. He had gone after Raleigh, but he had not killed him. And if he had wanted to kill Jasmine, he would have done it cleanly, probably with his bare hands. Brandy knew him well enough to believe him perfectly capable of that, whatever the consequences. She also knew him well enough to know that he would never burn down a stableful of prize animals to accomplish the death of one worthless human being.

Then who had started the fire? "I've got to get Melissa away from here. I hear her c..." Calling? Crying? Why so late at night? Had Missy heard the fury between Grey and Jasmine? Perhaps Jasmine had caused her own death, taking Missy and going to the stables and inadvertently tipping over a lantern. Or perhaps one of the horses had kicked her, and she had fallen unconscious, spilling oil and flame into the hay. It did not satisfy Brandy. Jasmine had been a good horsewoman, albeit more timid than Grey would have liked, so she had probably been a careful one, too. Anyone who had been around stables knew the danger of fire.

Brandy felt as if some important information were prowling around in her mind, staying just out of her grasp. She searched through the pages again, and this time the phrases leaped at her with stunning force: "I think the old witch knows we are lovers"; "She'd like to see him dead, too. Then Raleigh would inherit"; "Mrs. Bailey is in a rage of jealousy, one more to come between the fortune and her favorite."

Competent Margaret Bailey who had run King's Inland for so many years? Yes, Mrs. Bailey whose face was alight with love every time Raleigh arrived, never when Grey came home. Mrs. Bailey who remembered and tried to speak casually of Grey's always making the distinction between the "woman who takes good care of me and my real mother." Mrs. Bailey who was constantly fondling the treasures of the house as though they were living things; Mrs. Bailey who had nearly had heart failure when she had lost her hold on the piece of jade. Mrs. Bailey who got along well with Ruth Collins because Ruth had no intention of having children, because Ruth would let her continue her rule, because Ruth hated Missy as much as Mrs. Bailey did. Margaret Bailey who had little to do with Missy, not because she was too old, but because she loathed the child.

Brandy was terrified. She felt as if the bottom had just dropped out of the world, leaving her falling slowly after it. She tried to attribute the words to Jasmine's spite, but she did not succeed because the attempts on her own life were flashing before her. The futile but frightening attempts at smothering, the cut girth, the fire, all things a woman could do with stealth and little strength. And had the house burned, Mrs. Bailey had had an easy way out through the back, and Raleigh had not been there to worry about. It had been worth it to her to risk the loss of the house on the chance of killing all three—Brandy, Missy, Grey. And the day in the snow, not too difficult if Margaret Bailey had come home early and gotten Missy out, hiding her in her own apartment if not the music room; she would have been sure that Brandy would take the bait. But Missy, why hadn't she struggled? Too terrified probably, or too sleepy; Brandy remembered the drugged feeling she'd had. A careful dose in something they'd eaten? Had Mrs. Bailey lured Jasmine out—"I hear her c . . ."—to kill her before she could tell much and endanger Raleigh? Perhaps she had known that Grey had ridden off after an argument but had not realized the full extent of his knowledge. Why hadn't she killed Missy then? Because no matter how much she hated her, there was a chance that Missy was the child of her beloved Raleigh.

"But why me? Why should she want to kill me?" Brandy asked aloud, and had the answer—because she was making progress with Missy and the child might soon tell what she'd seen that night. And the half-told tale of Rafe's crime—the child left out, no mention of the fact that Rafe had found his wife with her lover, that fitted the sly, malicious way. Make Brandy distrust everyone. She saw the pattern with Grey too. No doubt with a great show of innocent concern, Mrs. Bailey had planted the suggestion that Brandy and Raleigh were involved with each other, and no doubt Brandy had been pictured as the improper one. And Ruth had been told by someone that Brandy and Grey were carrying on. Make everyone distrust Brandy. With grim amusement, Brandy admitted to herself that her usual lack of decorum had undoubtedly made the housekeeper's job easier. But she reflected with no amusement at all that Mrs. Bailey must have heard her struggle with Grey and ignored it. Another way to make her leave. Another way to destroy lives.

Her longing for Grey was so intense that she sobbed. Even with Jasmine's account, she did not think anyone else would believe her. She wanted to spirit Missy away, but she could imagine how insane Rafe or the Cowperwaithes would think her story; they had all known and trusted Margaret Bailey for too long. And they would not want to face Grey's anger if he came home to find that his daughter had been kidnapped by her governess.

She had never felt so cornered. She buried her face in her hands and then froze as she heard a faint sound at her door. It seemed an age before she made herself move, but then she went swiftly to the door and opened it. There was no one in the hall, and Missy's door was closed.

Stop it this instant! If you can behave normally until

Grey gets home, everything will be all right. No on
else knows the diary exists. She drew a deep breath
and the world refocused. She was late for supper, an
she hurried to freshen up, trying to erase all evidenc
of tears, and go downstairs; no sense in doing anythin
out of the ordinary.

Mrs. Bailey greeted her pleasantly, and Brandy real
ized how difficult it was going to be to maintain her ai
of innocence; even the older woman's smile gave he
gooseflesh. She wished the weather had been sever
enough to keep Persia from going home except that
might delay Grey's return. She was afraid to ask if Mr
Bailey had heard from him since even that now sounde
suspicious, but the housekeepr volunteered th
information.

"I received word from Grey today. Poor man, h
seems to be having difficulty completing some chore
but he said to expect him night after tomorrow."

Not so long to wait. *Why has she told me? Is
because Rafe picked up the letter for her and she
afraid he might have mentioned it? Or is it just to tes
my reaction?* The questions were shouting in Brandy
brain, and she felt the creeping paralysis of fear trium
phant. She forced herself to look straight at Mrs. Bailey
wondering if she ought to provide herself with extr
protection by telling her she could be leaving soon
deciding not to because it could be used as anothe
weapon against Missy's sanity. Instead, she sai
noncommittally, "Oh, so soon? He certainly doesn
seem to mind the rigors of winter travel."

The bright-blue eyes watching her from behind thei
spectacles seemed more intense than usual.

She excused herself as soon as the meal was finished
saying that Missy had been very restless and she hope
she wasn't coming down with anything. Mrs. Baile
expressed her concern, and Brandy hated her.

She tried to compose herself before she went int
Missy's room; the last thing the child needed was t
know that she was afraid. But she had no intention

letting Missy sleep alone. She didn't think Mrs. Bailey would attempt anything—why should she when there was no reason to suspect that Brandy knew?—but she wasn't going to take any chances. She had thought of moving Missy in with her because her door had a latch on it while Missy's did not. But she feared the change would upset the child and warn the housekeeper. On the other hand, if she stayed with Missy while she slept and then just neglected to leave until early morning, the child might never know, and if Mrs. Bailey checked on her, it would appear that nothing was out of the ordinary save for Brandy's worry that Missy might be sickening for something. She devoutly hoped that Missy would not be in one of her wakeful moods for the next two nights.

She put on her night rail and took down her hair in her own room and went back to the child. Missy stirred but did not awaken, and even Panza went back to sleep after one lazy wag of his tail. Brandy spent the night awake in the chair by the fire and slipped back to her room at sunrise, feeling a little foolish and very tired besides. There had been no sound of anyone prowling, no creaking boards or doors softly opened, and Brandy thought the vigil had probably been a waste. She still could not believe that Mrs. Bailey would try anything violent so close to Grey's homecoming, but if she did, Brandy was certain it would be by stealth at night since face to face she was easily stronger than the older woman. The important thing was not to leave Missy unprotected.

By the time she went downstairs Persia was there, and Brandy was so glad to see her that she nearly blurted out a plea for her to stay the night. But she stopped herself in time; she had no adequate reason to give Persia, and it would warn Mrs. Bailey that something was afoot.

Persia eyed her with concern. "You're lookin' peaky again. Is somethin' wrong?"

"No," Brandy assured her. "I just need more fresh air. I'll take Missy for a walk this afternoon."

"That's a splendid idea. You do look pale and tired." Brandy had not seen Mrs. Bailey come in, and she barely restrained herself from jumping like a startled rabbit at the sound of her voice. She wondered if she imagined the sarcasm underlying the cheerful tones.

The day passed with agonizing slowness, but a long walk helped and served a useful purpose besides—Brandy wanted Missy to be tired enough to sleep the whole night through again. On their way home, she saw Rafe in the distance and waved to him but continued toward the house, curbing her desire to run to him and beg him to take them both away.

She could hardly bear it when Persia called her happy good-night and left at dusk. She felt utterly forsaken by all save the evil force at King's Inland. Then her chin went up, and she thought: *Come on, Brandy, just one more night, and then Grey will be here*. She even managed to chat naturally with Mrs. Bailey during dinner, and the housekeeper made no protest when she again excused herself right after.

She checked on Missy and saw with satisfaction that she was sleeping soundly. Then she went to her own room and changed into what she now considered her disguise, since the last thing she intended to do was to sleep. She looked longingly at her bed, knowing that if she lay on it even for a minute, she would probably sleep for a week. She decided to take the book from Pearl and the letter to Hugh with her to keep her occupied and awake. The letter would be particularly useful for that, she thought ruefully, for now that she knew so much about Grey's past and present motives, now that she knew her love was justified, it was going to be doubly difficult to write to Hugh. She opened the writing box to take out the fragment she already had written.

Her mouth was instantly dry; her voice echoed oddly

in her ears. "Very stupid, very untidy, Mrs. Bailey, or do you want me to *know* you've read them?"

The locket lay on top of Hugh's letter, not under where it had been, and she knew she had put the papers back and closed the panel carefully though now it was slightly awry and the corner of one of the thin sheets protruded through the crack, probably from being crammed half in half out of the drawer behind. Perhaps Persia had surprised Mrs. Bailey in her reading, and she had had to put everything back quickly. But how had she known? Brandy remembered the sound at her door, the sound she had discounted as the product of overnight nerves. She had been late, and the housekeeper had come to see what she was up to.

Her skin prickled as if ants were walking in legions over her, but she did not seem to be able to move or think at all. Then she heard the sharp echo of a self-given command. "Move, damn it, move, get to Missy!"

Even as she wrenched open her door, she heard the front door slamming shut. She grabbed up the trailing skirt of her night dress and ran, slipping and sliding on the stairs, cursing in desperation as she stopped to open the heavy door. She made it outside in time to see Mrs. Bailey dragging Missy into the barn. "I'm coming, Missy!" she screamed as she saw the door close.

She ran through the snow to the door and swung it open, stopping dead. The bar had been left off on purpose, of course. She was doing everything according to Mrs. Bailey's plan. The barn and the stable wings were in complete darkness, but the horses were stamping and nickering nervously. She was in there somewhere, waiting for her. But all of Brandy's caution left her when she heard Missy crying, and she headed for the sound, stumbling over things she couldn't see.

The sobbing was coming from one of the empty box stalls. Brandy called as she came, "It's all right, darling, I'll be there in a minute." She found the entrance to the stall, and in the next instant, Missy was in her arms.

The double door slammed shut behind them, and she heard both bolts go home. The housekeeper's voice was muffled by the heavy doors, but its eerie quality came through. "Nicely done, Mrs. Bailey, an end to all of this, a beginning for my Raleigh, my own Raleigh. He liked people to think I was his mother, oh, yes, he did, not like the other one. She should have died, useless woman, but not him, that was mean; he should have lived to make pretty Margaret into Mrs. King, into Raleigh's mother. Oh, this is much better than burning the house down; that was a silly thing to think of." It was as if she were crooning to a separate part of herself, to pretty Margaret whose plans for becoming mistress of King's Inland had been blighted by the random chance of the master's death by disease. Light and dark, not in Ruth or Rafe or Raleigh, not in Grey or Missy, but in Margaret Bailey.

Brandy's flesh crawled, but she made her voice strong. "Mrs. Bailey, you can't get away with this. Let us out!"

The laugh cackled hysterically. "No, I can't do that. I have you right where I want you. That damned Jasmine, she left things for you to read. And I didn't tell you the truth—Grey will be home late tonight, not tomorrow night, late enough to find you both in ashes. And who will believe he didn't do it? It happened once before, you know. I wish he'd died then too. They'll get rid of him, and my Raleigh will have everything."

"You *are* mad! Grey will know you did it. He'll kill you for it. Or Rafe will come." Keep her talking, please God, let one of them arrive in time.

The ugly laughter assaulted her ears again. "Rafe won't be out on a night like this, last time was a lot more risky. And Grey might think Missy did it, but I don't care if he knows the truth; it would be better if he kills me. The loyal housekeeper murdered, the governess and his child burned to death. Bad boy to do all that. He'll be hung for it, and Raleigh will be king. Oh, clever, pretty Margaret."

The voice became querulous. "It's all your fault; you

were making Missy well again. I *promised* her nothing
would happen to her father if she kept still about how
her mother died. But she won't keep her part of the
bargain. It's only fair she should pay."

The key to Missy's terrible silence, the blinding
revelation that the child had given up the world not
because she feared her father, but because she loved
him enough to destroy herself to keep him safe. What
little hope Brandy had died in that knowledge; anyone
insane enough to so abuse a child was capable of any
evil. Keep her talking.

"What about Raleigh? You know what this will mean to
him."

"He'll hate Grey for it, not me. It's sad, but he
wouldn't like it if he knew I killed Jasmine, and now
Missy might tell him."

"Mrs. Bailey . . . Margaret . . . what if we promise not
to tell about tonight? Will you let us go?" There was no
answer. "Margaret, are you still there?" Brandy tried to
keep the rising panic out of her voice. No response.
Margaret Bailey was too clever to be delayed by such a
simple ruse.

She made her voice steady. "Stay here, darling. I'm
going to see if I can get the door open." She hugged
Missy convulsively and moved the short pace to the
door. She threw her weight against it again and again;
she tore the ends of her fingers trying to pry open a
crack so she could lift the bolts. It was no use; the stall
had been built of the finest wood to hold even the most
unmanageable horse; her puny strength didn't even
make it creak. She slumped against the door, panting,
and then held her breath and tried to hear any noises
from outside. There was silence, and then a horse
screamed and others answered. She heard a crash and
another scream which sounded human. She hoped
viciously that Mrs. Bailey had had her skull caved in by
a pair of hooves. It wouldn't do them any good, though,
for the noise of the terrified animals was increasing,
accompanied by the sound of crashing timber and a

strange roaring. Brandy caught the first odor of smoke. So this is the way it's going to be, she thought, such a horrid, wasteful way to die. She ceased to be afraid; all she felt was overwhelming sorrow for what Grey must now bear and for Missy who had just found life again and was now to lose it forever.

She went back and cradled her. She expected she would be in such shock by now that she wouldn't know what was happening, but Missy was renewing her contact with the world with a vengeance. Her body, completely pliable and responsive, pressed against Brandy, her hands touched and soothed with an eloquence which said clearly, *Don't worry about me; I fear for you.*

Brandy made no attempt to lie to her. "Missy," she said, "we aren't dead until we both stop breathing. Maybe we'll have a better chance when the fire reaches us, maybe the door will burn enough for us to get it open. Maybe not. But we have to try to stay alive. Your father needs us." She choked on the last words; smoke was beginning to fill the stall.

She took Missy's hand. "Come on, we're going to get close to the door so I'll know if I can open it." Brandy had to shout because suddenly the roar was all around them. She shoved Missy to the floor. "Better to breathe there, stay down!" she gasped, and knew Missy understood, for her hands told her the child was staying put.

She began to push and claw frantically at the door, and she thought it might be giving way a little, perhaps from the flames on the other side, when she heard the creaking above her and looked up into the hellish glow of the first flames eating the beams. She saw a section begin to sag, and she threw herself on Missy. She managed to say clearly, "I love you, Missy," and she heard Missy say her first word after the long silence, "Brandy," before the world caved in.

CHAPTER XIII

Sounds. "Brandy, love, can you hear me?" a man's voice kept repeating, and a strangely pitched child's voice begged insistently, "Wake, please, Papa needs, don't leave," abbreviating the connections, speaking only the heart words.

Brandy opened her eyes slowly. She was lying on her stomach. The snow was cold beneath the material against her skin, and she wrinkled her nose against the sour, scorched smell of the air. How odd to be lying naked outdoors—well, not entirely, something covered her back. Her head was cradled in someone's lap. They would fire her from Greenfield Academy for this. She started to laugh, but pain exploded in her rib cage and rippled along her back and legs, and the sound came out as a whimper. A confusion of hands were stroking her head, two large, two small. "Missy?" she croaked.

The man's voice again, Grey's, curiously husky. "Don't try to talk or move, sweetheart. Missy's fine. You protected her; the fire didn't touch her. But you've got some burns, and I think you've broken a couple of ribs. Rafe has gone to get a big blanket so we can carry you in safely."

Despite the pain, she worked desperately to turn her head enough to look up, and she saw the tear streaks on his soot-stained face. "Even the devil cries sometimes," he said, and then his voice broke, and his hard body

217

trembled. "Brandy, Brandy, I came so close to losing you tonight."

"But we found Missy! Grey, she's home again. She always loved you."

"Yes," said Missy, and kissed Brandy on the cheek. "Now you Mama?"

Grey's voice answered for her, hesitant, humble. "She will be if she wants to. Bad things have happened to her at King's Inland, and she may want to leave." But then he ruffled Brandy's hair and said to Missy, "But the fire cut her hair so short, if she leaves right away, someone might think she's a boy and kidnap her for a sailor."

Missy giggled, a melodious child's sound, and observed wisely, "No, there's girl under coat."

Brandy gasped and would have managed to laugh this time if she hadn't caught sight of Grey's hands and arms. He had been holding her as if completely unaware of the burns he'd got. "Grey, your poor hands!"

"It's not serious. Looks worse than it is," he said briefly.

Everything rushed back. "Mrs. Bailey? The horses?"

Grey's voice was steady. "Margaret is dead. We got Pete, Polly, one of the colts, and Lady out. We can talk about it later, when you're better."

Rafe appeared with the blanket, and when they slid her onto it and lifted her, she could see the glow of the still-burning stables. She shut her eyes and concentrated on keeping silent. Rafe and Grey were being as gentle as they could; crying out would only make it harder for them. She found it curiously easy to keep still; anything was better than death.

She drifted in and out of consciousness, but she was aware in flashes of Rafe and Grey taking care of her, putting something which smelled strongly of tea on her burns, salving her torn hands, binding her ribs. She tried to say something about how many things Maine men knew how to do, but she lost the words and slept instead.

Missy was often present and so was Persia when Brandy opened her eyes, but Grey seemed to be forever there, his own hands bandaged, his face weary but peaceful, the old harshness gone as if it had never been.

Finally, after what seemed an eternity of drifting, Brandy wakened fully. Her body hurt in a thousand places, but she was clearheaded. It was evening, and Grey was sleeping exhaustedly, hunched in the chair beside her bed, but he felt her gaze and opened his eyes.

"Go to bed right now," she commanded.

She watched the dawning of his smile in wonder, no longer a brief twisting of the lips but a full acknowledgment of joy flowing to light the midnight eyes. "Now I know you will be all right, bossy Brandy." Tenderness had replaced the mockery in his voice, and Brandy resigned herself to spending the rest of her life feeling weak-kneed and fluttery every time he smiled or spoke to her.

His expression sobered as he asked, "Do you want to talk about it now?"

"No. I want you to get some sleep first." What she really wanted was for him never to have to read Jasmine's hateful words, but since they existed, she did not feel she had the right to keep them from him.

He went and got Persia and then hovered until Persia shooed him away, assuring him that Brandy's fever had broken and that she was perfectly capable of taking care of her. He kissed Brandy before he left, not at all embarrassed by Persia's presence.

Persia looked so pleased about the whole thing that Brandy laughed, and Persia said, "Well, I do like things to work out, an' I never could abide that Collins woman."

She was as competent as she claimed, bringing Brandy a light meal, fluffing pillows and deftly rearranging the bed clothes to make her more comfortable. She chattered away, and Brandy was content to listen to her account of Missy's amazing talents. "Why, she's just as bright as a button, always was, just took you to know it." She hesitated and then went on. "That wicked, wicked woman, it's still past believin'. Did you reckon it was her?"

"Not until it was almost too late."

"Why ever didn't you come to Rafe or me as soon as you knew?"

"Because, as you said, it was past believing." There was no accusation in Brandy's voice, but Persia said contritely, "You're right. We'd known her for so long it would've been a goodly fish to swallow."

When Brandy woke again, it was morning, and Missy came to visit her. Brandy thought the child's voice the best music she had ever heard. Her inflections were close to normal now, her sentences were filling out, and Brandy was amused by this proof that Missy had been doing a lot of practicing. She found to her relief that Missy could talk about "bad Mrs. Bailey" and the fire with no qualms; she had been through so much before that the terrifying way her silence had ended seemed to have left no additional scars.

"Darling, I know everything you did was to protect your father, but why didn't you just tell him about Mrs. Bailey?" Brandy asked.

Missy looked at her, obviously surprised an adult could be so foolish. "I saw what she did to Mama. She said would do to Papa if I told." Brandy saw the terrible logic of it; Margaret Bailey had killed Jasmine, had destroyed the security of Missy's world; how was the child to know that Grey was strong enough to prevent the same thing from happening to himself? Missy's voice went steadily on. "She was bad. She came at nighttime to your room. I watched. I was afraid for you."

Brandy swallowed the lump in her throat at the thought of this tiny child staying awake, helpless, but still trying to protect someone she loved. "Missy," she asked gently, "that day when I went out in the snow, were you in the music room?"

Missy shook her head. "No, I went to sleep in my room. You were there. When I woke up, Papa was there." Brandy's suspicions were confirmed—undoubtedly they had both eaten something which had contained a sleeping draft. Had Missy not been drugged when Mrs. Bailey picked her up, she might have screamed in terror. And Brandy was sure that Missy had been taken to Mrs. Bailey's quarters, a truly safe hiding place, not the music room. No wonder the housekeeper had so kindly prepared that nice meal with many of their favorite dishes. What an evil woman to risk poisoning a child with too much of some drug, probably laudanum, so easily obtainable for the headache.

"You are the bravest person I know, Missy, but now you don't have to be so brave anymore; you've got your father to be brave for you."

Missy twisted a thread on her dress and asked anxiously, "Will you stay? He can be brave for you, too."

Brandy smiled at her. "Your father and I have many things to talk about, but I expect I'll be here for a very long time."

Grey appeared at the door, and Missy ran to him, squeaking excitedly as he lifted her in his arms. "She *will* stay. I told you!"

Grey's eyes met Brandy's, and Missy said, "Put me down now. I will go to my room so you can talk grown-up." She bustled out with Panza at her heels.

Grey shook his head in mock despair. "Heaven help me! I've got two females giving me orders." His expression was suddenly as anxious and appealing as Missy's had been. "Did she get it right? Did you say you would stay?" His voice grew ragged. "Brandy, I'd be lying if I claimed I was a better man than Hugh Adams. I'm not. I am ruthless, arrogant, and cruel, you know that better than anyone." He swallowed audibly before he could continue. "But I swear I'll spend the rest of my life trying to make up for what I did to you."

Brandy couldn't bear it. "You will not, Grey King! We'll mark that off as a bad beginning, and we'll make a

new one together. I love you as you are; and I don'
want you to be like Hugh Adams. You are the only mar
I know who could survive such tragedies as you've had
as well. And I discovered long ago that it makes me
absolutely miserable when you're humble!"

He was beside the bed, trying to temper his urgen
strength as he held her. "Damn your broken ribs," he
groaned, and cut off her laugh with a long kiss for which
she thought breathing well lost.

She would have been content to let the moment spir
out forever, but she still feared Jasmine's power to
destroy them. She pulled away a little and said, "I wan
to talk about it now." He nodded.

She began by repeating all the signs which had led
her to believe that Missy's reaction to him was no'
caused by hatred and fear as everyone assumed. "And c
course, the stronger my love for you became, the less
able I was to believe you were responsible for you
wife's death, your child's silence, or any of the things
which happened to me." She stated it as a simple fact,
but it didn't strike Grey as simple, and she had to look
away from his fierce joy before she could go on. "Then I
found something and through me, Margaret Bailey did,
too. She even talked about them in the barn, along with
all the other crazy things she said." Brandy related
snatches of Mrs. Bailey's mad monologue, putting the
time off, but then her voice faltered. "Grey, I . . . maybe
I should have burned them. I don't know. But I think
you have the right to read them. Will you bring me the
writing box from the desk, please?"

Grey had listened in stunned silence to Brandy's
account of Mrs. Bailey's mad speech, and he was puzzled by her request, but he complied and set the box
on the bed within Brandy's reach. But she didn't touch
it. "Was it always kept in this room, or was it in
Jasmine's room before?"

He understood. "No, it was kept in here. I didn't
know that Jasmine ever used it, and I guess Margaret
didn't either because she knew of the secret drawer;

she showed it to Raleigh and me once. It was something to amuse two restless boys on a rainy afternoon. We even used it for a while for hiding special treasures until its novelty wore off."

Brandy had tripped it accidentally with the locket chain, but now she saw how it worked. Grey opened the box and pulled out one of the small drawers, reached into the empty space and pushed something at the back. The panel under the writing surface clicked open. Grey's hands were steady as he straightened the sheets, and his face was very still as he read. Brandy watched anxiously, afraid she would see pain flash in his face, confirming Jasmine's eternal ability to hurt him, but his expression did not alter, and when he was finished, he rose and put the sheets into the fire and returned to her, meeting her eyes squarely.

"There wasn't much in those that I didn't know except for Margaret's treachery, but that blindness was enough; it nearly cost you your life, nearly ruined Missy forever. I knew Raleigh was Margaret's favorite, but I didn't know he was her obsession, didn't know how much she hated me or how jealous she was of my love for my mother. Pitiful woman, she was wrong about my father; he would never have married her, even had he lost my mother. He adored my mother, who, frail as she was, was always full of laughter and love for him. And I never saw that Margaret's attachment to King's Inland, to the house itself, was a sickness. And Jasmine was right about my intentions that night." His voice did not falter. "I did want to kill Raleigh, but the distance between us was enough to blunt my rage. I realized that killing my brother would accomplish nothing except perhaps to separate me from Missy for the rest of my life. I turned back and found the stable in flames, Jasmine dead. I knew I hadn't done it; I thought it was an accident. But then the change in Missy was so devastating I felt I was to blame because I had started the whole disaster by quarreling with Jasmine. Perhaps I was a little mad with guilt. And then, God forgive me, when things started happening to you, I truly believed they were Missy's doing, and I was helpless against it; I couldn't bear the idea of putting her away. And I thought if anyone could change her, you could. I risked your life for it. For that I will never forgive myself. As for the rest of it, the affair between Jasmine and Raleigh, that had nothing to do with you and will have nothing to do with our life together."

Brandy knew he believed it, and she wanted to believe it with him, but she had to be sure all the ghosts had been exorcised. "My darling, I am a strong-willed woman; I stayed in spite of your protests. The risk was mine and worth it; any risk will always be worth it because I love you so. But I must ask—what about Raleigh, now that you know so much, do you blame him? And what of Missy, seeing it written, knowing it may very well be true, does that make you love her less?"

He winced at the harshness of the questions, but he understood her need. "I blame Raleigh for committing adultery with my wife. But he was young, foolish, and jealous of me; all dangerous things to be with a woman like Jasmine. He and Jasmine paid much too heavy a price—Jasmine with her death; Raleigh by a loss of self-respect and knowing that though Missy may be his child, he will never be more than an uncle to her. I don't blame him for Margaret's crimes; it would destroy him completely to know he was the twisted root of them. I will tell him that she was mad, nothing more. As for Missy, I will never know whether or not I am her father by blood, but in every other way I am, and nothing on earth could make me love her any more than I do.

"There, love, don't cry," he said, brushing the tears from her cheeks.

"For joy," she managed to whisper before he kissed her again.

Neither of them heard Missy when she stopped at

the door, peeked in, and proceeded down the hall, explaining things to Panza. "Grown-ups talk funny ways, but it's all right, now she'll stay." Word perfect, she sang one of Brandy's songs as she skipped down the stairs.

ABOUT THE AUTHOR

CELESTE DE BLASIS, a native Californian, lives on a ranch high in the Mojave Desert. She is the author of such memorable novels as *The Proud Breed, The Tiger's Woman, The Night Child,* and the acclaimed Swan Trilogy.

THE LATEST IN BOOKS
AND AUDIO CASSETTES

Paperbacks

] 28416 **RIGHTFULLY MINE** Doris Mortman $5.95

] 27032 **FIRST BORN** Doris Mortman $4.95

] 27283 **BRAZEN VIRTUE** Nora Roberts $4.50

] 25891 **THE TWO MRS. GRENVILLES**
Dominick Dunne $4.95

] 27891 **PEOPLE LIKE US** Dominick Dunne $4.95

] 27260 **WILD SWAN** Celeste De Blasis $4.95

] 25692 **SWAN'S CHANCE** Celeste De Blasis $4.95

] 26543 **ACT OF WILL**
Barbara Taylor Bradford $5.95

] 27790 **A WOMAN OF SUBSTANCE**
Barbara Taylor Bradford $5.95

] 27197 **CIRCLES** Doris Mortman $5.95

Audio

] **SEPTEMBER** by Rosamunde Pilcher
Performance by Lynn Redgrave
180 Mins. Double Cassette   45241-X $15.95

] **THE SHELL SEEKERS** by Rosamunde Pilcher
Performance by Lynn Redgrave
180 Mins. Double Cassette   48183-9 $14.95

] **THE EVENING NEWS** by Arthur Hailey
Performance by Fritz Weaver
180 Mins. Double Cassette   45223-1 $14.95

] **COLD SASSY TREE** by Olive Ann Burns
Performance by Richard Thomas
180 Mins. Double Cassette   45166-9 $14.95

Bantam Books, Dept. FBS, 414 East Golf Road, Des Plaines, IL 60016

Please send me the items I have checked above. I am enclosing $_____
(please add $2.00 to cover postage and handling). Send check or money
order, no cash or C.O.D.s please. (Tape offer good in USA only.)

Mr/Ms _____

Address _____

City/State _____ Zip_____

FBS—11/90

Please allow four to six weeks for delivery.
Prices and availability subject to change without notice.

DON'T MISS
THESE CURRENT
Bantam Bestsellers

☐	28390	**THE AMATEUR** Robert Littell	$4.95
☐	28525	**THE DEBRIEFING** Robert Littell	$4.95
☐	28362	**COREY LANE** Norman Zollinger	$4.50
☐	27636	**PASSAGE TO QUIVIRA** Norman Zollinger	$4.50
☐	27759	**RIDER TO CIBOLA** Norman Zollinger	$3.95
☐	27811	**DOCTORS** Erich Segal	$5.95
☐	28179	**TREVAYNE** Robert Ludlum	$5.95
☐	27807	**PARTNERS** John Martel	$4.95
☐	28058	**EVA LUNA** Isabel Allende	$4.95
☐	27597	**THE BONFIRE OF THE VANITIES** Tom Wolfe	$5.95
☐	27510	**THE BUTCHER'S THEATER** Jonathan Kellerman	$4.95
☐	27800	**THE ICARUS AGENDA** Robert Ludlum	$5.95
☐	27891	**PEOPLE LIKE US** Dominick Dunne	$4.95
☐	27953	**TO BE THE BEST** Barbara Taylor Bradford	$5.95
☐	26892	**THE GREAT SANTINI** Pat Conroy	$5.95
☐	26574	**SACRED SINS** Nora Roberts	$3.95
☐	28436	**PAYMENT IN BLOOD** Elizabeth George	$4.95

Buy them at your local bookstore or use this page to order.